SONIC
THE HEDGEHOG
ARCHIVES VOLUME 20

featuring the talents of
IAN FLYNN, PATRICK "SPAZ" SPAZIANTE, JIM AMASH, KARL BOLLERS,
ART MAWHINNEY, HARVEY MERCADOOCASIO, JOSH & AIMEE RAY, CHRIS ALLAN,
JAMES FRY, FRANK GAGLIARDO, KEN PENDERS, BARRY GROSSMAN, DICK AYERS,
ANDREW PEPOY, SUZANNE PADDOCK, PAM EKLUND, JEFF POWELL, & STEVEN BUTLER

cover by
PATRICK "SPAZ" SPAZIANTE

SPECIAL THANKS TO ANTHONY GACCIONE & CINDY CHAU @ SEGA LICENSING

ARCHIE COMIC PUBLICATIONS, INC.
JONATHAN GOLDWATER, publisher/co-ceo
NANCY SILBERKLEIT, co-ceo
MIKE PELLERITO, president
VICTOR GORELICK, co-president/e-i-c
JIM SOKOLOWSKI, senior vice president
sales/business development
HAROLD BUCHHOLZ, senior vice president
publishing/operations
PAUL KAMINSKI, executive director of
editorial/compilation editor
STEVEN SCOTT, director of publicity and marketing
...itor
...ger
...olers
...cant
...der/
...bark
...tern

TABLE OF CONTENTS

Sonic and his friends have finally returned to Knothole, but there's no peace to be found! King Acorn and Sonic clash over how to handle Dr. Eggman. The madman is barely held at bay by a computer virus. And deep in space, a new force rockets towards Mobius!

The past casts a dark shadow as Amy Rose and the Freedom Fighters learn the tragic story behind Sonic's father, Jules the Hedgehog. What happened during the Great War? What was it that pushed Sir Charles to use the roboticizer on his own brother?

After so much struggle and loss, it's about time Sonic got some good news! For all his valor, Sonic is being knighted! Friends and rivals line up to share the day with our true blue hero – all except for Uncle Chuck. Dr. Eggman still controls him and an army of Robian slaves, which will be sent to unearth the madman's newest discovery – Chaos!

Sonic's father lies at death's door, the Great War reaches its unthinkable climax, and all the while, the man who will become Dr. Eggman crafts his master plan from behind the scenes. Watch as the pieces fall into place to create Sonic's past!

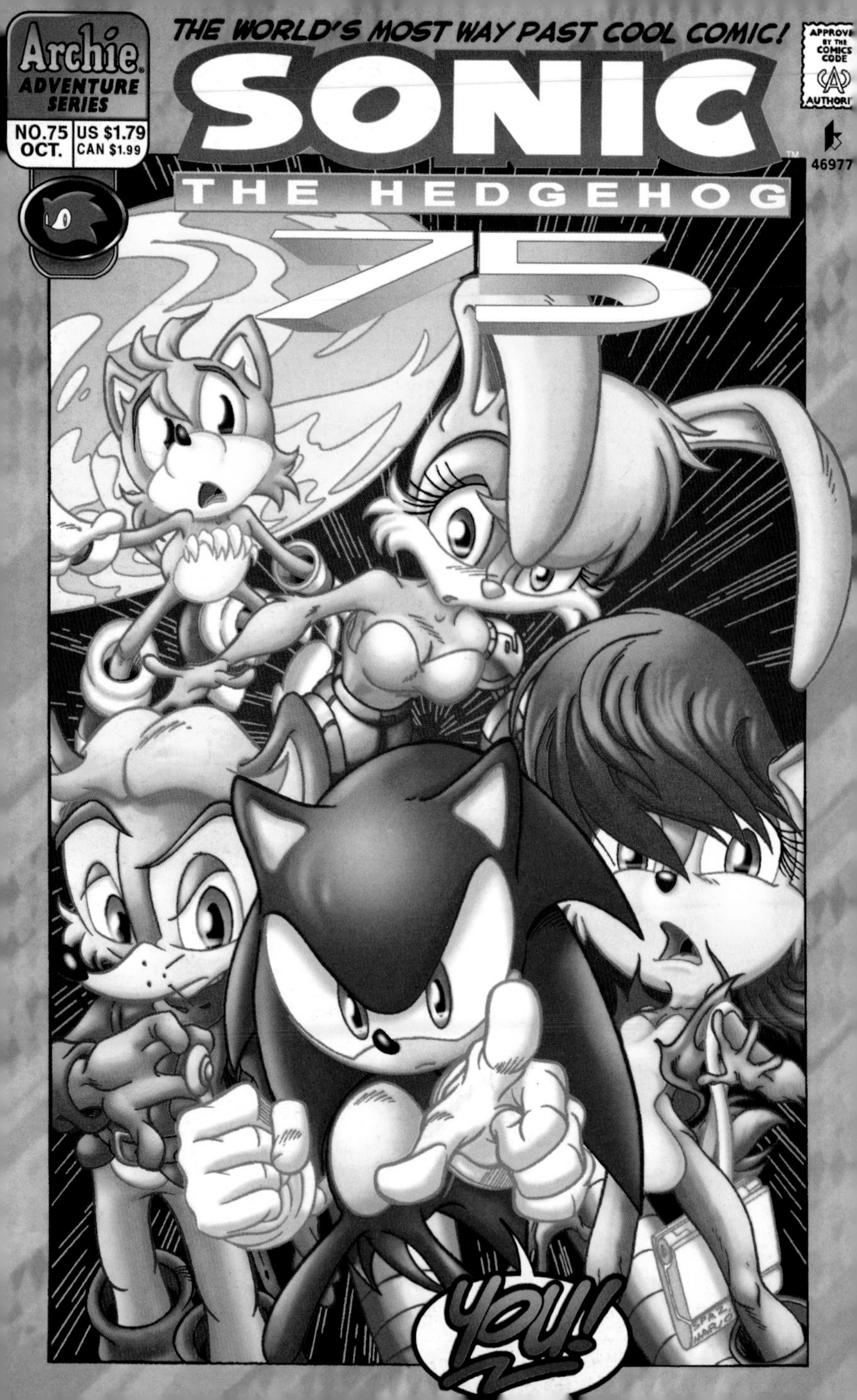
Archie
ADVENTURE SERIES
NO.75
OCT.
US $1.79
CAN $1.99
THE WORLD'S MOST WAY PAST COOL COMIC!
SONIC
THE HEDGEHOG
75
APPROV
BY THE
COMICS
CODE
AUTHORI
46977
YOU!!

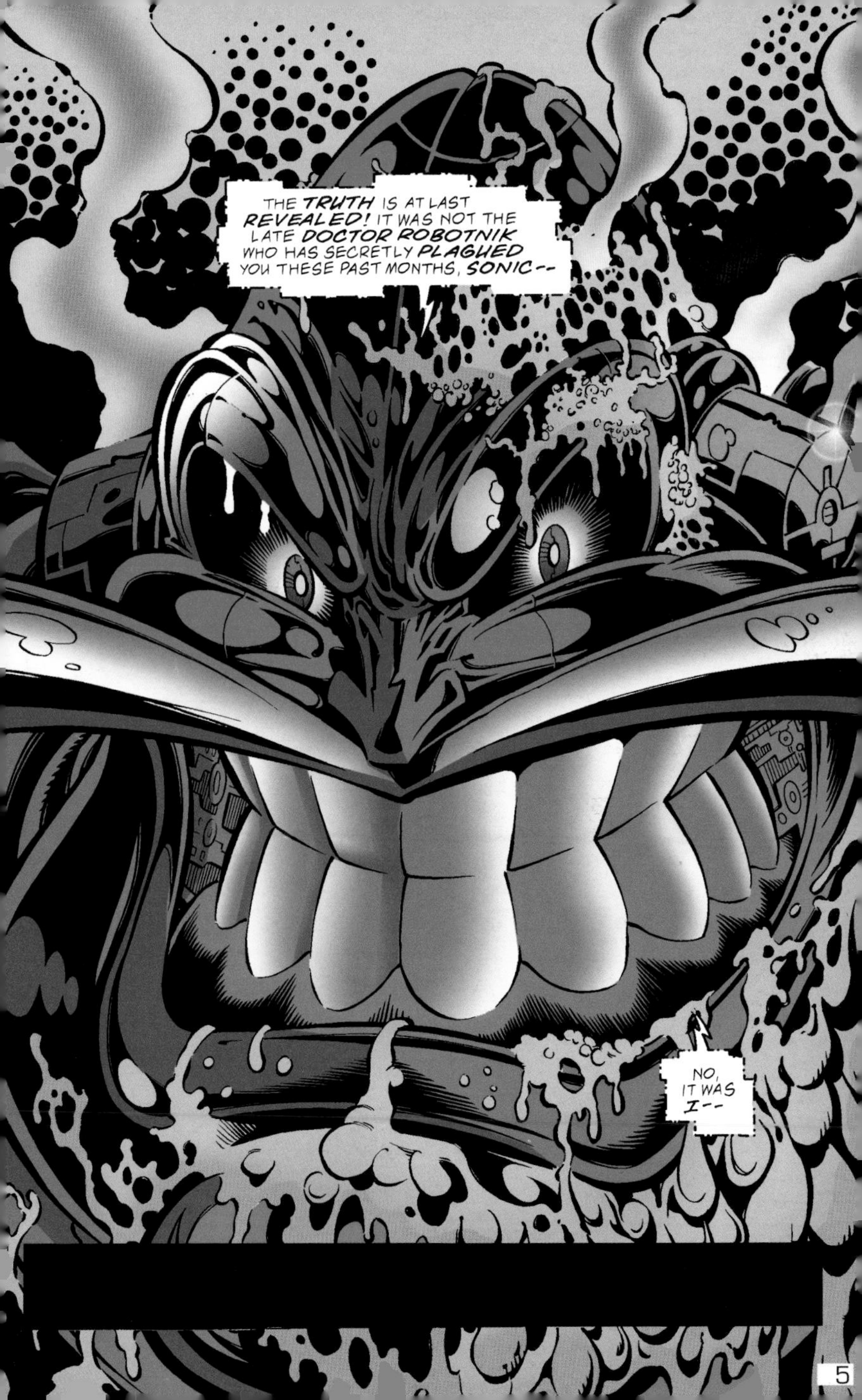
THE TRUTH IS AT LAST REVEALED! IT WAS NOT THE LATE DOCTOR ROBOTNIK WHO HAS SECRETLY PLAGUED YOU THESE PAST MONTHS, SONIC--
NO, IT WAS I--
[redacted]

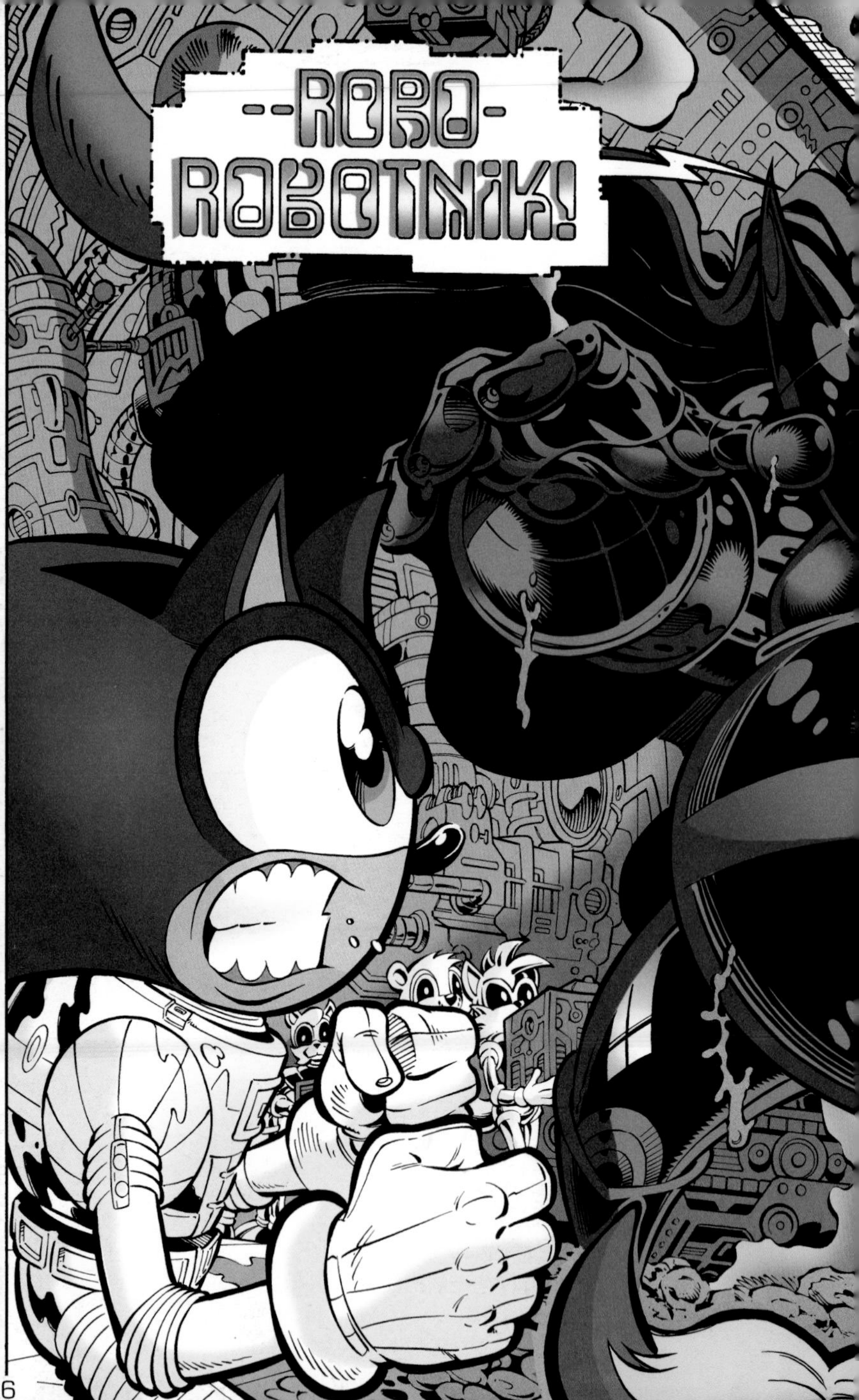
--ROBO-
ROBOTNIK!

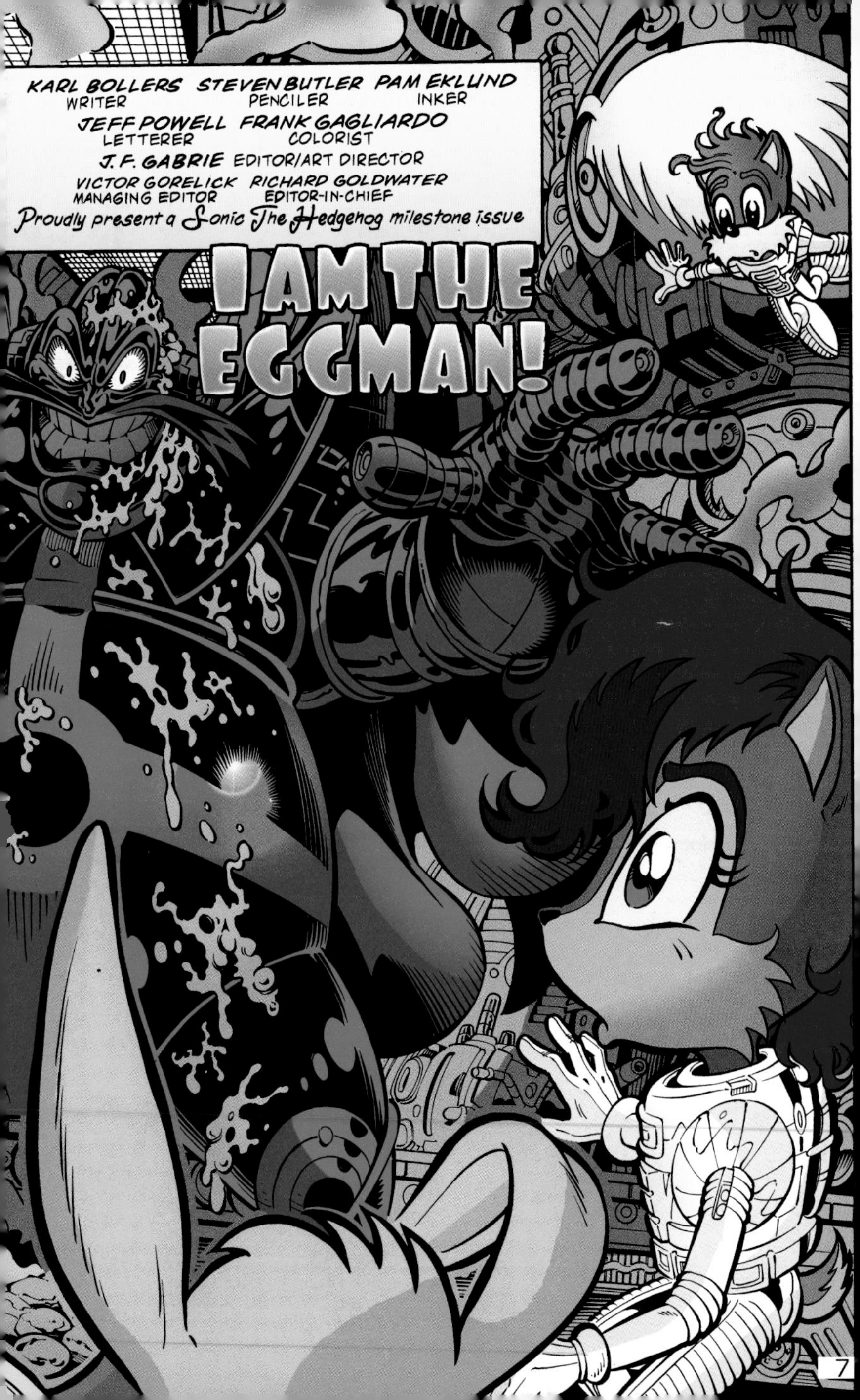
KARL BOLLERS WRITER
STEVEN BUTLER PENCILER
PAM EKLUND INKER
JEFF POWELL LETTERER
FRANK GAGLIARDO COLORIST
J. F. GABRIE EDITOR/ART DIRECTOR
VICTOR GORELICK MANAGING EDITOR
RICHARD GOLDWATER EDITOR-IN-CHIEF
Proudly present a Sonic The Hedgehog milestone issue
I AM THE EGGMAN!

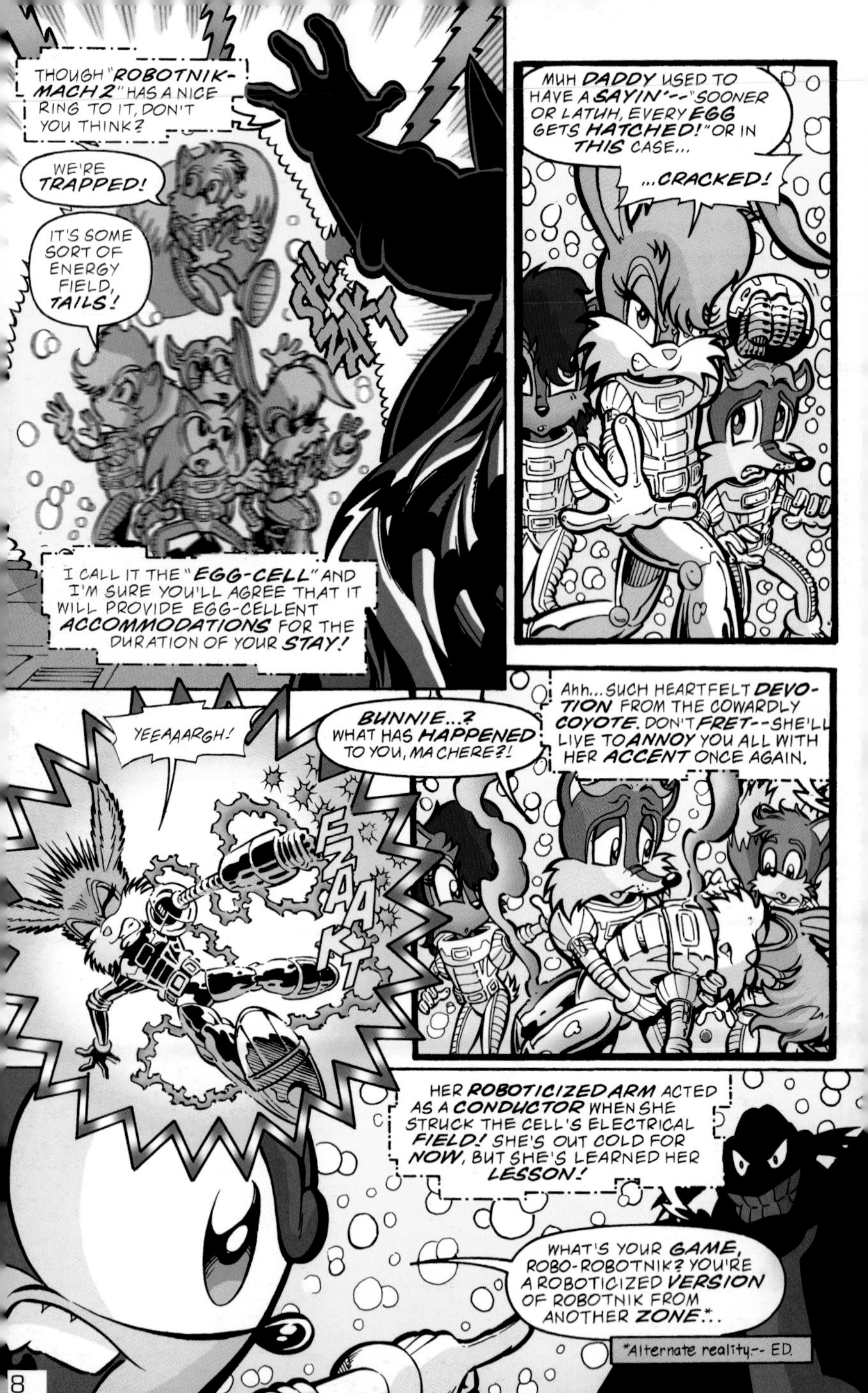

THOUGH "ROBOTNIK-MACH 2" HAS A NICE RING TO IT, DON'T YOU THINK?
WE'RE TRAPPED!
IT'S SOME SORT OF ENERGY FIELD, TAILS!
SH-SNAK-T
I CALL IT THE "EGG-CELL" AND I'M SURE YOU'LL AGREE THAT IT WILL PROVIDE EGG-CELLENT ACCOMMODATIONS FOR THE DURATION OF YOUR STAY!
MUH DADDY USED TO HAVE A SAYIN'-- "SOONER OR LATUH, EVERY EGG GETS HATCHED!" OR IN THIS CASE...
...CRACKED!
YEEAAARGH!
BUNNIE...? WHAT HAS HAPPENED TO YOU, MA CHERE?!
Ahh... SUCH HEARTFELT DEVOTION FROM THE COWARDLY COYOTE. DON'T FRET--SHE'LL LIVE TO ANNOY YOU ALL WITH HER ACCENT ONCE AGAIN.
FZAAKT
HER ROBOTICIZED ARM ACTED AS A CONDUCTOR WHEN SHE STRUCK THE CELL'S ELECTRICAL FIELD! SHE'S OUT COLD FOR NOW, BUT SHE'S LEARNED HER LESSON!
WHAT'S YOUR GAME, ROBO-ROBOTNIK? YOU'RE A ROBOTICIZED VERSION OF ROBOTNIK FROM ANOTHER ZONE*...
*Alternate reality.-- ED.

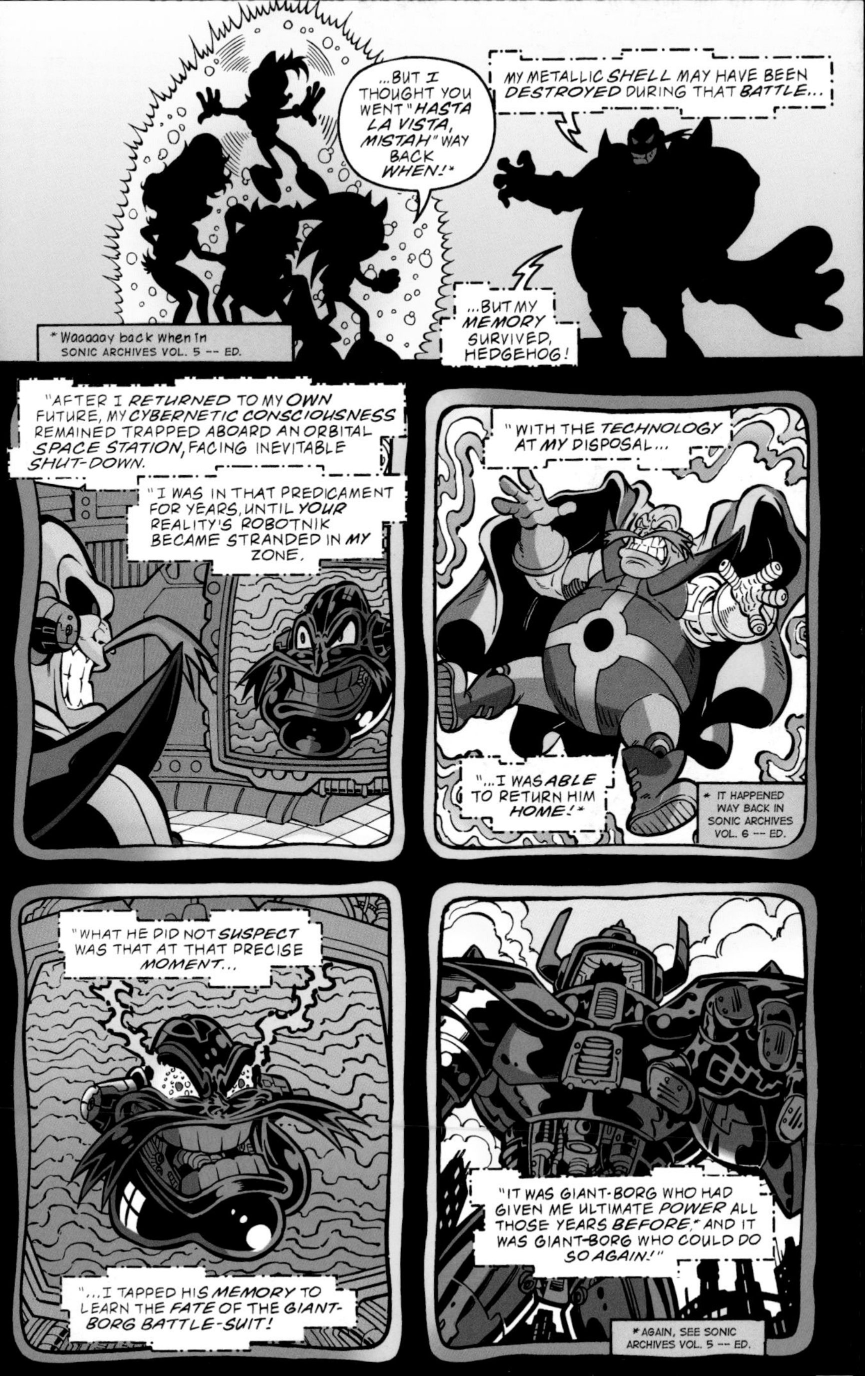
...BUT I THOUGHT YOU WENT "HASTA LA VISTA, MISTAH" WAY BACK WHEN!*
MY METALLIC SHELL MAY HAVE BEEN DESTROYED DURING THAT BATTLE...
...BUT MY MEMORY SURVIVED, HEDGEHOG!
* Waaaaay back when in SONIC ARCHIVES VOL. 5 -- ED.
"AFTER I RETURNED TO MY OWN FUTURE, MY CYBERNETIC CONSCIOUSNESS REMAINED TRAPPED ABOARD AN ORBITAL SPACE STATION, FACING INEVITABLE SHUT-DOWN.
"I WAS IN THAT PREDICAMENT FOR YEARS, UNTIL YOUR REALITY'S ROBOTNIK BECAME STRANDED IN MY ZONE.
"WITH THE TECHNOLOGY AT MY DISPOSAL...
"...I WAS ABLE TO RETURN HIM HOME!*
* IT HAPPENED WAY BACK IN SONIC ARCHIVES VOL. 6 -- ED.
"WHAT HE DID NOT SUSPECT WAS THAT AT THAT PRECISE MOMENT...
"...I TAPPED HIS MEMORY TO LEARN THE FATE OF THE GIANT-BORG BATTLE-SUIT!
"IT WAS GIANT-BORG WHO HAD GIVEN ME ULTIMATE POWER ALL THOSE YEARS BEFORE,* AND IT WAS GIANT-BORG WHO COULD DO SO AGAIN!"
* AGAIN, SEE SONIC ARCHIVES VOL. 5 -- ED.

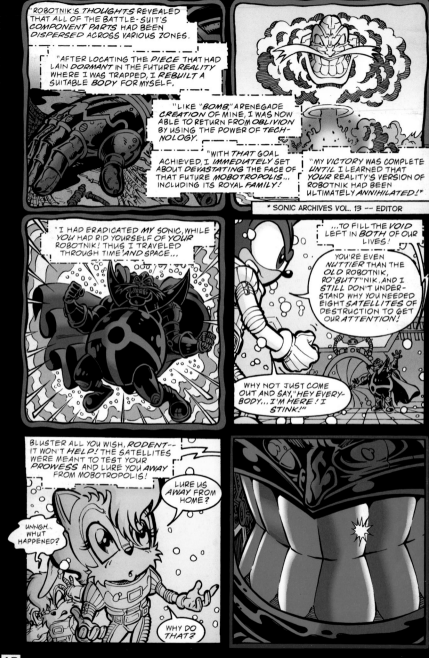

"ROBOTNIK'S *THOUGHTS* REVEALED THAT ALL OF THE BATTLE-SUIT'S *COMPONENT PARTS* HAD BEEN *DISPERSED* ACROSS VARIOUS ZONES.

"AFTER LOCATING THE *PIECE* THAT HAD LAIN *DORMANT* IN THE FUTURE *REALITY* WHERE I WAS TRAPPED, I *REBUILT* A SUITABLE *BODY* FOR MYSELF.

"LIKE "*BOMB*," A RENEGADE *CREATION* OF MINE, I WAS NOW ABLE TO RETURN FROM *OBLIVION* BY USING THE POWER OF *TECHNOLOGY*.

"WITH *THAT* GOAL ACHIEVED, I *IMMEDIATELY* SET ABOUT *DEVASTATING* THE FACE OF THAT FUTURE *MOBOTROPOLIS*... INCLUDING ITS ROYAL *FAMILY!*

"MY *VICTORY* WAS COMPLETE *UNTIL* I LEARNED THAT *YOUR* REALITY'S VERSION OF ROBOTNIK HAD BEEN ULTIMATELY *ANNIHILATED!*"

* SONIC ARCHIVES VOL. 13 -- EDITOR

"I HAD ERADICATED *MY* SONIC, WHILE *YOU* HAD RID YOURSELF OF *YOUR* ROBOTNIK! THUS I TRAVELED THROUGH TIME *AND* SPACE...

...TO FILL THE *VOID* LEFT IN *BOTH* OF OUR LIVES!

YOU'RE EVEN *NUTTIER* THAN THE *OLD* ROBOTNIK, RO"*BUTT*"NIK, AND I *STILL* DON'T UNDERSTAND WHY YOU NEEDED EIGHT *SATELLITES* OF DESTRUCTION TO GET OUR *ATTENTION!*

WHY NOT JUST COME OUT AND SAY, "HEY EVERYBODY... I'M *HERE! I STINK!*"

BLUSTER ALL YOU WISH, *RODENT*-- IT WON'T *HELP!* THE SATELLITES WERE MEANT TO TEST YOUR *PROWESS* AND LURE YOU *AWAY* FROM MOBOTROPOLIS!

LURE US *AWAY* FROM *HOME?*

UNNGH... WHUT HAPPENED?

WHY DO THAT?

10

SPECIAL ETCHED PIN-UP BY

PAM EKLUND.

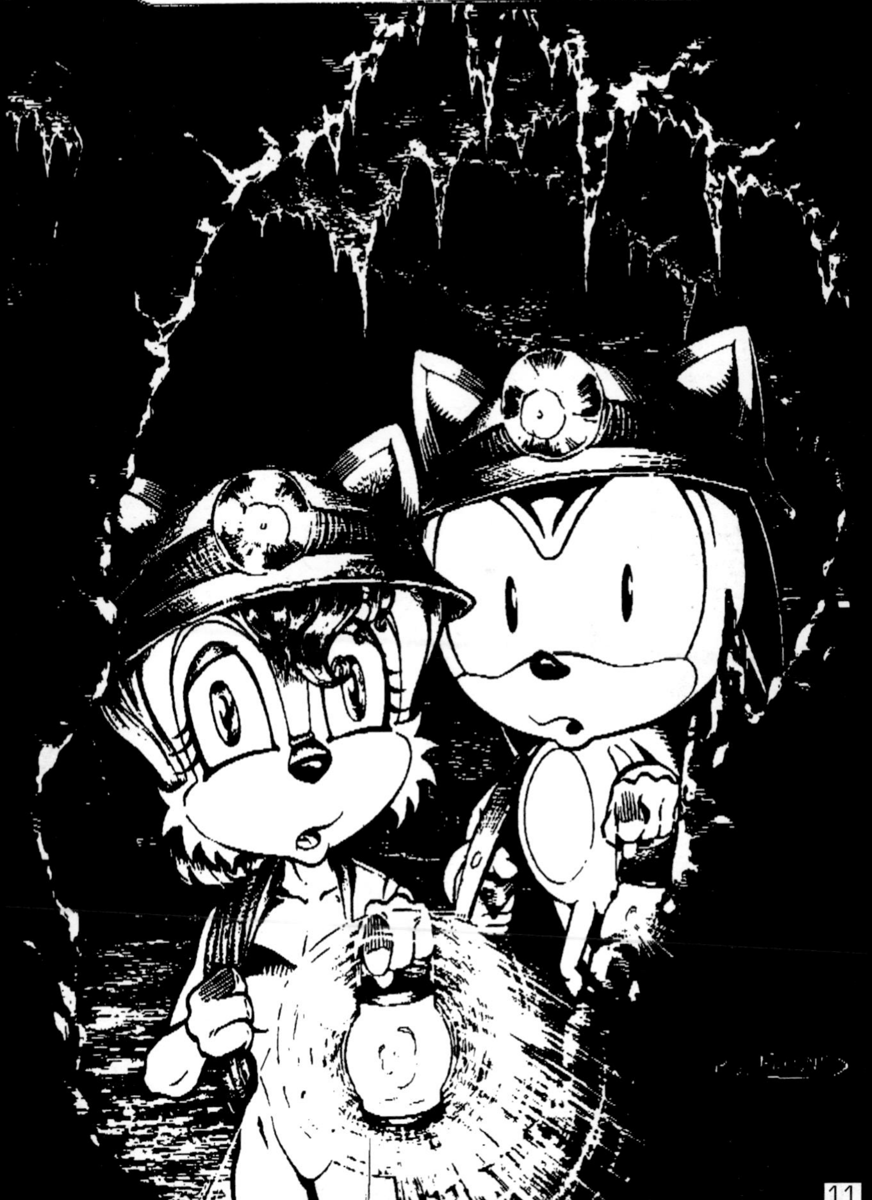

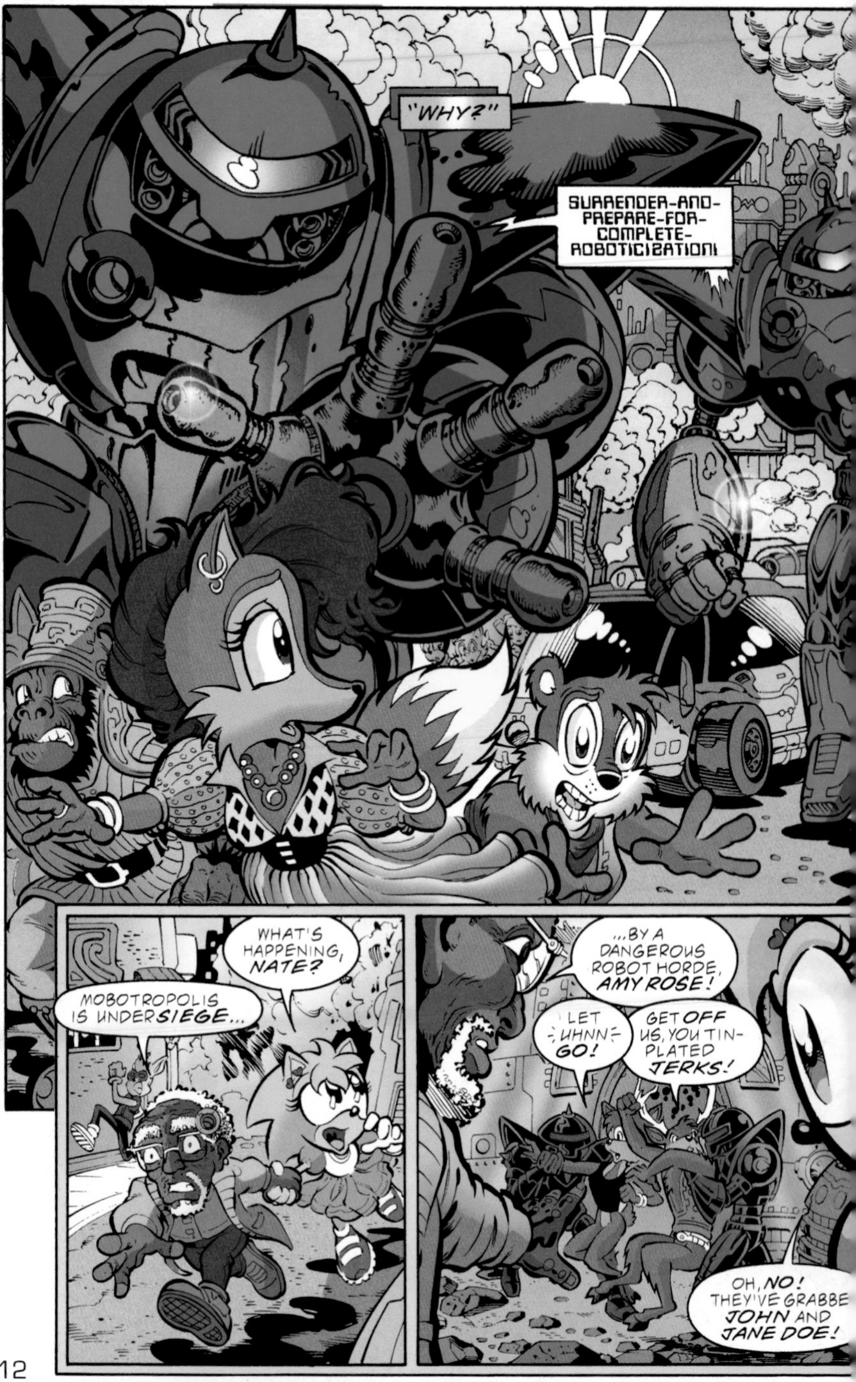
"WHY?"
SURRENDER-AND-PREPARE-FOR-COMPLETE-ROBOTICIZATION!
MOBOTROPOLIS IS UNDER SIEGE...
WHAT'S HAPPENING, NATE?
...BY A DANGEROUS ROBOT HORDE, AMY ROSE!
LET UHNN GO!
GET OFF US, YOU TIN-PLATED JERKS!
OH, NO! THEY'VE GRABBE JOHN AND JANE DOE!

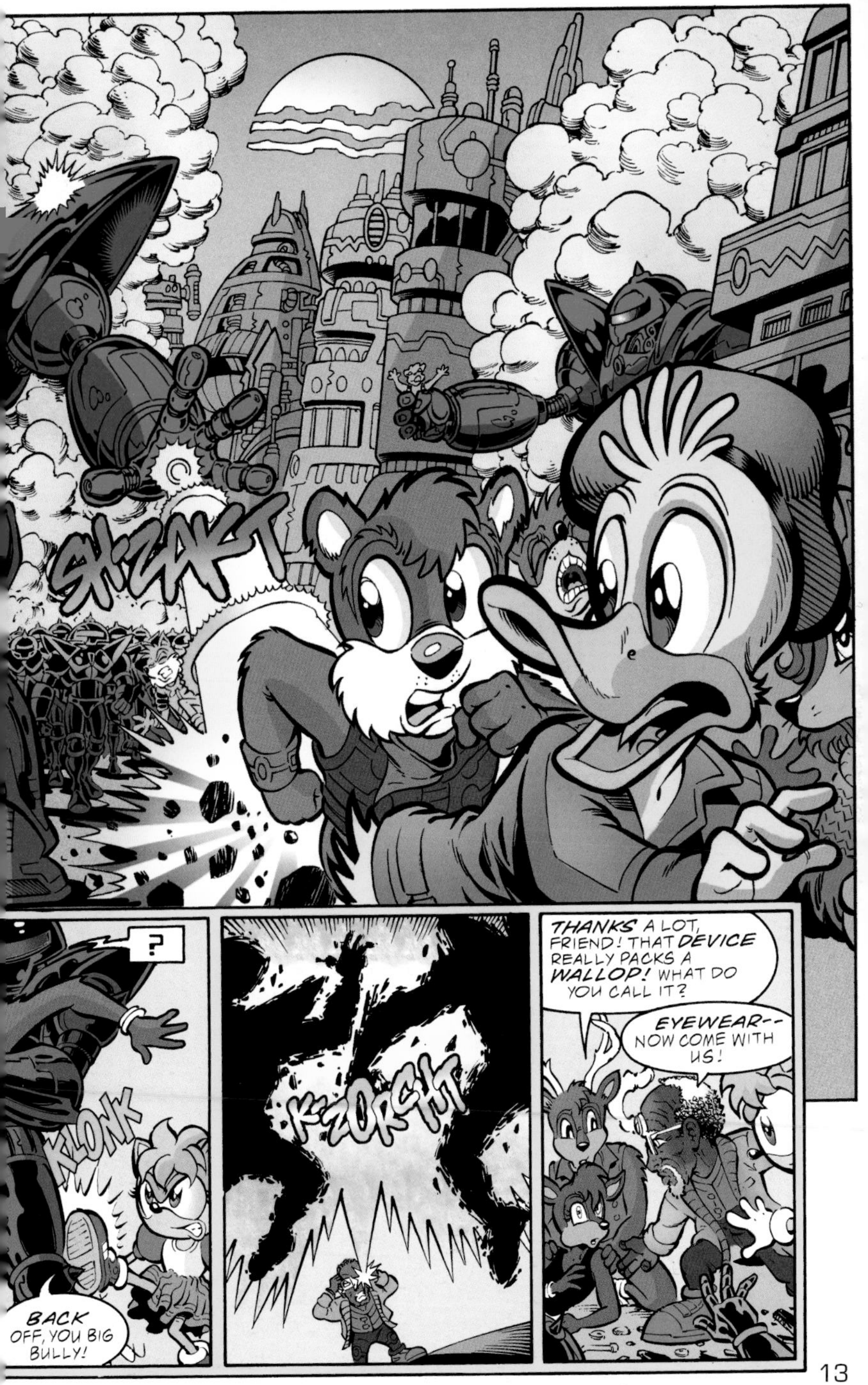
SHZAKT
?
KLONK
BACK OFF, YOU BIG BULLY!
K-ZORCHT
THANKS A LOT, FRIEND! THAT DEVICE REALLY PACKS A WALLOP! WHAT DO YOU CALL IT?
EYEWEAR-- NOW COME WITH US!

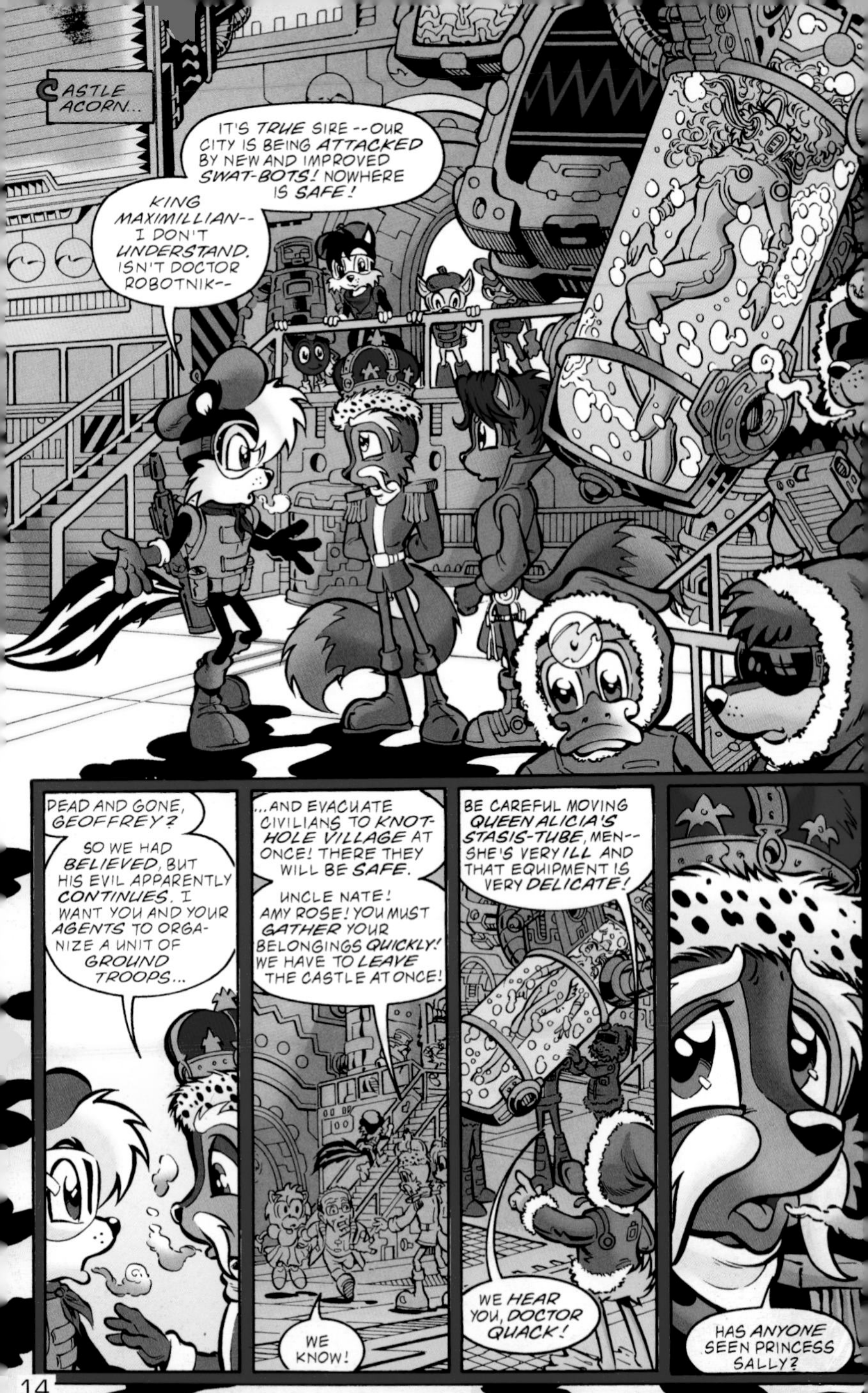
CASTLE ACORN...
IT'S TRUE SIRE --OUR CITY IS BEING ATTACKED BY NEW AND IMPROVED SWAT-BOTS! NOWHERE IS SAFE!
KING MAXIMILLIAN-- I DON'T UNDERSTAND. ISN'T DOCTOR ROBOTNIK--
DEAD AND GONE, GEOFFREY?
SO WE HAD BELIEVED, BUT HIS EVIL APPARENTLY CONTINUES. I WANT YOU AND YOUR AGENTS TO ORGANIZE A UNIT OF GROUND TROOPS...
...AND EVACUATE CIVILIANS TO KNOTHOLE VILLAGE AT ONCE! THERE THEY WILL BE SAFE.
UNCLE NATE! AMY ROSE! YOU MUST GATHER YOUR BELONGINGS QUICKLY! WE HAVE TO LEAVE THE CASTLE AT ONCE!
WE KNOW!
BE CAREFUL MOVING QUEEN ALICIA'S STASIS-TUBE, MEN-- SHE'S VERY ILL AND THAT EQUIPMENT IS VERY DELICATE!
WE HEAR YOU, DOCTOR QUACK!
HAS ANYONE SEEN PRINCESS SALLY?

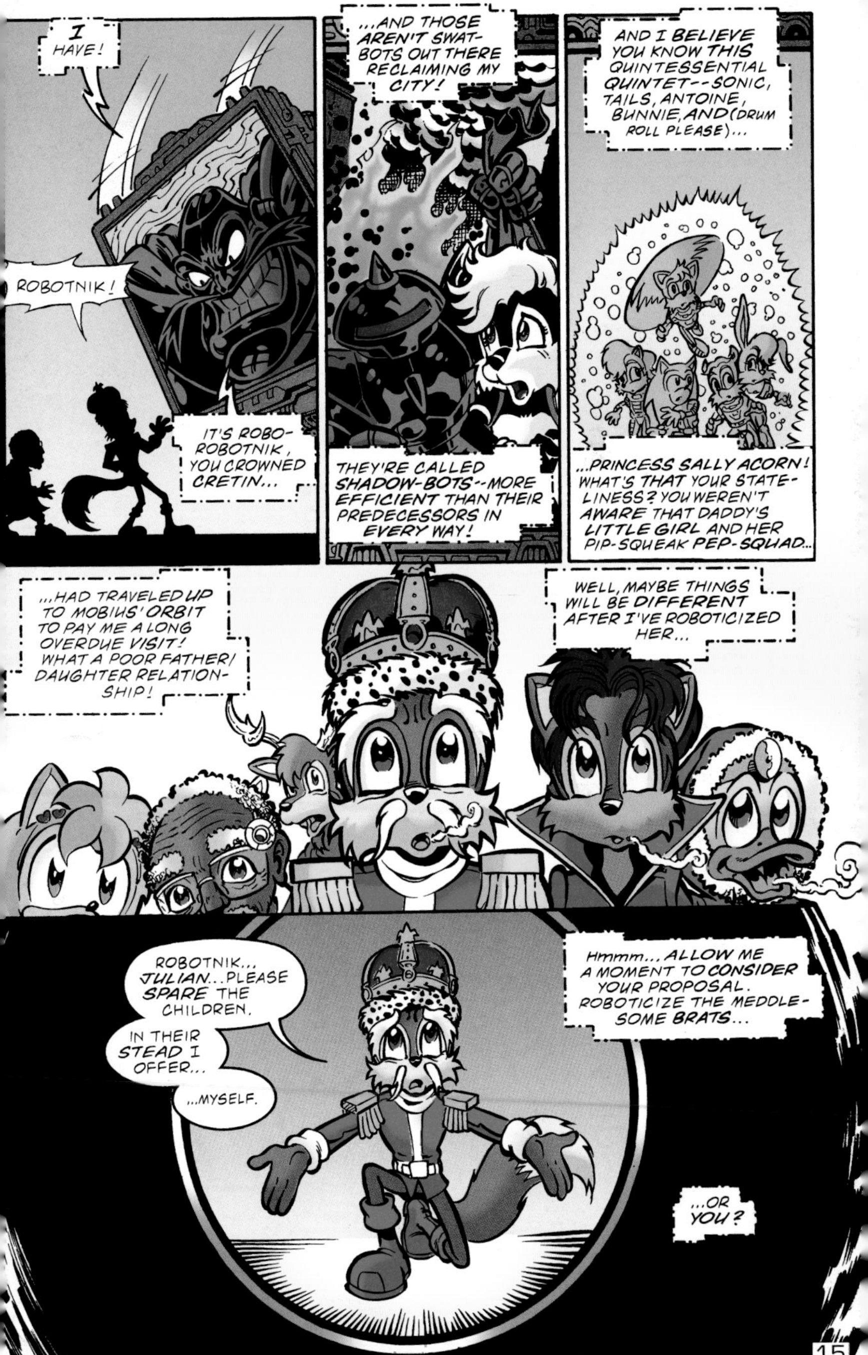

I HAVE!
ROBOTNIK!
IT'S ROBO-ROBOTNIK, YOU CROWNED CRETIN...
...AND THOSE AREN'T SWAT-BOTS OUT THERE RECLAIMING MY CITY!
THEY'RE CALLED SHADOW-BOTS--MORE EFFICIENT THAN THEIR PREDECESSORS IN EVERY WAY!
AND I BELIEVE YOU KNOW THIS QUINTESSENTIAL QUINTET--SONIC, TAILS, ANTOINE, BUNNIE, AND (DRUM ROLL PLEASE)...
...PRINCESS SALLY ACORN! WHAT'S THAT YOUR STATE-LINESS? YOU WEREN'T AWARE THAT DADDY'S LITTLE GIRL AND HER PIP-SQUEAK PEP-SQUAD...
...HAD TRAVELED UP TO MOBIUS' ORBIT TO PAY ME A LONG OVERDUE VISIT! WHAT A POOR FATHER/DAUGHTER RELATION-SHIP!
WELL, MAYBE THINGS WILL BE DIFFERENT AFTER I'VE ROBOTICIZED HER...
ROBOTNIK... JULIAN... PLEASE SPARE THE CHILDREN.
IN THEIR STEAD I OFFER...
...MYSELF.
Hmmm... ALLOW ME A MOMENT TO CONSIDER YOUR PROPOSAL. ROBOTICIZE THE MEDDLE-SOME BRATS...
...OR YOU?

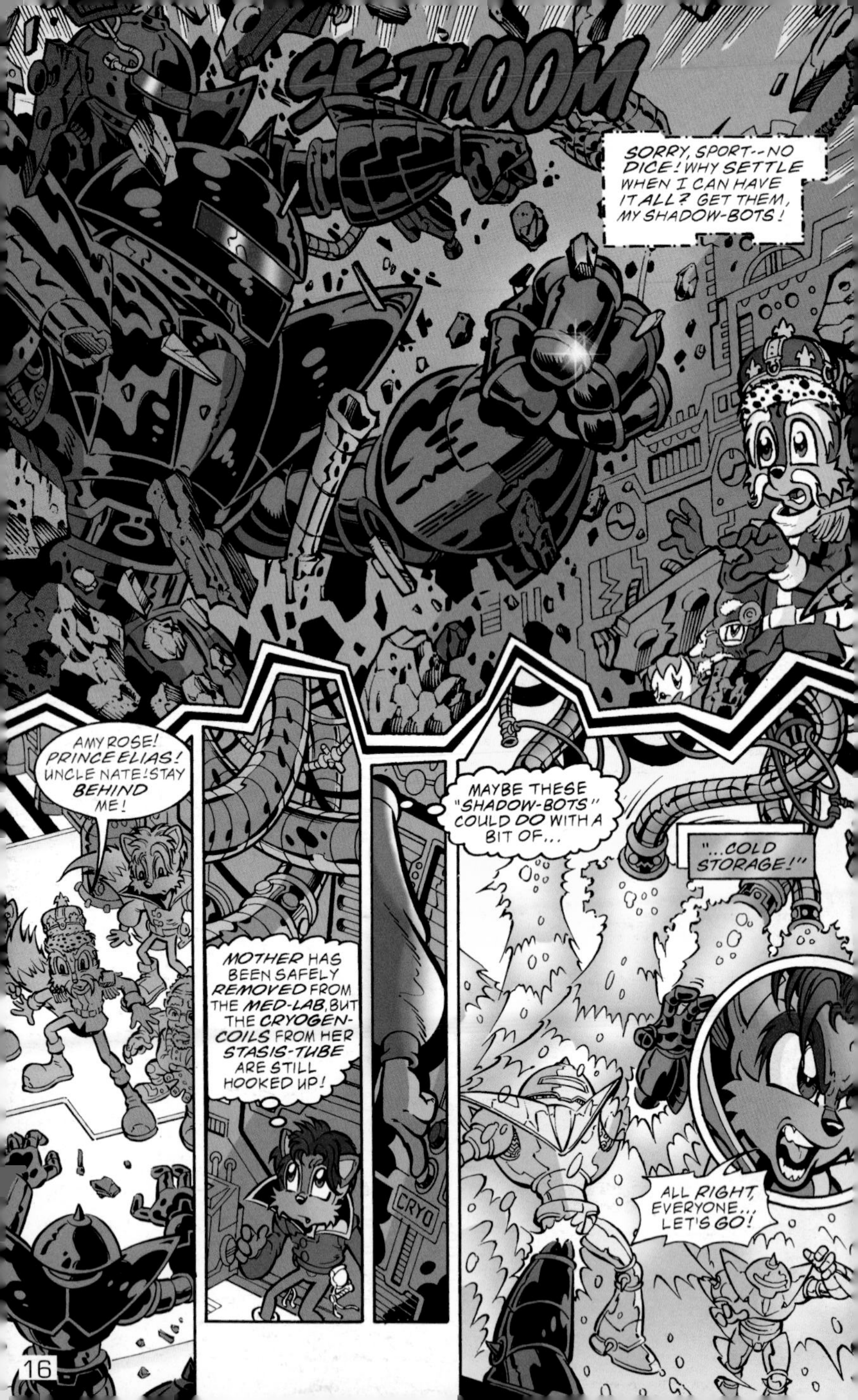
SK-THOOM
SORRY, SPORT--NO DICE! WHY SETTLE WHEN I CAN HAVE IT ALL? GET THEM, MY SHADOW-BOTS!
AMY ROSE! PRINCE ELIAS! UNCLE NATE! STAY BEHIND ME!
MOTHER HAS BEEN SAFELY REMOVED FROM THE MED-LAB, BUT THE CRYOGEN-COILS FROM HER STASIS-TUBE ARE STILL HOOKED UP!
CRYO
MAYBE THESE "SHADOW-BOTS" COULD DO WITH A BIT OF...
"...COLD STORAGE!"
ALL RIGHT, EVERYONE... LET'S GO!

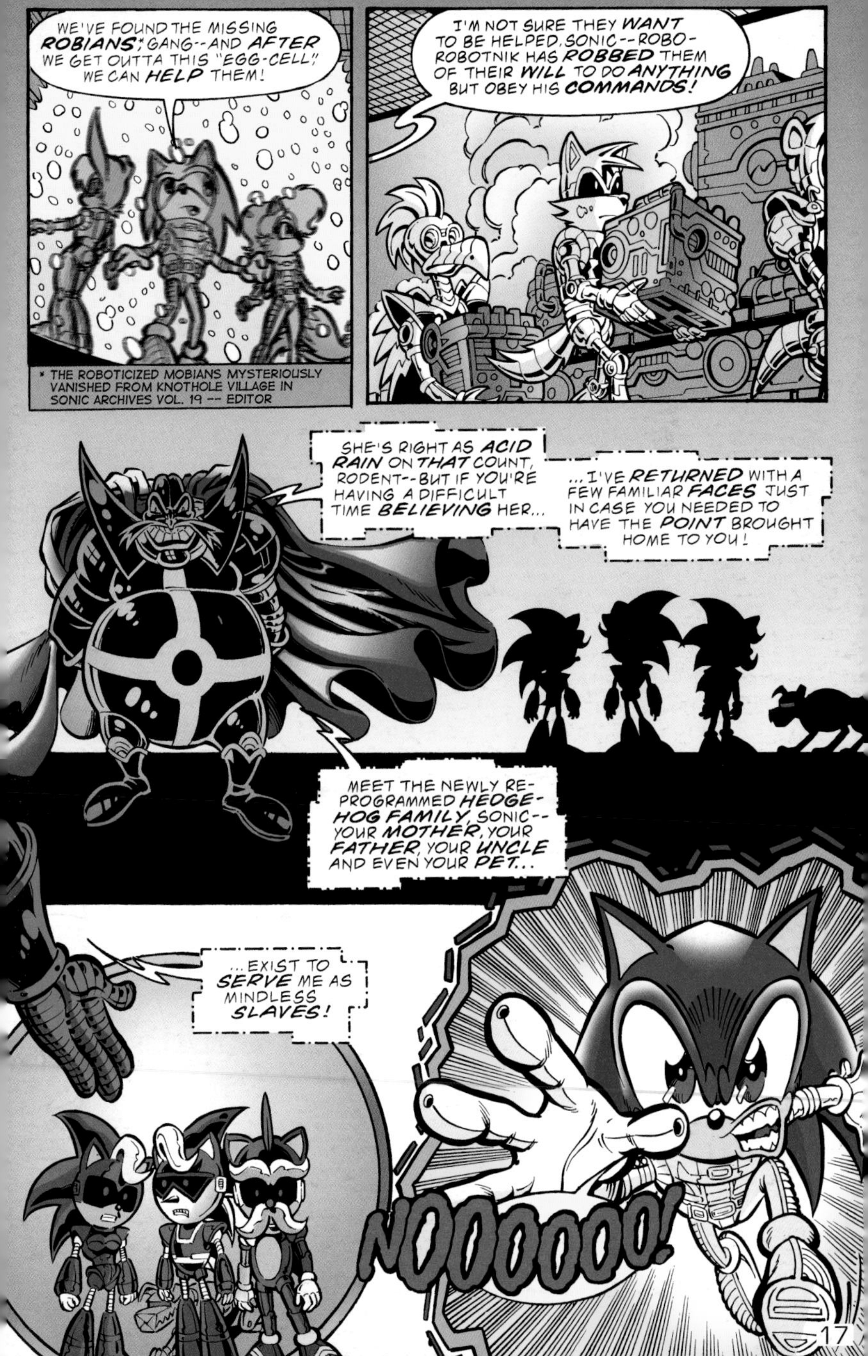
WE'VE FOUND THE MISSING ROBIANS;* GANG--AND AFTER WE GET OUTTA THIS "EGG-CELL," WE CAN HELP THEM!
* THE ROBOTICIZED MOBIANS MYSTERIOUSLY VANISHED FROM KNOTHOLE VILLAGE IN SONIC ARCHIVES VOL. 19 -- EDITOR
I'M NOT SURE THEY WANT TO BE HELPED, SONIC--ROBO-ROBOTNIK HAS ROBBED THEM OF THEIR WILL TO DO ANYTHING BUT OBEY HIS COMMANDS!
SHE'S RIGHT AS ACID RAIN ON THAT COUNT, RODENT--BUT IF YOU'RE HAVING A DIFFICULT TIME BELIEVING HER...
...I'VE RETURNED WITH A FEW FAMILIAR FACES JUST IN CASE YOU NEEDED TO HAVE THE POINT BROUGHT HOME TO YOU!
MEET THE NEWLY RE-PROGRAMMED HEDGE-HOG FAMILY, SONIC--YOUR MOTHER, YOUR FATHER, YOUR UNCLE AND EVEN YOUR PET...
...EXIST TO SERVE ME AS MINDLESS SLAVES!
NOOOOOO!

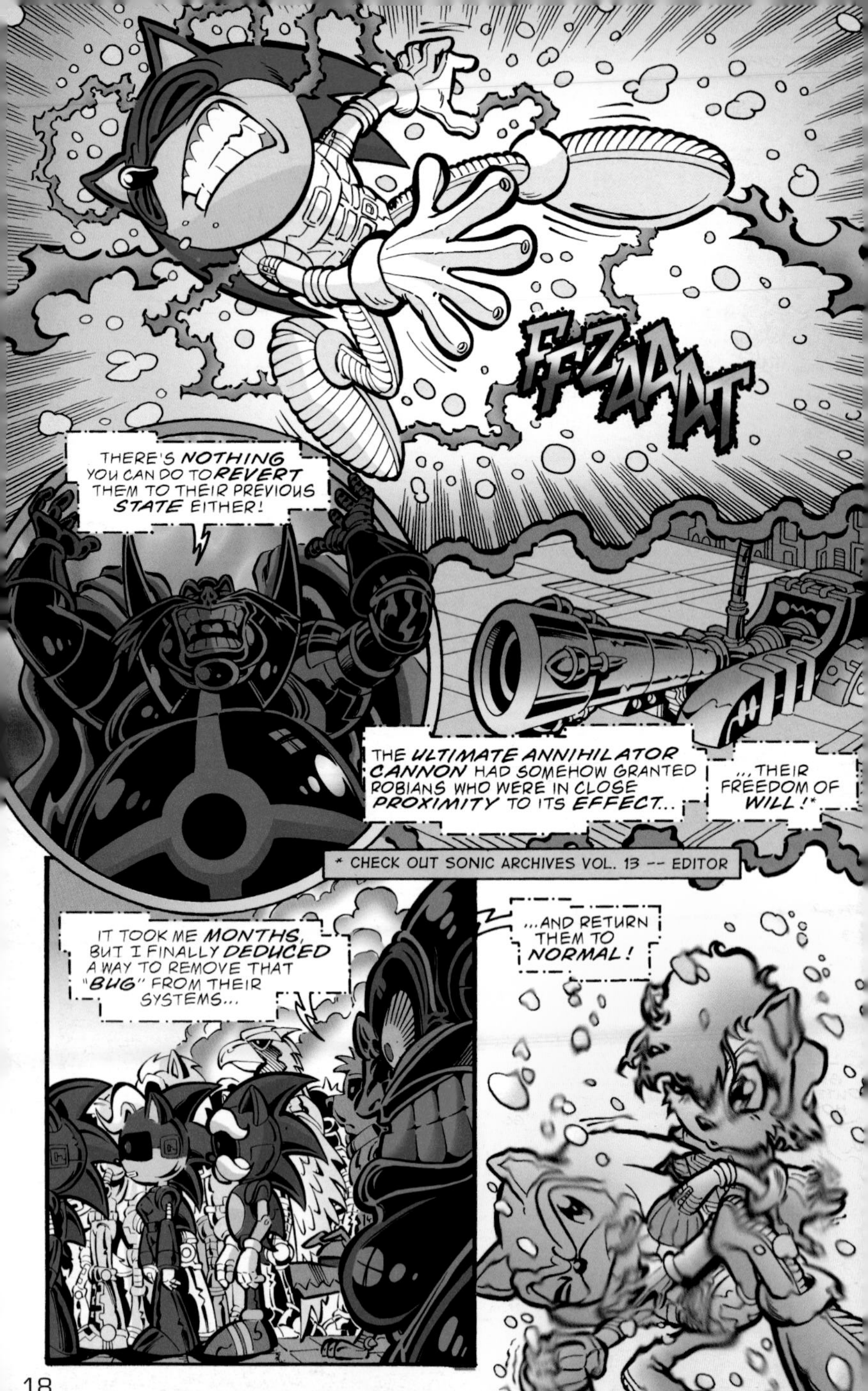
FFZAAAT
THERE'S NOTHING YOU CAN DO TO REVERT THEM TO THEIR PREVIOUS STATE EITHER!
THE ULTIMATE ANNIHILATOR CANNON HAD SOMEHOW GRANTED ROBIANS WHO WERE IN CLOSE PROXIMITY TO ITS EFFECT...
...THEIR FREEDOM OF WILL!*
* CHECK OUT SONIC ARCHIVES VOL. 13 -- EDITOR
IT TOOK ME MONTHS, BUT I FINALLY DEDUCED A WAY TO REMOVE THAT "BUG" FROM THEIR SYSTEMS...
...AND RETURN THEM TO NORMAL!

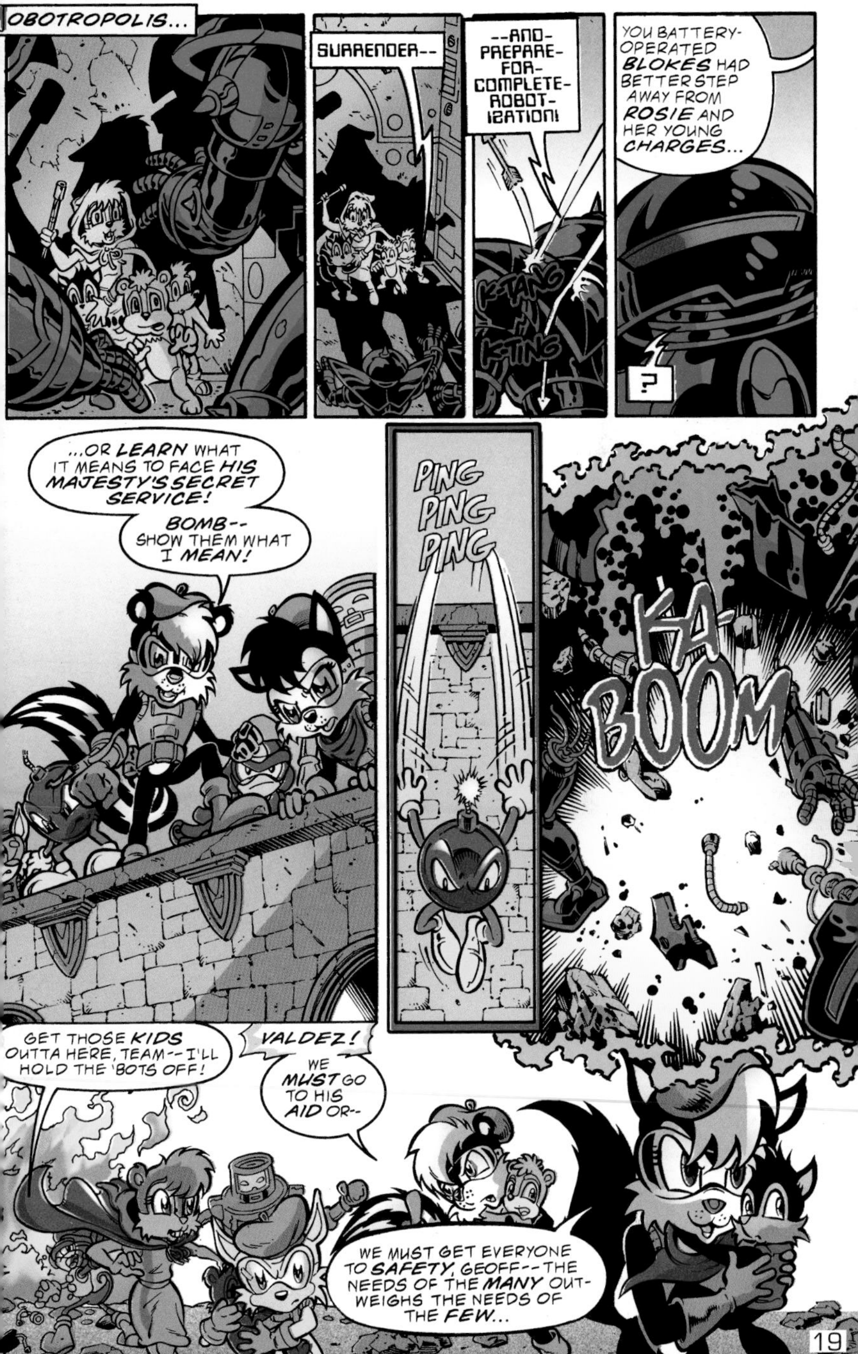
OBOTROPOLIS...
SURRENDER--
--AND-PREPARE-FOR-COMPLETE-ROBOT-IZATION!
YOU BATTERY-OPERATED BLOKES HAD BETTER STEP AWAY FROM ROSIE AND HER YOUNG CHARGES...
K-TANG
K-TING
?
...OR LEARN WHAT IT MEANS TO FACE HIS MAJESTY'S SECRET SERVICE!
BOMB-- SHOW THEM WHAT I MEAN!
PING PING PING
KA-BOOM
GET THOSE KIDS OUTTA HERE, TEAM--I'LL HOLD THE 'BOTS OFF!
VALDEZ!
WE MUST GO TO HIS AID OR--
WE MUST GET EVERYONE TO SAFETY, GEOFF--THE NEEDS OF THE MANY OUTWEIGHS THE NEEDS OF THE FEW...

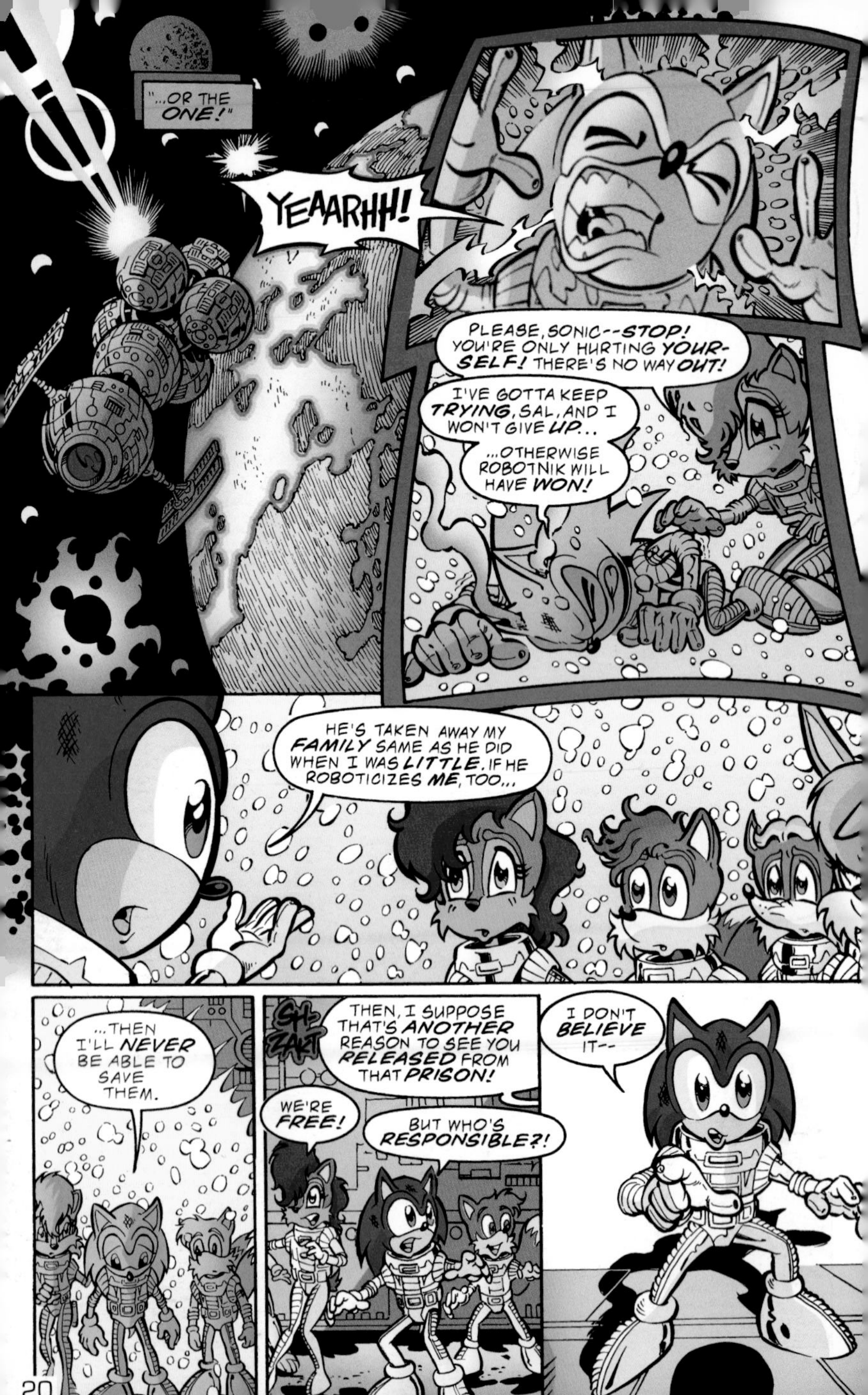
"...OR THE ONE!"
YEAARHH!
PLEASE, SONIC--STOP! YOU'RE ONLY HURTING YOURSELF! THERE'S NO WAY OUT!
I'VE GOTTA KEEP TRYING, SAL, AND I WON'T GIVE UP...
...OTHERWISE ROBOTNIK WILL HAVE WON!
HE'S TAKEN AWAY MY FAMILY SAME AS HE DID WHEN I WAS LITTLE. IF HE ROBOTICIZES ME, TOO...
...THEN I'LL NEVER BE ABLE TO SAVE THEM.
SH-ZAKT
THEN, I SUPPOSE THAT'S ANOTHER REASON TO SEE YOU RELEASED FROM THAT PRISON!
WE'RE FREE!
BUT WHO'S RESPONSIBLE?!
I DON'T BELIEVE IT--

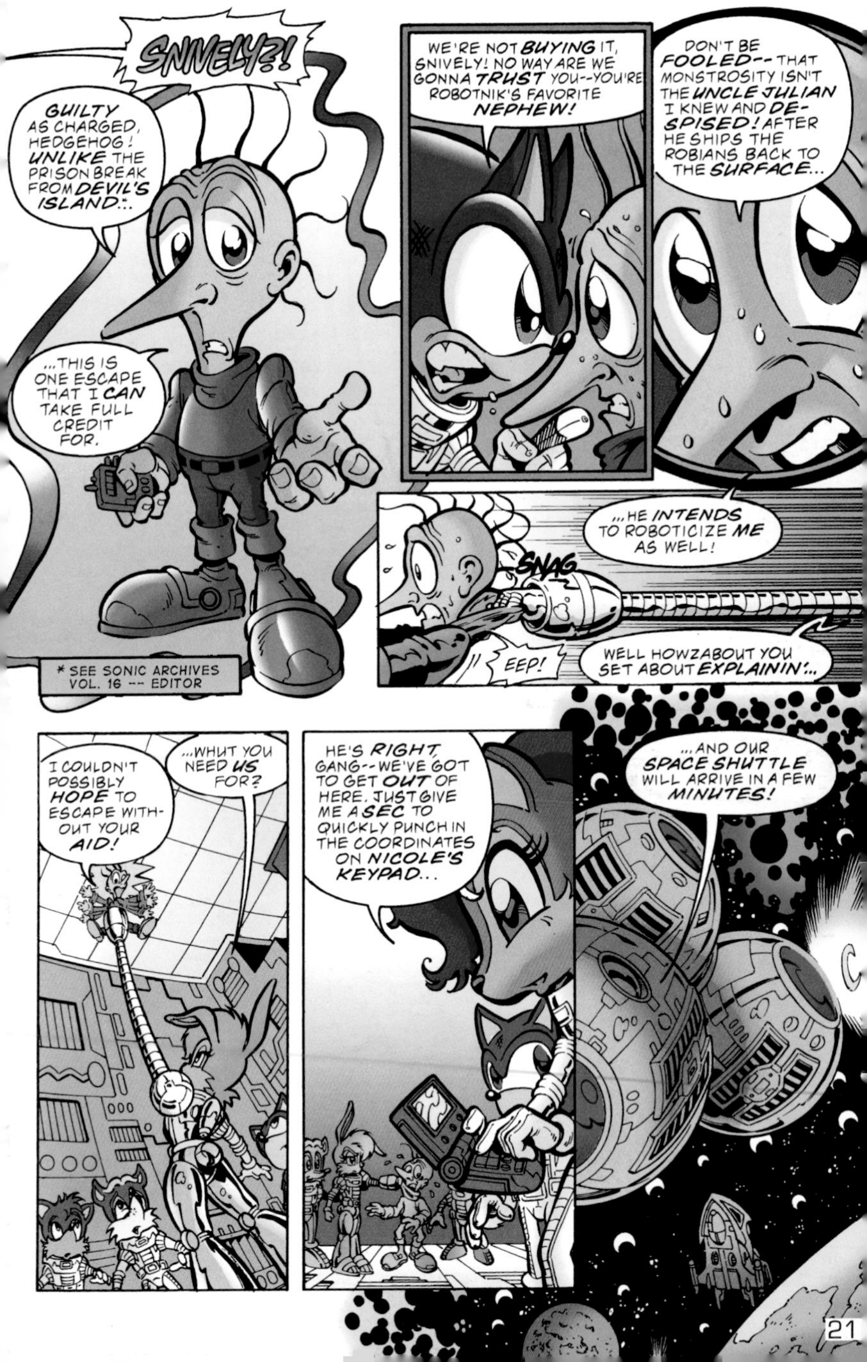
SNIVELY?!
GUILTY AS CHARGED, HEDGEHOG! UNLIKE THE PRISON BREAK FROM DEVIL'S ISLAND*...
...THIS IS ONE ESCAPE THAT I CAN TAKE FULL CREDIT FOR.
* SEE SONIC ARCHIVES VOL. 16 -- EDITOR
WE'RE NOT BUYING IT, SNIVELY! NO WAY ARE WE GONNA TRUST YOU--YOU'RE ROBOTNIK'S FAVORITE NEPHEW!
DON'T BE FOOLED--THAT MONSTROSITY ISN'T THE UNCLE JULIAN I KNEW AND DESPISED! AFTER HE SHIPS THE ROBIANS BACK TO THE SURFACE...
...HE INTENDS TO ROBOTICIZE ME AS WELL!
SNAG
EEP!
WELL HOWZABOUT YOU SET ABOUT EXPLAININ'...
...WHUT YOU NEED US FOR?
I COULDN'T POSSIBLY HOPE TO ESCAPE WITHOUT YOUR AID!
HE'S RIGHT, GANG--WE'VE GOT TO GET OUT OF HERE. JUST GIVE ME A SEC TO QUICKLY PUNCH IN THE COORDINATES ON NICOLE'S KEYPAD...
...AND OUR SPACE SHUTTLE WILL ARRIVE IN A FEW MINUTES!

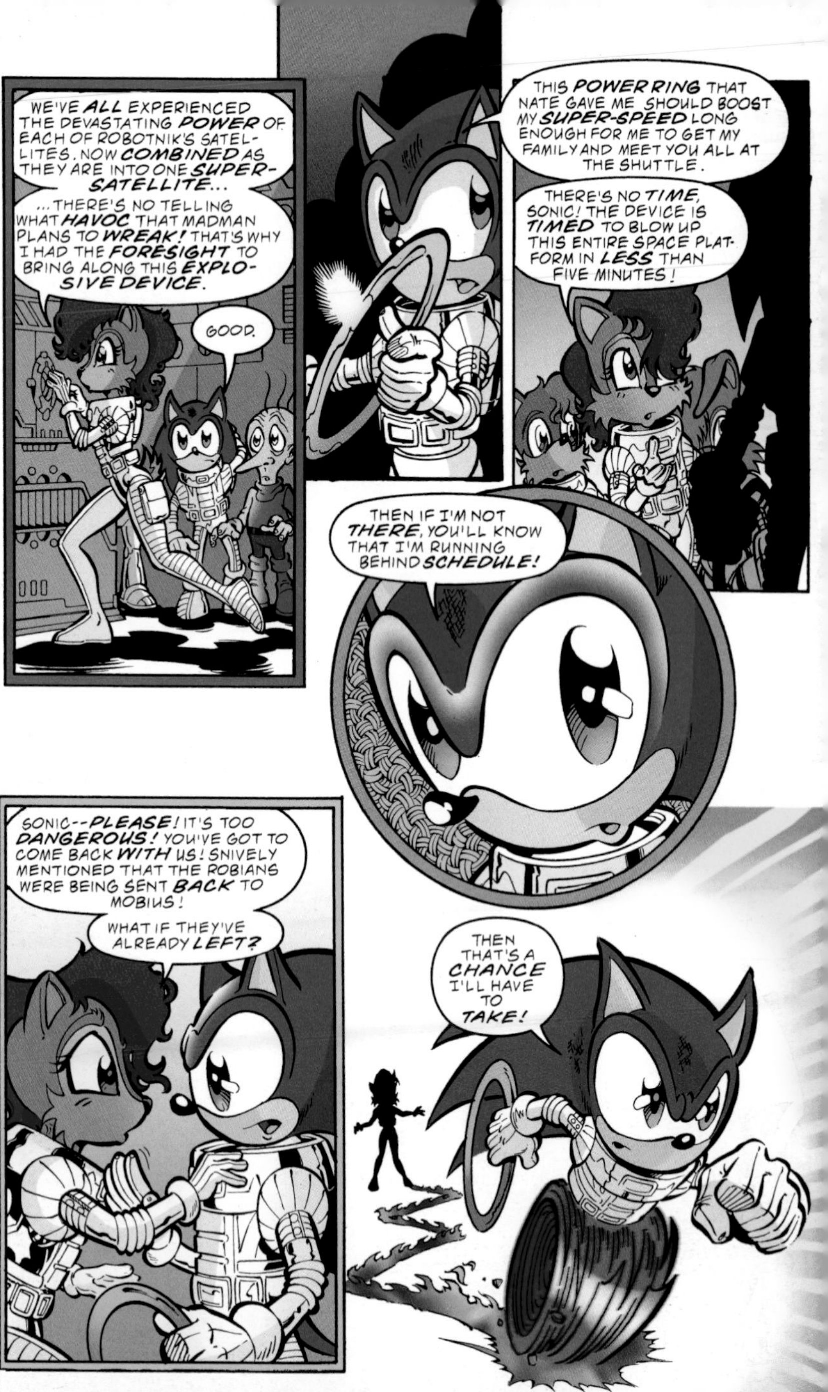
WE'VE ALL EXPERIENCED THE DEVASTATING POWER OF EACH OF ROBOTNIK'S SATEL-LITES. NOW COMBINED AS THEY ARE INTO ONE SUPER-SATELLITE...
...THERE'S NO TELLING WHAT HAVOC THAT MADMAN PLANS TO WREAK! THAT'S WHY I HAD THE FORESIGHT TO BRING ALONG THIS EXPLO-SIVE DEVICE.
GOOD.
THIS POWER RING THAT NATE GAVE ME SHOULD BOOST MY SUPER-SPEED LONG ENOUGH FOR ME TO GET MY FAMILY AND MEET YOU ALL AT THE SHUTTLE.
THERE'S NO TIME, SONIC! THE DEVICE IS TIMED TO BLOW UP THIS ENTIRE SPACE PLAT-FORM IN LESS THAN FIVE MINUTES!
THEN IF I'M NOT THERE, YOU'LL KNOW THAT I'M RUNNING BEHIND SCHEDULE!
SONIC--PLEASE! IT'S TOO DANGEROUS! YOU'VE GOT TO COME BACK WITH US! SNIVELY MENTIONED THAT THE ROBIANS WERE BEING SENT BACK TO MOBIUS!
WHAT IF THEY'VE ALREADY LEFT?
THEN THAT'S A CHANCE I'LL HAVE TO TAKE!

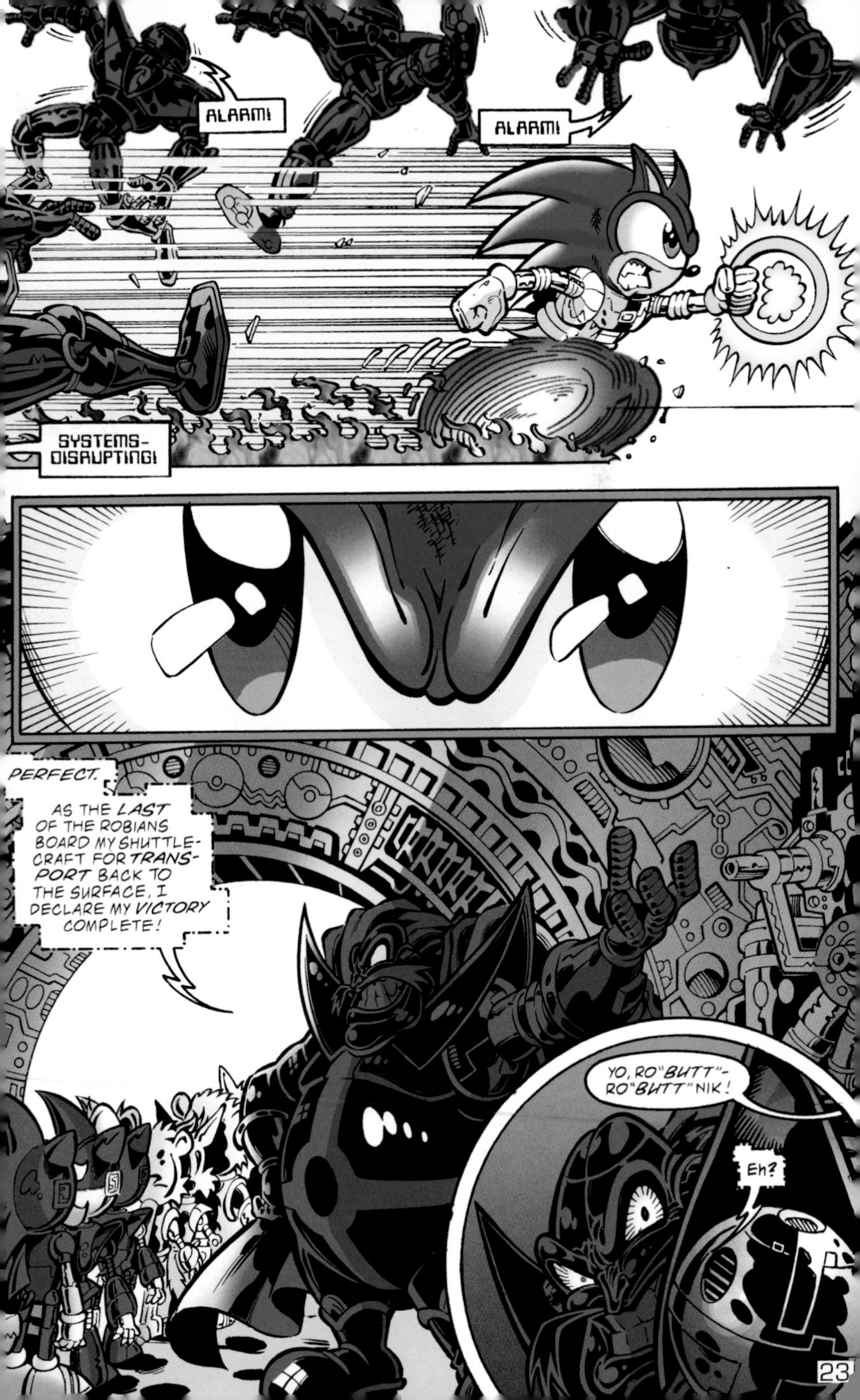
ALARM!
ALARM!
SYSTEMS-DISRUPTING!
PERFECT.
AS THE LAST OF THE ROBIANS BOARD MY SHUTTLE-CRAFT FOR TRANS-PORT BACK TO THE SURFACE, I DECLARE MY VICTORY COMPLETE!
YO, RO"BUTT"-RO"BUTT"NIK!
Eh?

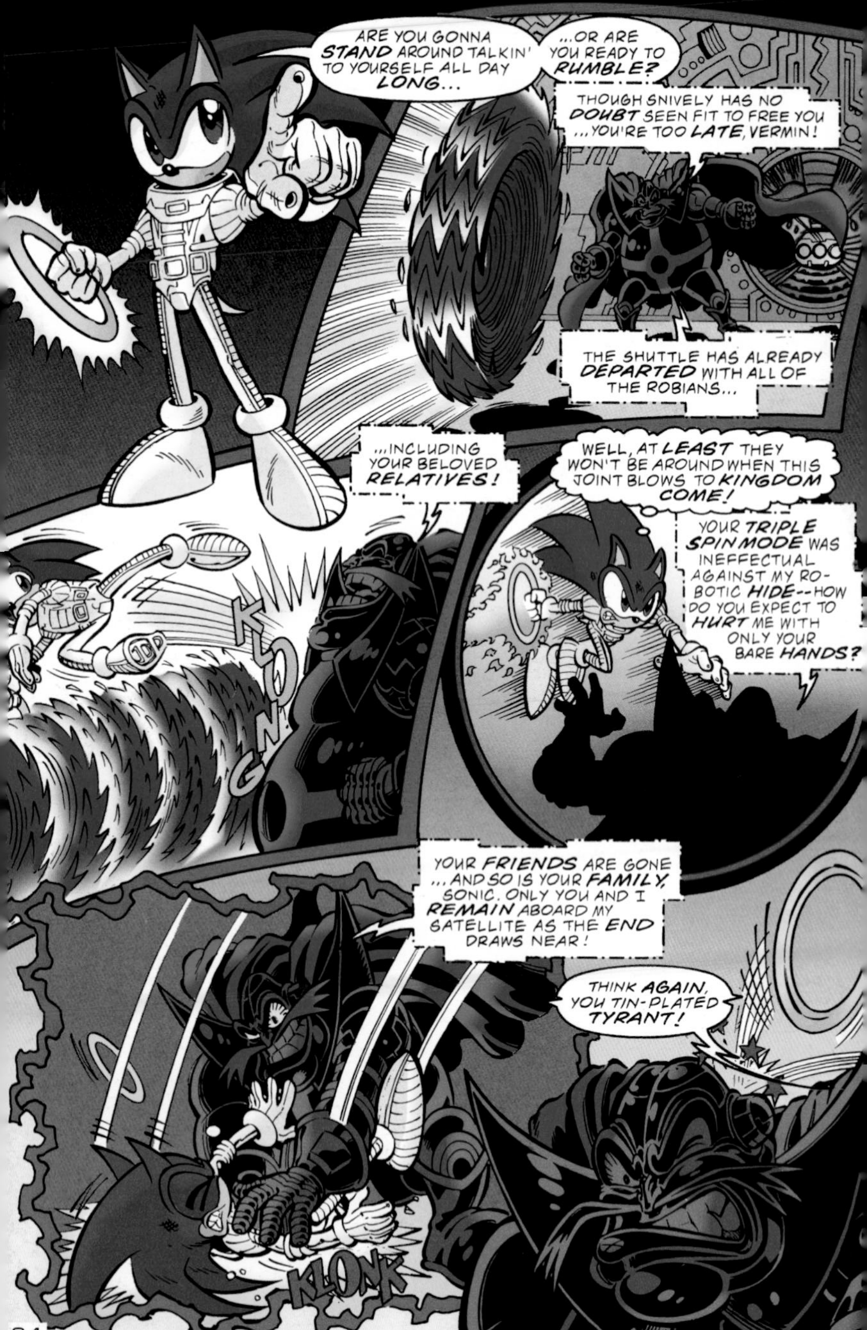
ARE YOU GONNA STAND AROUND TALKIN' TO YOURSELF ALL DAY LONG...
...OR ARE YOU READY TO RUMBLE?
THOUGH SNIVELY HAS NO DOUBT SEEN FIT TO FREE YOU ...YOU'RE TOO LATE, VERMIN!
THE SHUTTLE HAS ALREADY DEPARTED WITH ALL OF THE ROBIANS...
...INCLUDING YOUR BELOVED RELATIVES!
WELL, AT LEAST THEY WON'T BE AROUND WHEN THIS JOINT BLOWS TO KINGDOM COME!
YOUR TRIPLE SPIN MODE WAS INEFFECTUAL AGAINST MY RO-BOTIC HIDE--HOW DO YOU EXPECT TO HURT ME WITH ONLY YOUR BARE HANDS?
KLONNNG
YOUR FRIENDS ARE GONE ...AND SO IS YOUR FAMILY, SONIC. ONLY YOU AND I REMAIN ABOARD MY SATELLITE AS THE END DRAWS NEAR!
THINK AGAIN, YOU TIN-PLATED TYRANT!
KLONK

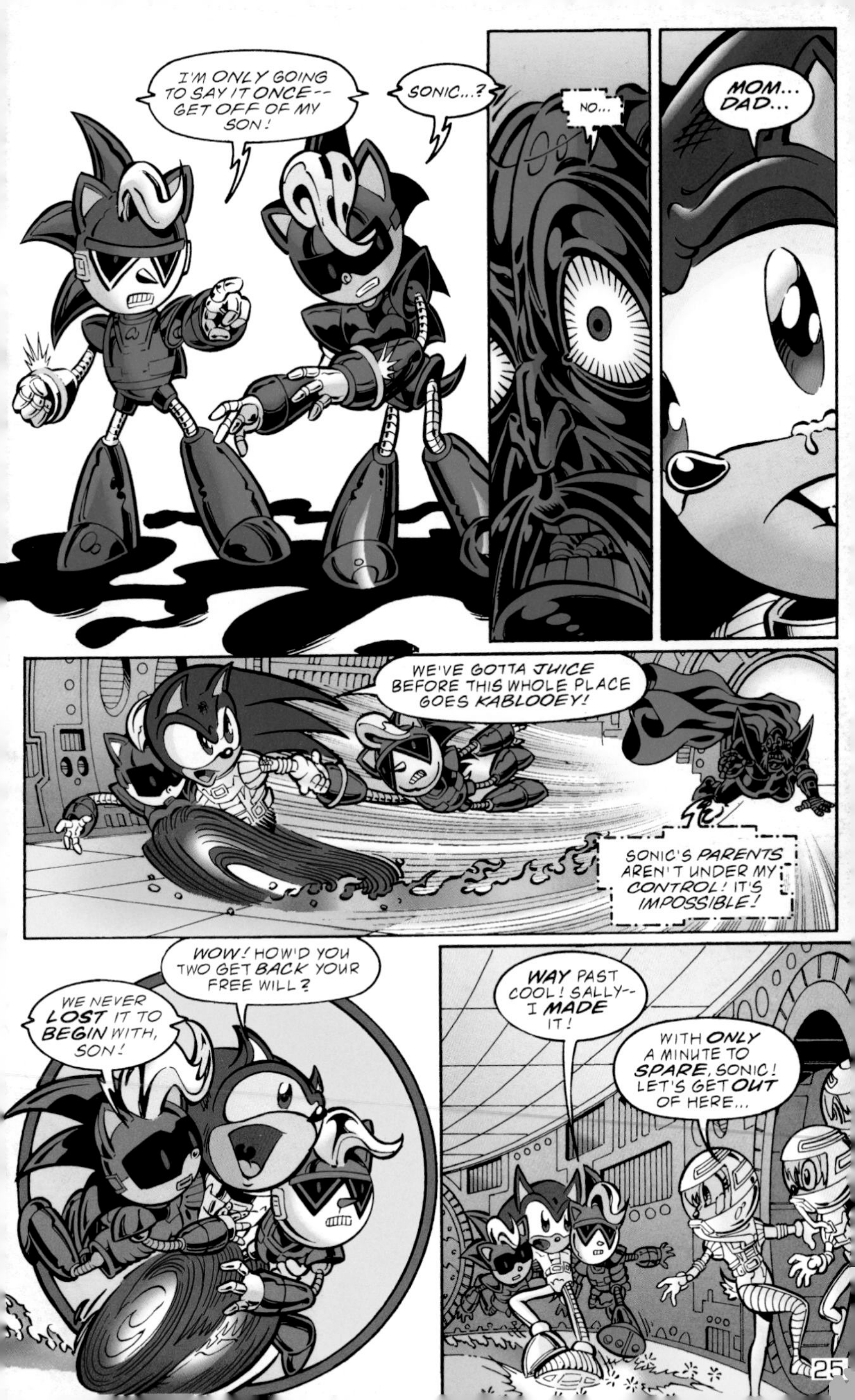
I'M ONLY GOING TO SAY IT ONCE-- GET OFF OF MY SON!
SONIC...?
NO...
MOM... DAD...
WE'VE GOTTA JUICE BEFORE THIS WHOLE PLACE GOES KABLOOEY!
SONIC'S PARENTS AREN'T UNDER MY CONTROL! IT'S IMPOSSIBLE!
WOW! HOW'D YOU TWO GET BACK YOUR FREE WILL?
WE NEVER LOST IT TO BEGIN WITH, SON!
WAY PAST COOL! SALLY-- I MADE IT!
WITH ONLY A MINUTE TO SPARE, SONIC! LET'S GET OUT OF HERE...

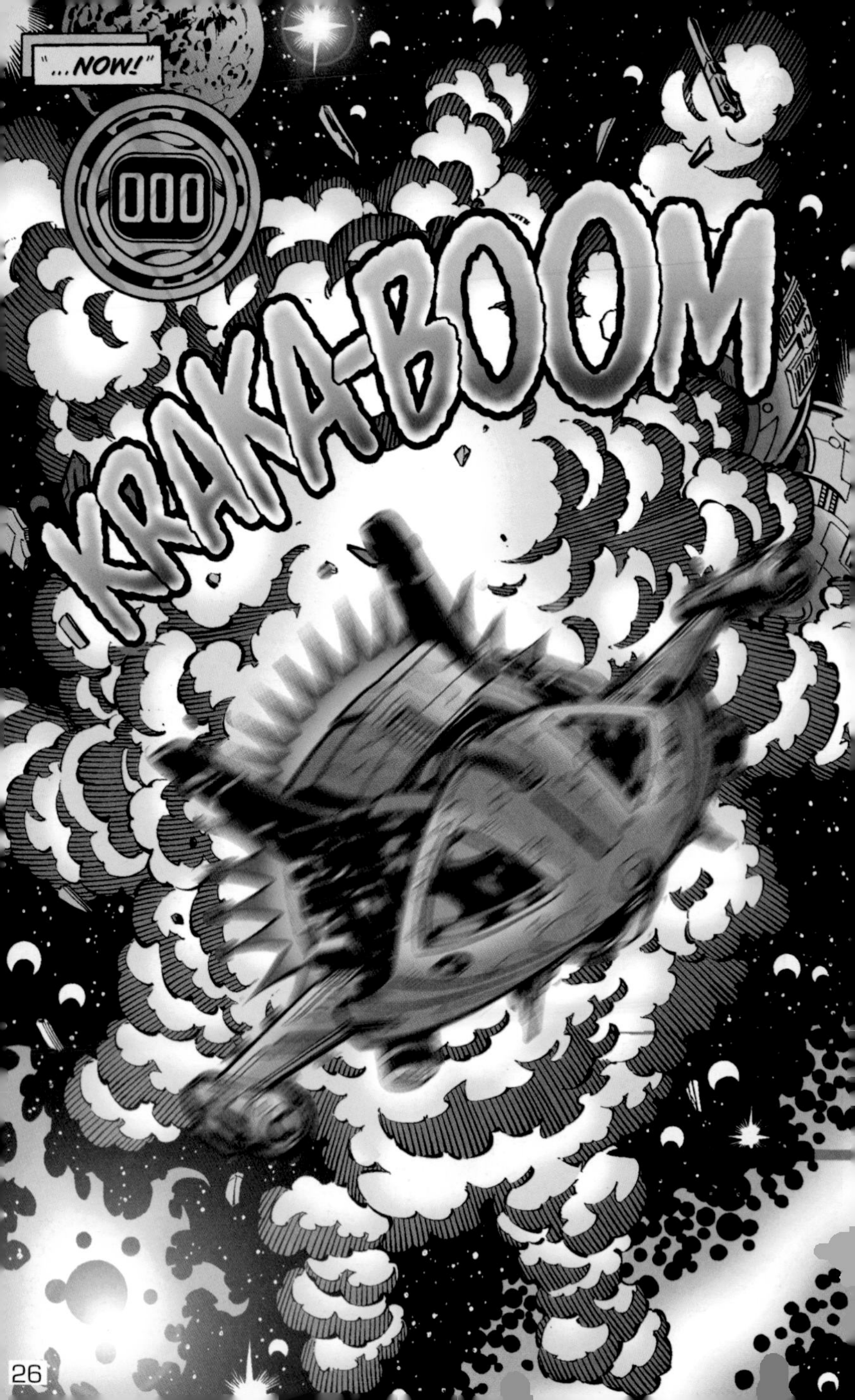
"...NOW!"
000
KRAKA-BOOM

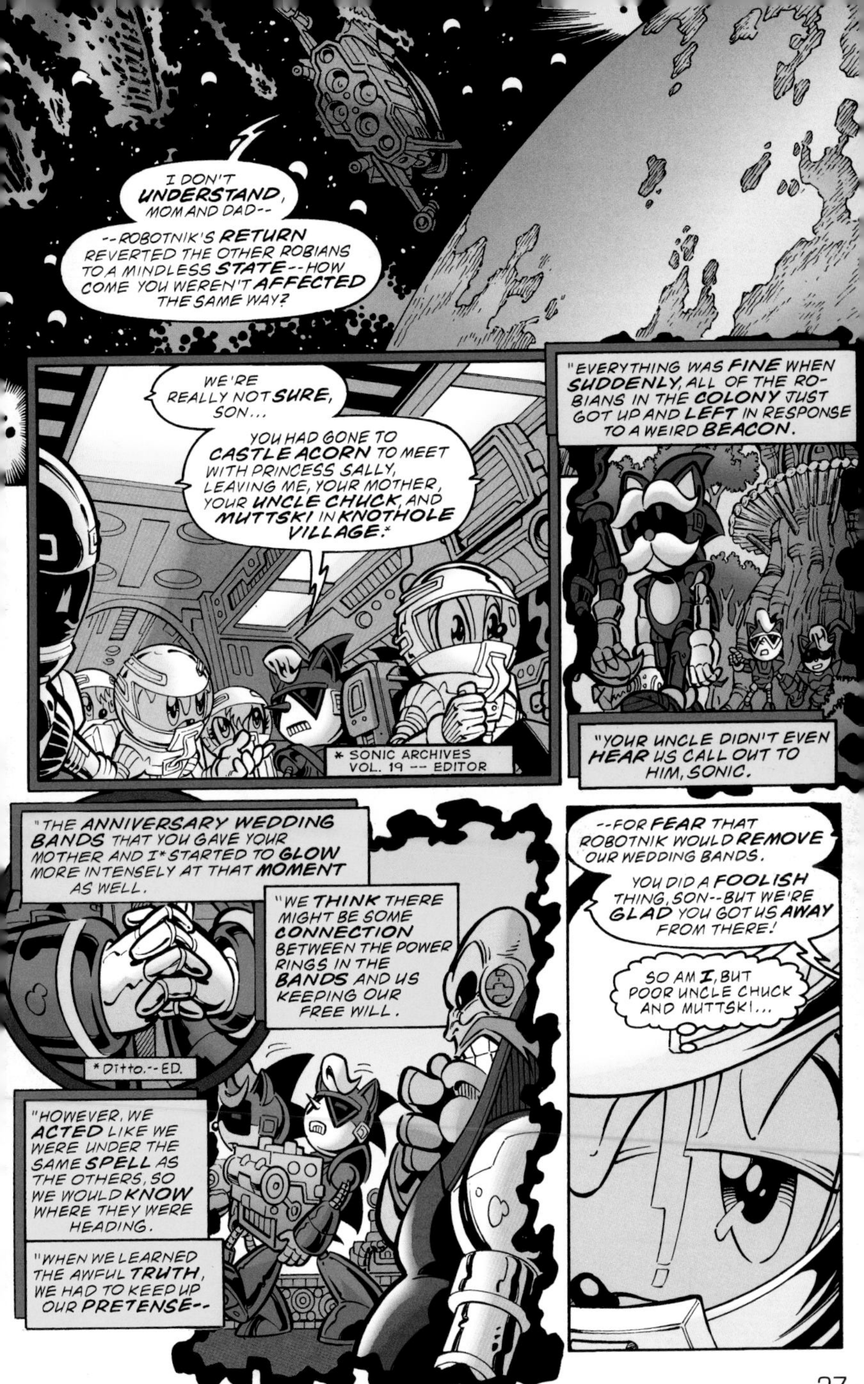
I DON'T UNDERSTAND, MOM AND DAD--
--ROBOTNIK'S RETURN REVERTED THE OTHER ROBIANS TO A MINDLESS STATE--HOW COME YOU WEREN'T AFFECTED THE SAME WAY?
WE'RE REALLY NOT SURE, SON...
YOU HAD GONE TO CASTLE ACORN TO MEET WITH PRINCESS SALLY, LEAVING ME, YOUR MOTHER, YOUR UNCLE CHUCK, AND MUTTSKI IN KNOTHOLE VILLAGE.*
* SONIC ARCHIVES VOL. 19 -- EDITOR
"EVERYTHING WAS FINE WHEN SUDDENLY, ALL OF THE ROBIANS IN THE COLONY JUST GOT UP AND LEFT IN RESPONSE TO A WEIRD BEACON.
"YOUR UNCLE DIDN'T EVEN HEAR US CALL OUT TO HIM, SONIC.
"THE ANNIVERSARY WEDDING BANDS THAT YOU GAVE YOUR MOTHER AND I* STARTED TO GLOW MORE INTENSELY AT THAT MOMENT AS WELL.
"WE THINK THERE MIGHT BE SOME CONNECTION BETWEEN THE POWER RINGS IN THE BANDS AND US KEEPING OUR FREE WILL.
*Ditto.--ED.
"HOWEVER, WE ACTED LIKE WE WERE UNDER THE SAME SPELL AS THE OTHERS, SO WE WOULD KNOW WHERE THEY WERE HEADING.
"WHEN WE LEARNED THE AWFUL TRUTH, WE HAD TO KEEP UP OUR PRETENSE--
--FOR FEAR THAT ROBOTNIK WOULD REMOVE OUR WEDDING BANDS.
YOU DID A FOOLISH THING, SON--BUT WE'RE GLAD YOU GOT US AWAY FROM THERE!
SO AM I, BUT POOR UNCLE CHUCK AND MUTTSKI...

'T IS *DUSK* IN THE NEWLY RE-CHRISTENED *ROBOTROPOLIS.*

AND, IN A SECRET *SUB-BASEMENT* LOCATED ONE HALF *MILE* BENEATH THE *NOW-ABANDONED CORRIDORS* OF *CASTLE ACORN*--

--AN ASSORTMENT OF *ROBOTIC BODIES* LIE DORMANT--

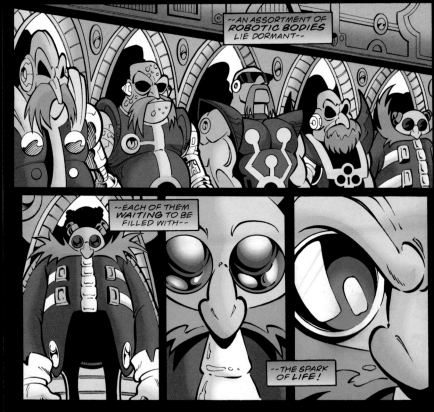

--EACH OF THEM WAITING TO BE FILLED WITH--

--THE SPARK OF LIFE!

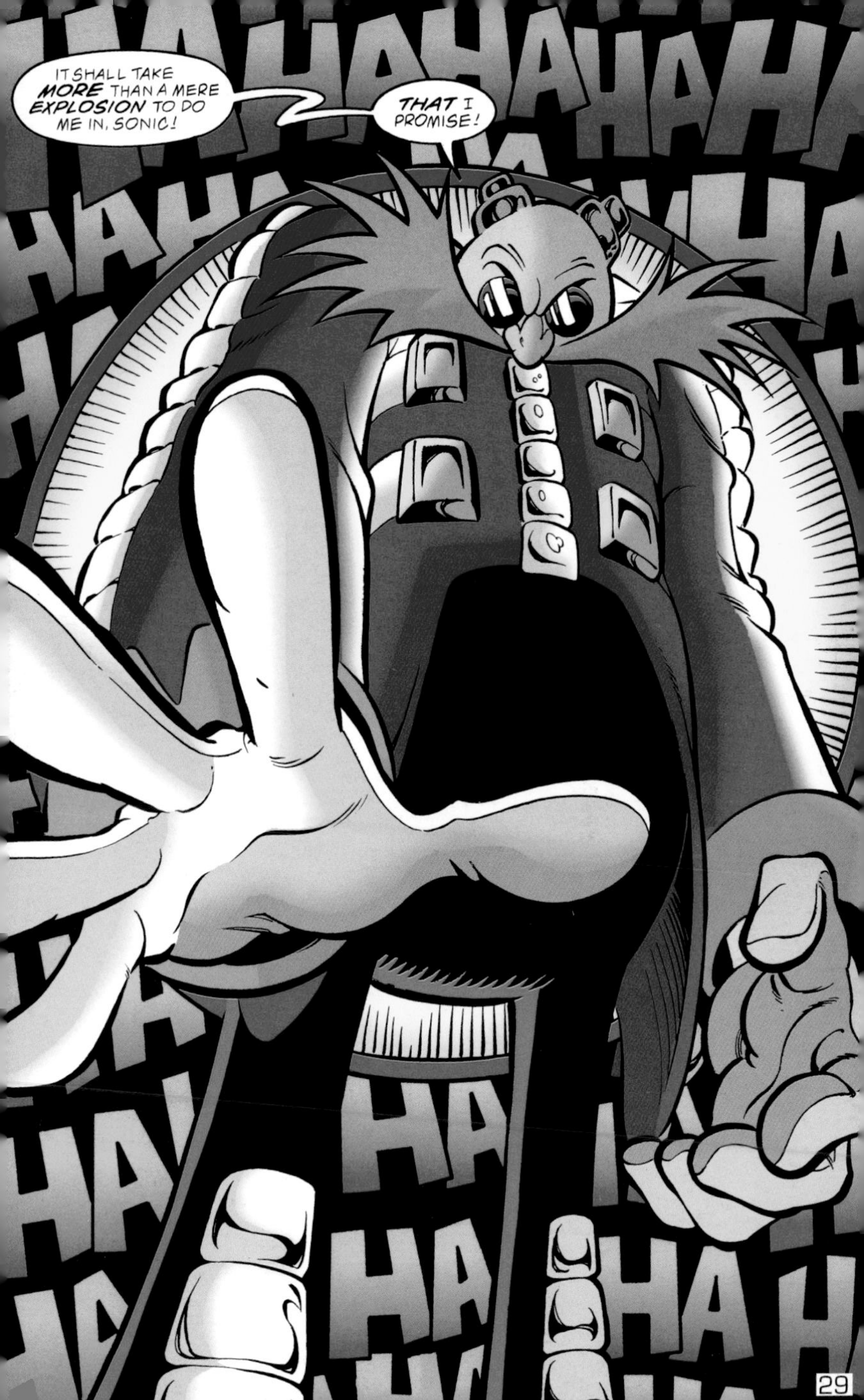
IT SHALL TAKE MORE THAN A MERE EXPLOSION TO DO ME IN, SONIC!
THAT I PROMISE!
HAHAHAHAHAHA

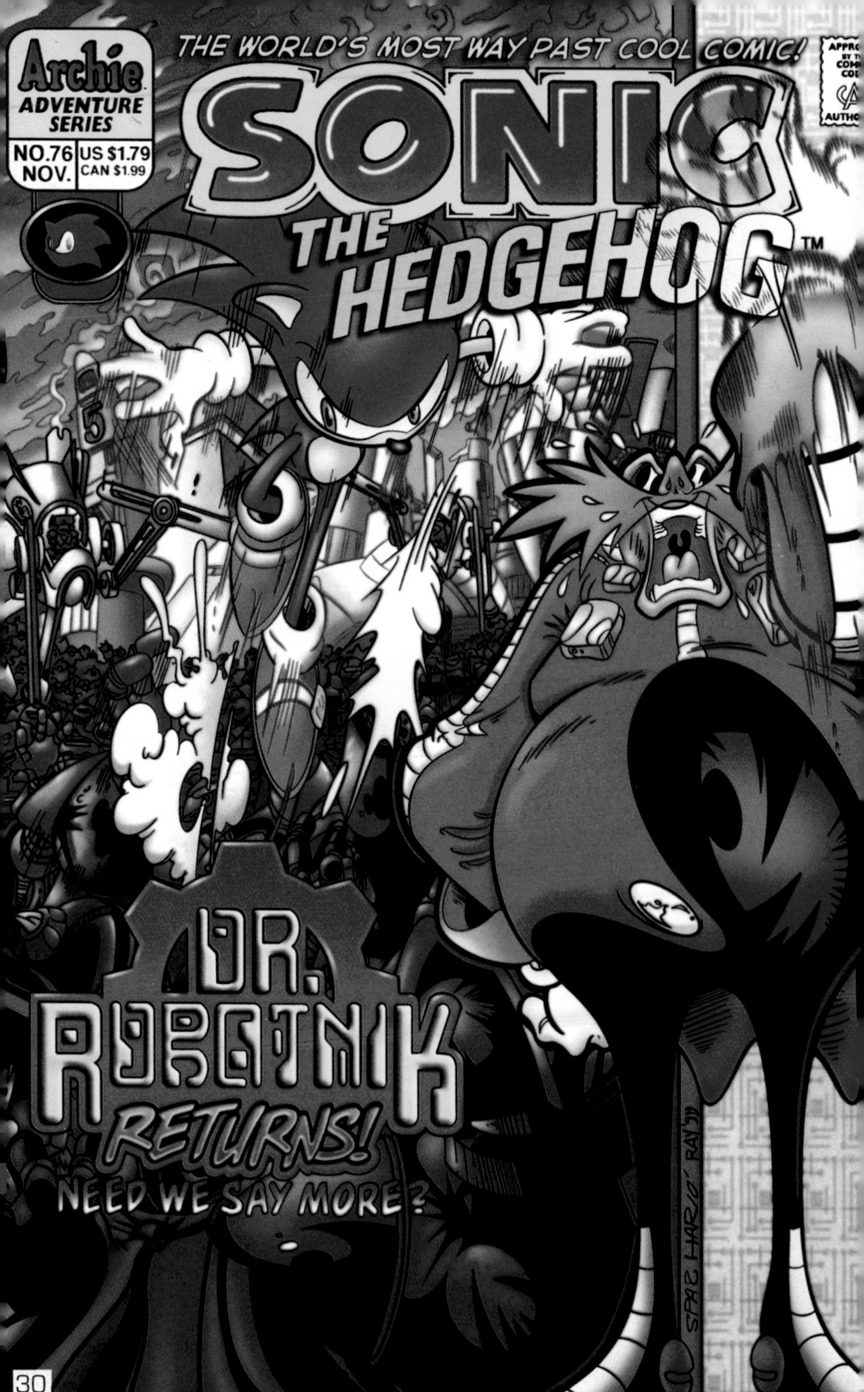

Archie
ADVENTURE SERIES
NO.76 NOV.
US $1.79
CAN $1.99
THE WORLD'S MOST WAY PAST COOL COMIC!
SONIC THE HEDGEHOG™
DR. ROBOTNIK RETURNS!
NEED WE SAY MORE?

After ten long years, the iron-fisted rule of DOCTOR ROBOTNIK over planet MOBIUS was believed to have finally ended! With the technological tyrant vanquished and his smelly factories shut down, order and beauty were restored to the city of MOBOTROPOLIS. Now the villain has returned to wreak havoc once more, but there are many who are willing to stand against him in the fight for freedom. The bravest among them is a brash, blue streak who just happens to be the fastest thing alive! ***ARCHIE COMICS AND SEGA PRESENT... SONIC THE HEDGEHOG!***

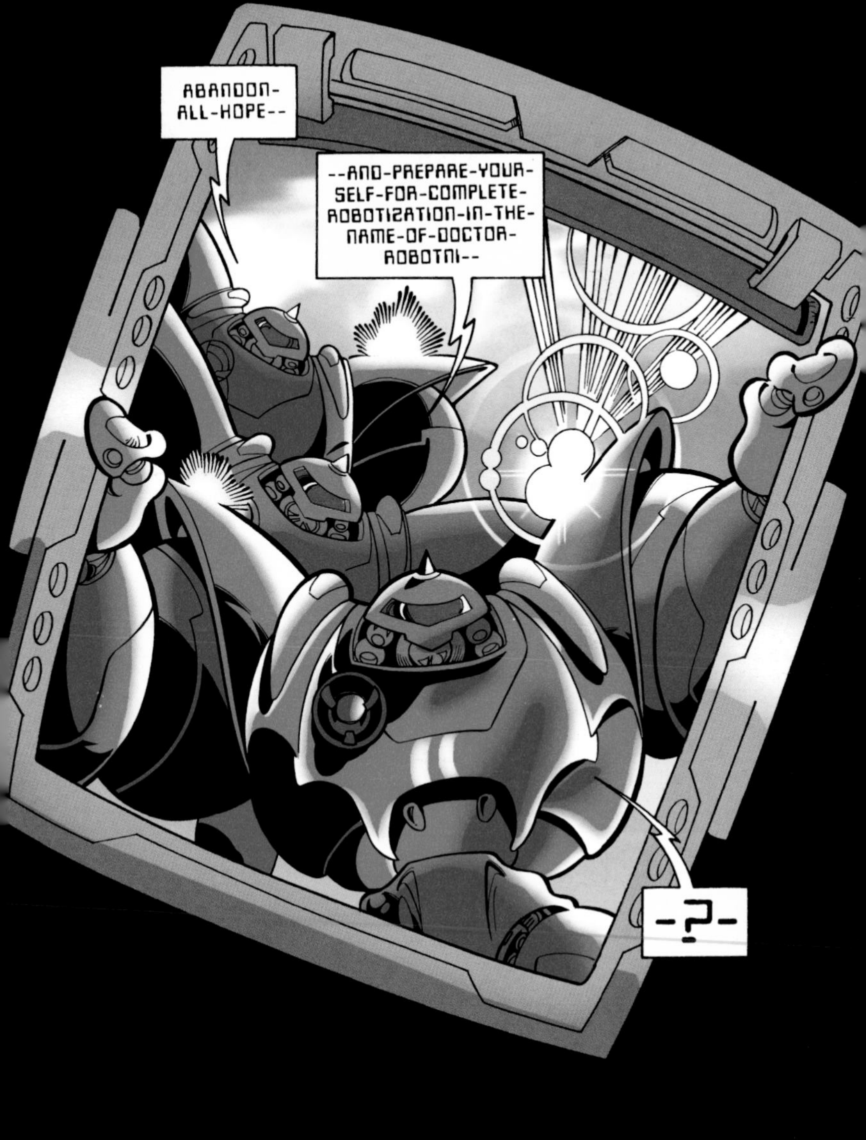
ABANDON-ALL-HOPE--
--AND-PREPARE-YOUR-SELF-FOR-COMPLETE-ROBOTIZATION-IN-THE-NAME-OF-DOCTOR-ROBOTNI--
-?-

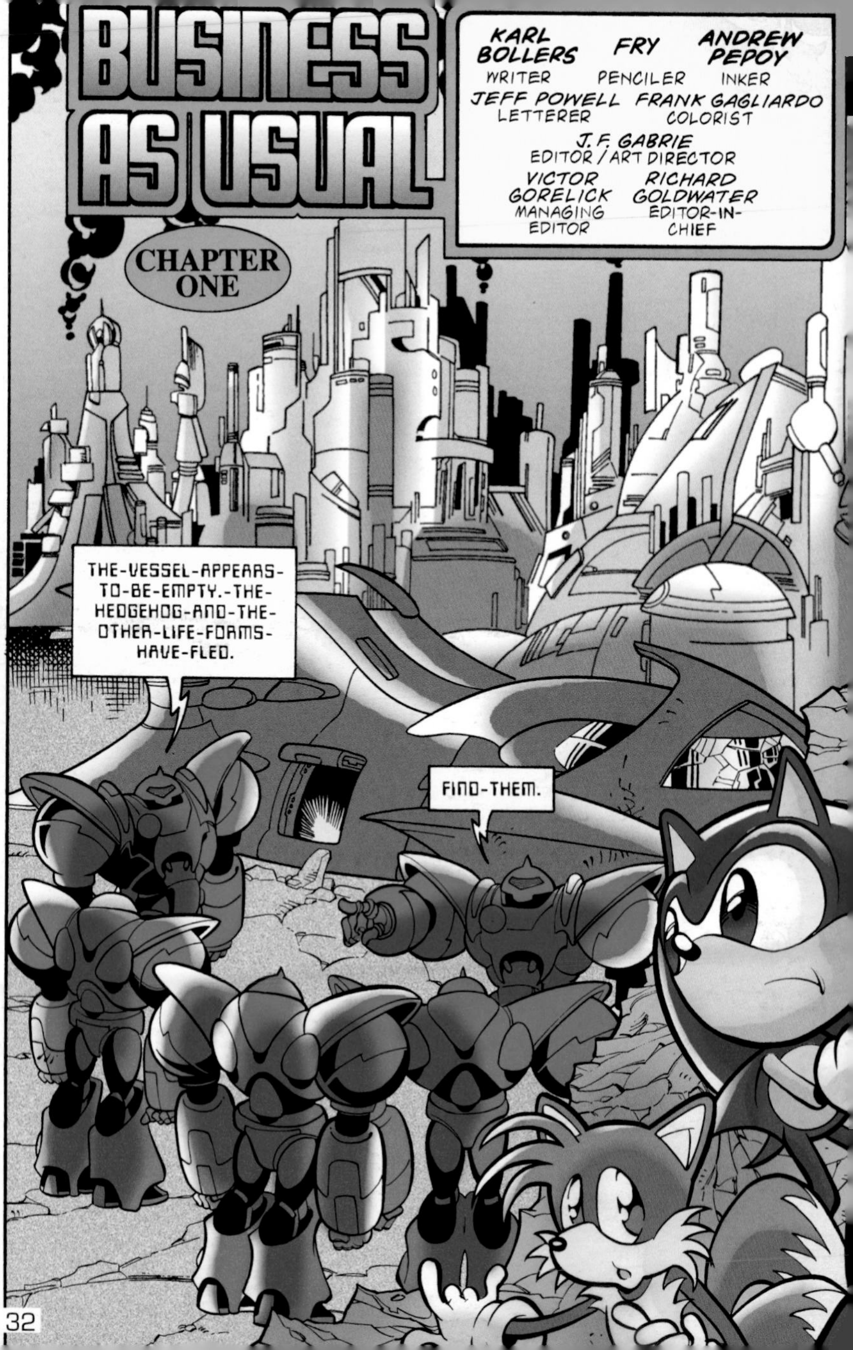
BUSINESS AS USUAL
KARL BOLLERS
WRITER
FRY
PENCILER
ANDREW PEPOY
INKER
JEFF POWELL
LETTERER
FRANK GAGLIARDO
COLORIST
J. F. GABRIE
EDITOR / ART DIRECTOR
VICTOR GORELICK
MANAGING EDITOR
RICHARD GOLDWATER
EDITOR-IN-CHIEF
CHAPTER ONE
THE-VESSEL-APPEARS-TO-BE-EMPTY.-THE-HEDGEHOG-AND-THE-OTHER-LIFE-FORMS-HAVE-FLED.
FIND-THEM.

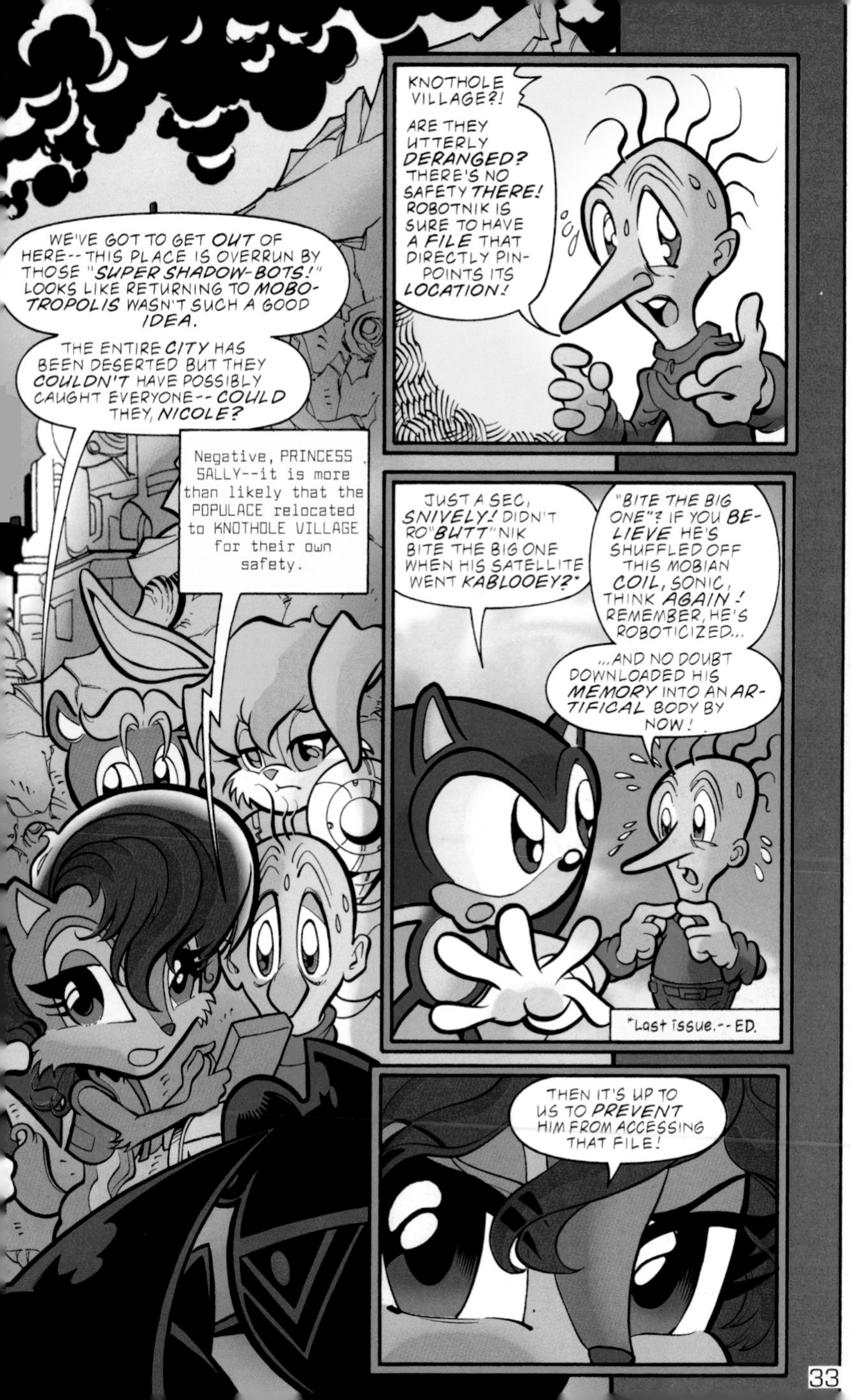
WE'VE GOT TO GET OUT OF HERE-- THIS PLACE IS OVERRUN BY THOSE "SUPER SHADOW-BOTS!" LOOKS LIKE RETURNING TO MOBOTROPOLIS WASN'T SUCH A GOOD IDEA.
THE ENTIRE CITY HAS BEEN DESERTED BUT THEY COULDN'T HAVE POSSIBLY CAUGHT EVERYONE-- COULD THEY, NICOLE?
Negative, PRINCESS SALLY--it is more than likely that the POPULACE relocated to KNOTHOLE VILLAGE for their own safety.
KNOTHOLE VILLAGE?!
ARE THEY UTTERLY DERANGED? THERE'S NO SAFETY THERE! ROBOTNIK IS SURE TO HAVE A FILE THAT DIRECTLY PINPOINTS ITS LOCATION!
JUST A SEC, SNIVELY! DIDN'T RO"BUTT"NIK BITE THE BIG ONE WHEN HIS SATELLITE WENT KABLOOEY?*
"BITE THE BIG ONE"? IF YOU BELIEVE HE'S SHUFFLED OFF THIS MOBIAN COIL, SONIC, THINK AGAIN! REMEMBER, HE'S ROBOTICIZED...
...AND NO DOUBT DOWNLOADED HIS MEMORY INTO AN ARTIFICAL BODY BY NOW!
*Last issue.--ED.
THEN IT'S UP TO US TO PREVENT HIM FROM ACCESSING THAT FILE!

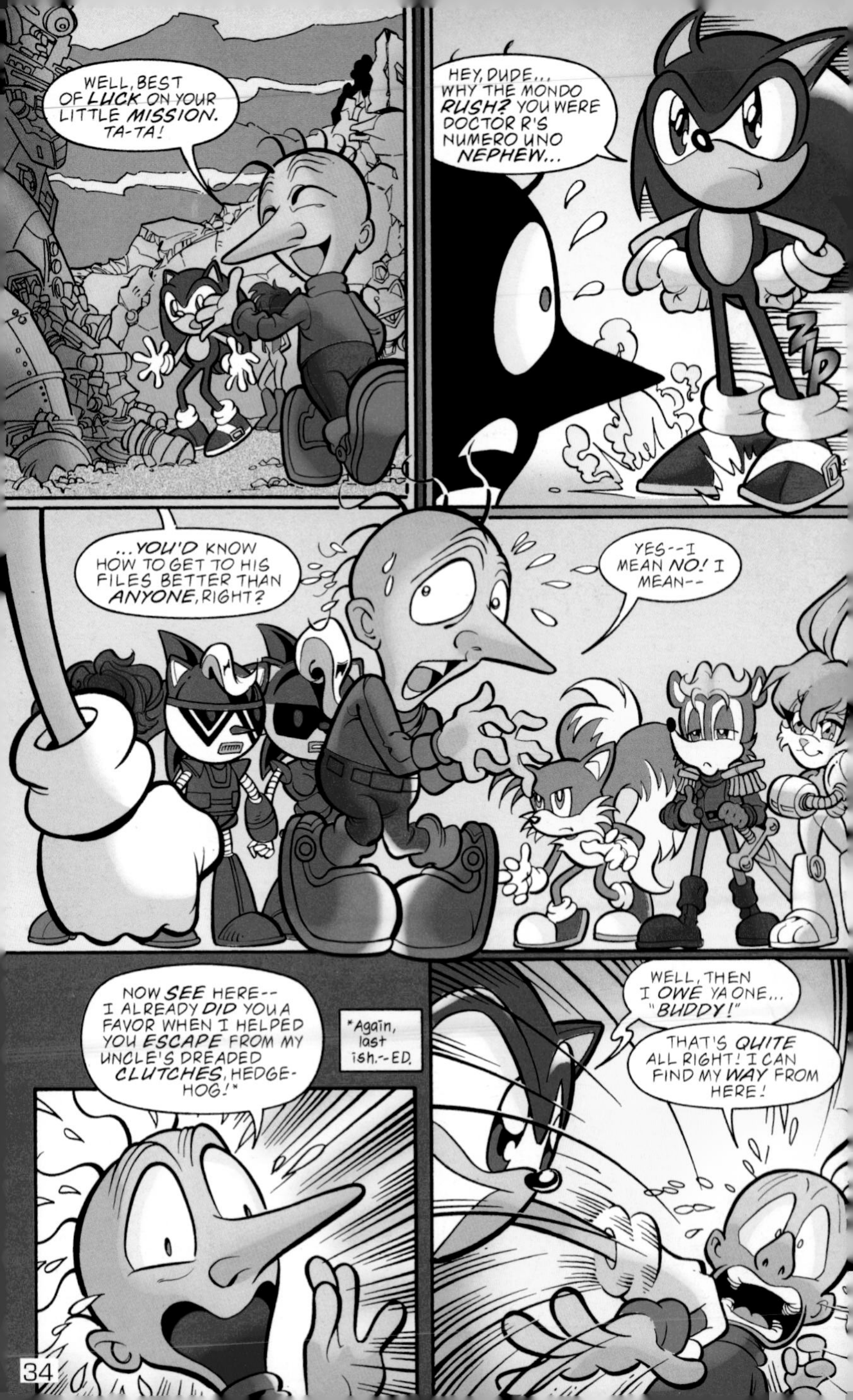
WELL, BEST OF LUCK ON YOUR LITTLE MISSION. TA-TA!
HEY, DUDE... WHY THE MONDO RUSH? YOU WERE DOCTOR R'S NUMERO UNO NEPHEW...
ZIP
...YOU'D KNOW HOW TO GET TO HIS FILES BETTER THAN ANYONE, RIGHT?
YES--I MEAN NO! I MEAN--
NOW SEE HERE-- I ALREADY DID YOU A FAVOR WHEN I HELPED YOU ESCAPE FROM MY UNCLE'S DREADED CLUTCHES, HEDGE-HOG!*
*Again, last ish.--ED.
WELL, THEN I OWE YA ONE... "BUDDY!"
THAT'S QUITE ALL RIGHT! I CAN FIND MY WAY FROM HERE!

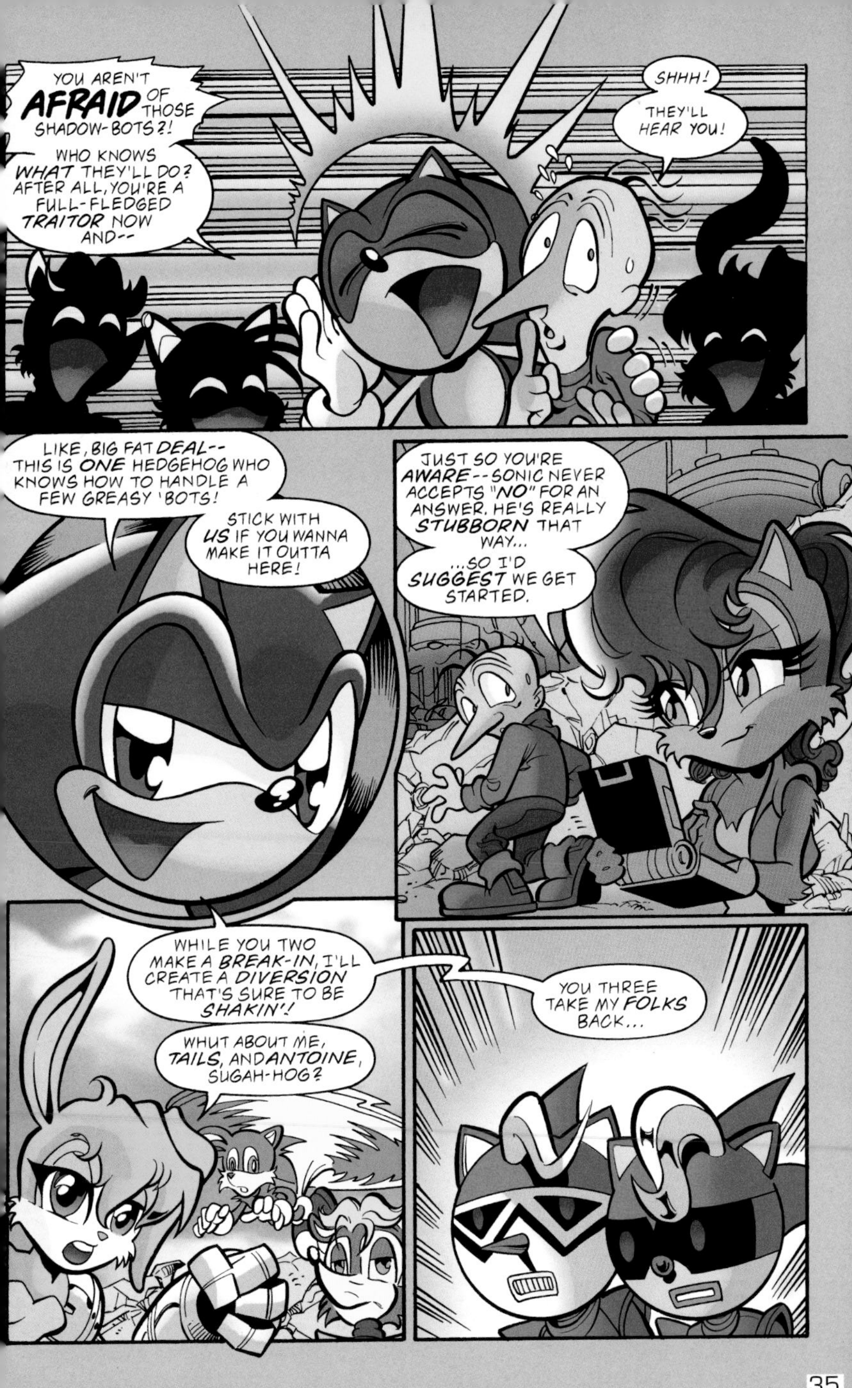
YOU AREN'T AFRAID OF THOSE SHADOW-BOTS?!
WHO KNOWS WHAT THEY'LL DO? AFTER ALL, YOU'RE A FULL-FLEDGED TRAITOR NOW AND--
SHHH!
THEY'LL HEAR YOU!
LIKE, BIG FAT DEAL-- THIS IS ONE HEDGEHOG WHO KNOWS HOW TO HANDLE A FEW GREASY 'BOTS!
STICK WITH US IF YOU WANNA MAKE IT OUTTA HERE!
JUST SO YOU'RE AWARE--SONIC NEVER ACCEPTS "NO" FOR AN ANSWER. HE'S REALLY STUBBORN THAT WAY...
...SO I'D SUGGEST WE GET STARTED.
WHILE YOU TWO MAKE A BREAK-IN, I'LL CREATE A DIVERSION THAT'S SURE TO BE SHAKIN'!
WHUT ABOUT ME, TAILS, ANDANTOINE, SUGAH-HOG?
YOU THREE TAKE MY FOLKS BACK...

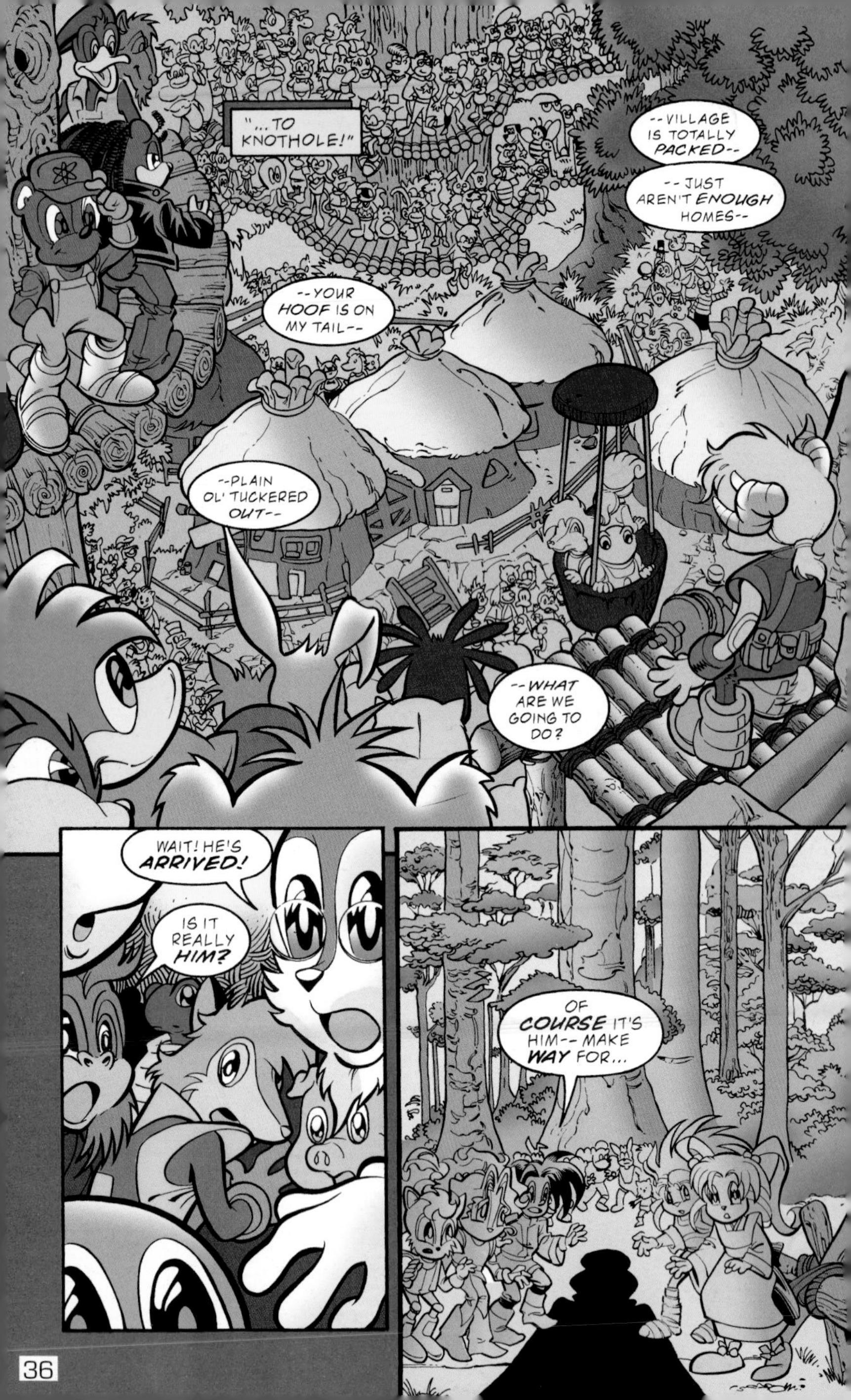
"...TO KNOTHOLE!"
--VILLAGE IS TOTALLY PACKED--
--JUST AREN'T ENOUGH HOMES--
--YOUR HOOF IS ON MY TAIL--
--PLAIN OL' TUCKERED OUT--
--WHAT ARE WE GOING TO DO?
WAIT! HE'S ARRIVED!
IS IT REALLY HIM?
OF COURSE IT'S HIM--MAKE WAY FOR...

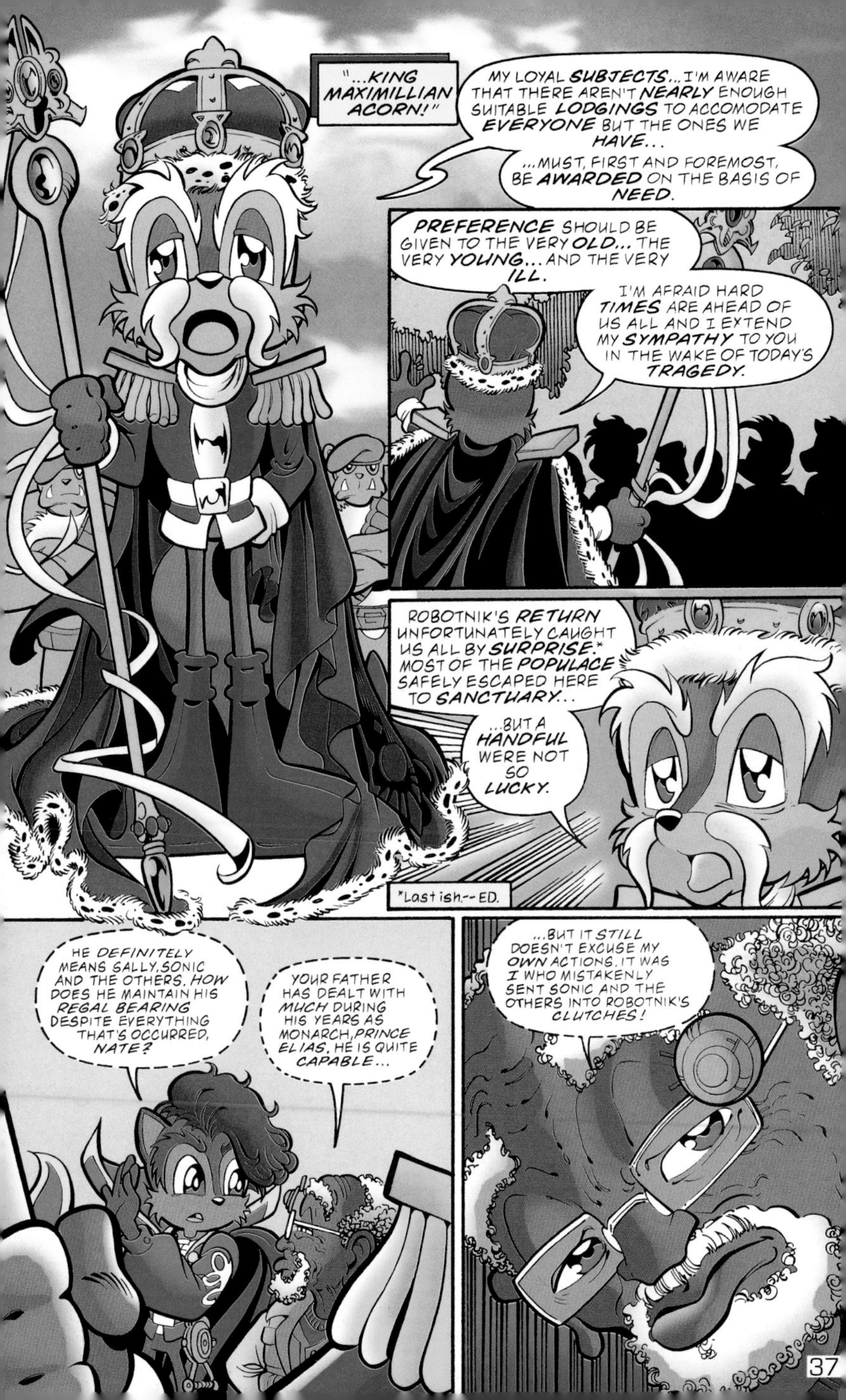
"...KING MAXIMILLIAN ACORN!"
MY LOYAL SUBJECTS... I'M AWARE THAT THERE AREN'T NEARLY ENOUGH SUITABLE LODGINGS TO ACCOMODATE EVERYONE BUT THE ONES WE HAVE...
...MUST, FIRST AND FOREMOST, BE AWARDED ON THE BASIS OF NEED.
PREFERENCE SHOULD BE GIVEN TO THE VERY OLD... THE VERY YOUNG... AND THE VERY ILL.
I'M AFRAID HARD TIMES ARE AHEAD OF US ALL AND I EXTEND MY SYMPATHY TO YOU IN THE WAKE OF TODAY'S TRAGEDY.
ROBOTNIK'S RETURN UNFORTUNATELY CAUGHT US ALL BY SURPRISE.* MOST OF THE POPULACE SAFELY ESCAPED HERE TO SANCTUARY...
...BUT A HANDFUL WERE NOT SO LUCKY.
*Last ish.-- ED.
HE DEFINITELY MEANS SALLY, SONIC AND THE OTHERS. HOW DOES HE MAINTAIN HIS REGAL BEARING DESPITE EVERYTHING THAT'S OCCURRED, NATE?
YOUR FATHER HAS DEALT WITH MUCH DURING HIS YEARS AS MONARCH, PRINCE ELIAS. HE IS QUITE CAPABLE...
...BUT IT STILL DOESN'T EXCUSE MY OWN ACTIONS. IT WAS I WHO MISTAKENLY SENT SONIC AND THE OTHERS INTO ROBOTNIK'S CLUTCHES!

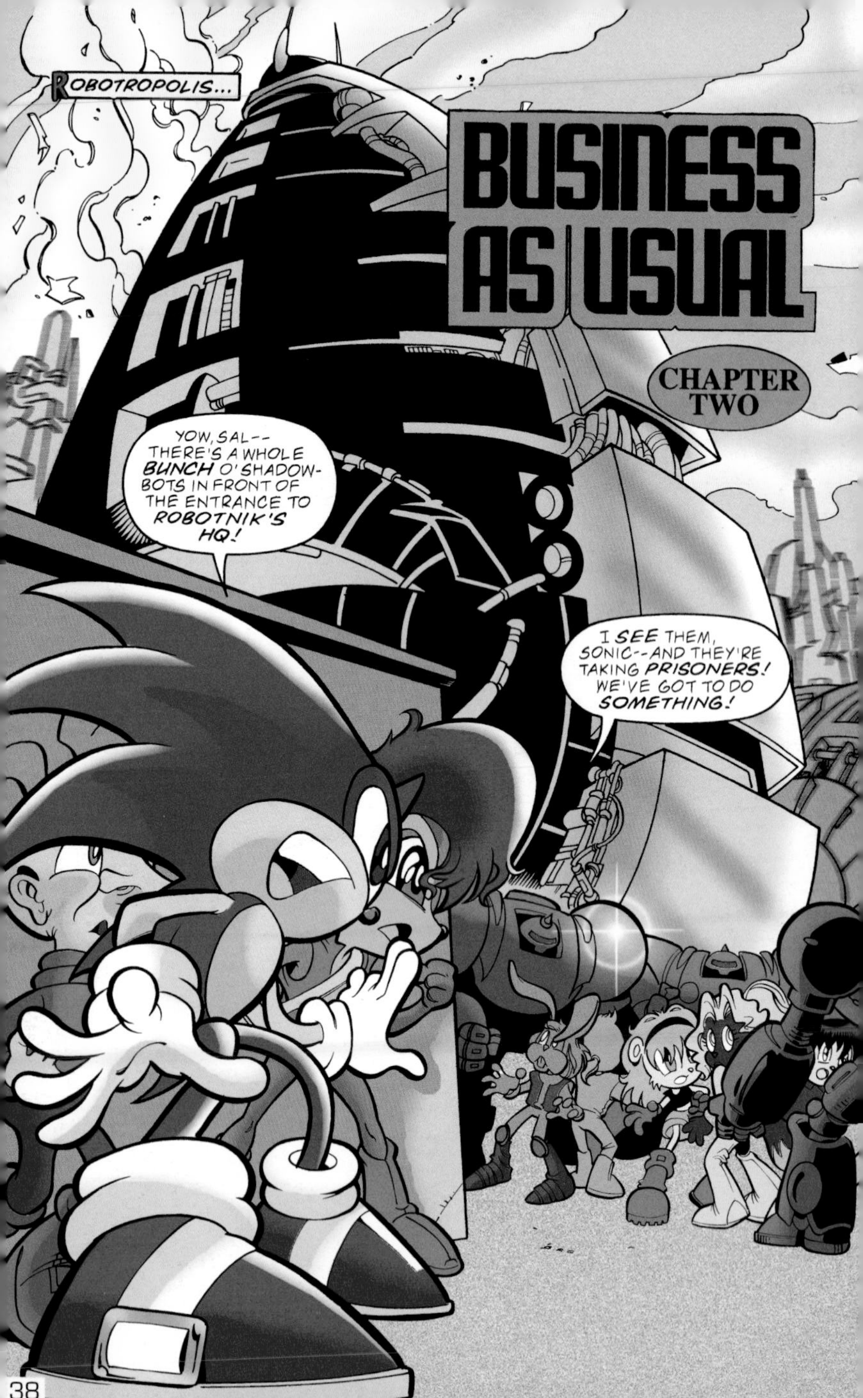
ROBOTROPOLIS...
BUSINESS AS USUAL
CHAPTER TWO
YOW, SAL-- THERE'S A WHOLE BUNCH O' SHADOW-BOTS IN FRONT OF THE ENTRANCE TO ROBOTNIK'S HQ!
I SEE THEM, SONIC--AND THEY'RE TAKING PRISONERS! WE'VE GOT TO DO SOMETHING!

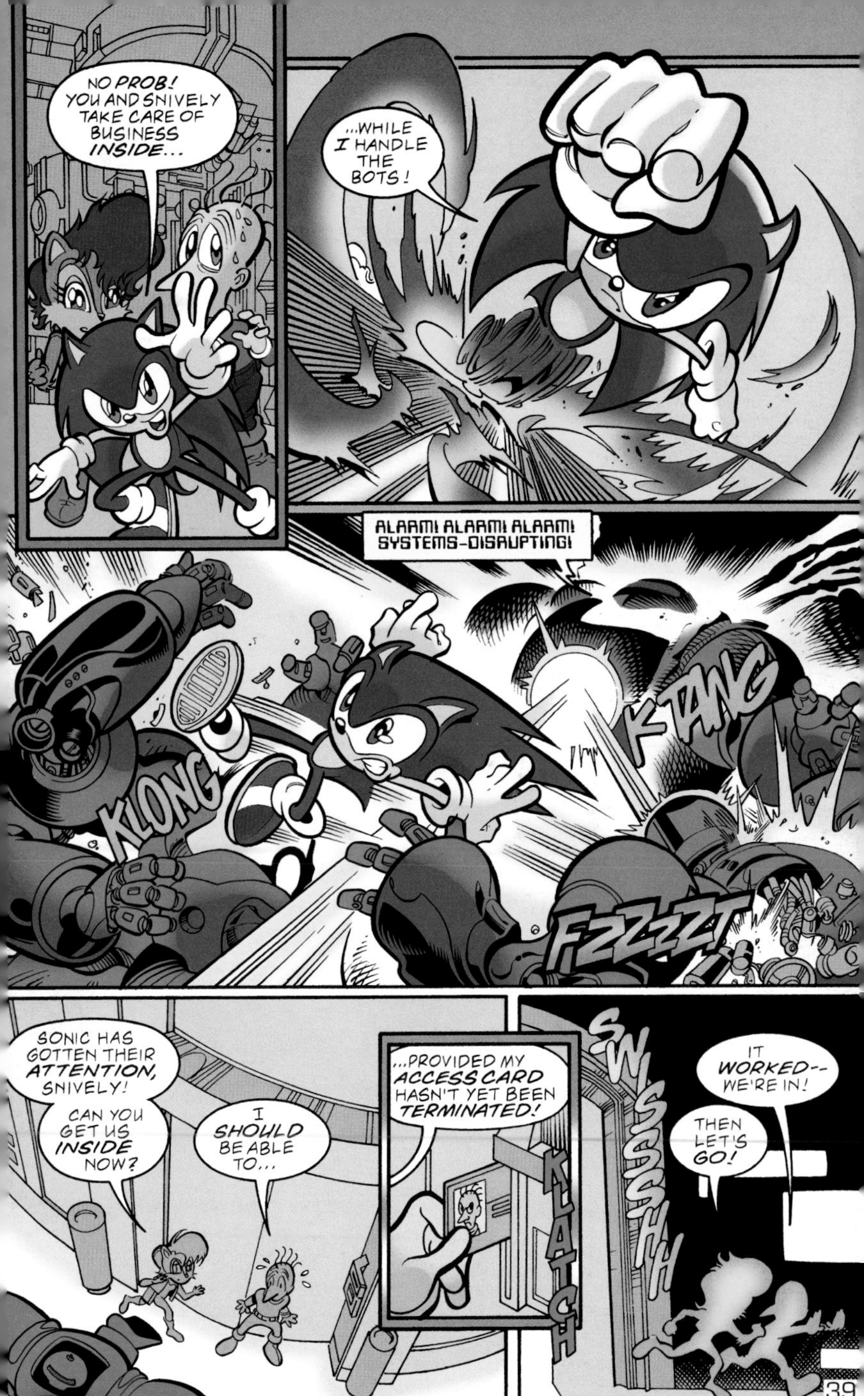
NO PROB! YOU AND SNIVELY TAKE CARE OF BUSINESS INSIDE...
...WHILE I HANDLE THE BOTS!
ALARM! ALARM! ALARM! SYSTEMS-DISRUPTING!
KLONG
K TANG
FZZZZT
SONIC HAS GOTTEN THEIR ATTENTION, SNIVELY!
CAN YOU GET US INSIDE NOW?
I SHOULD BE ABLE TO...
...PROVIDED MY ACCESS CARD HASN'T YET BEEN TERMINATED!
KLATCH
SWISSSHH
IT WORKED-- WE'RE IN!
THEN LET'S GO!

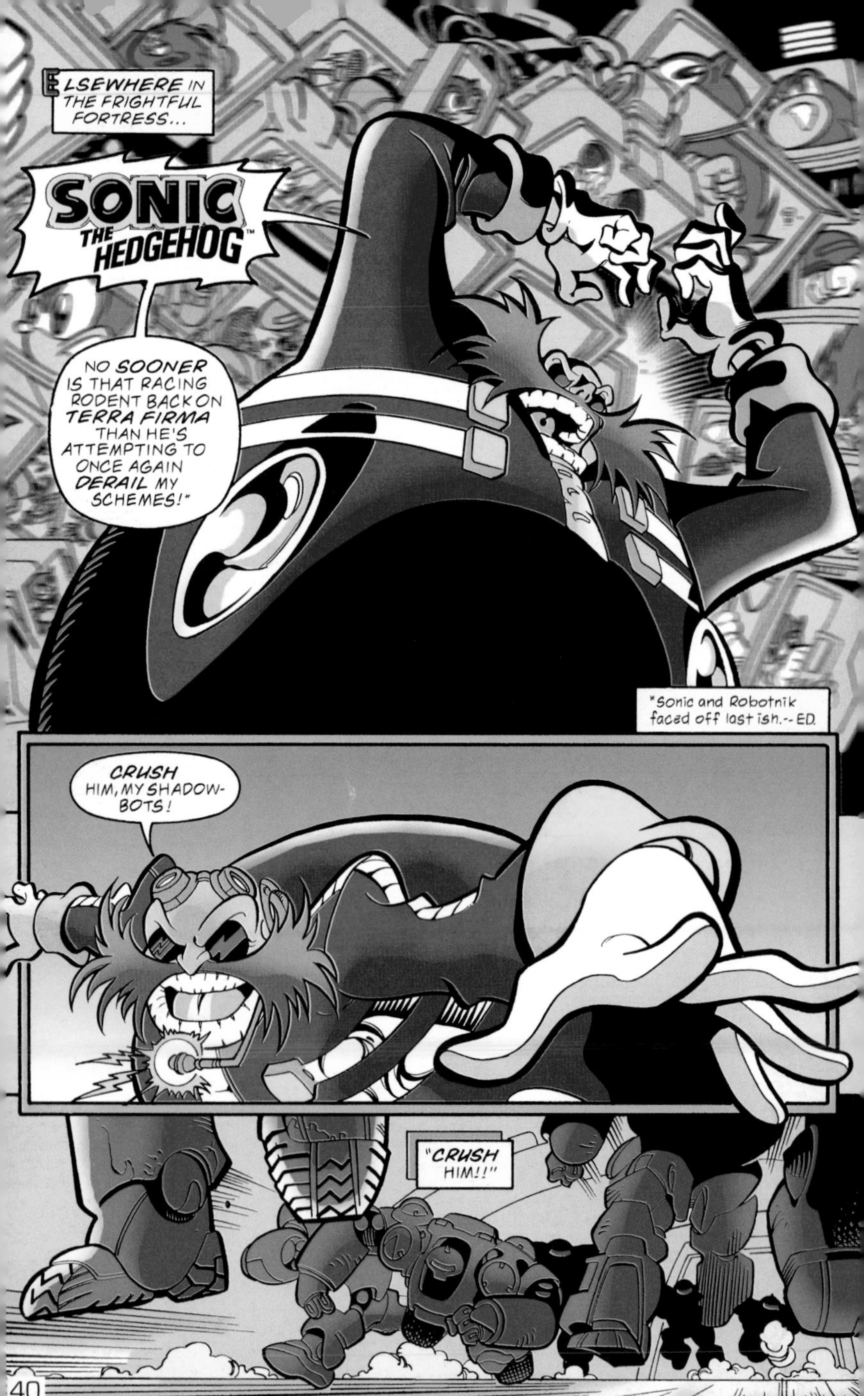
ELSEWHERE IN THE FRIGHTFUL FORTRESS...
SONIC THE HEDGEHOG™
NO SOONER IS THAT RACING RODENT BACK ON TERRA FIRMA THAN HE'S ATTEMPTING TO ONCE AGAIN DERAIL MY SCHEMES!*
*Sonic and Robotnik faced off last ish.-- ED.
CRUSH HIM, MY SHADOW-BOTS!
"CRUSH HIM!!"

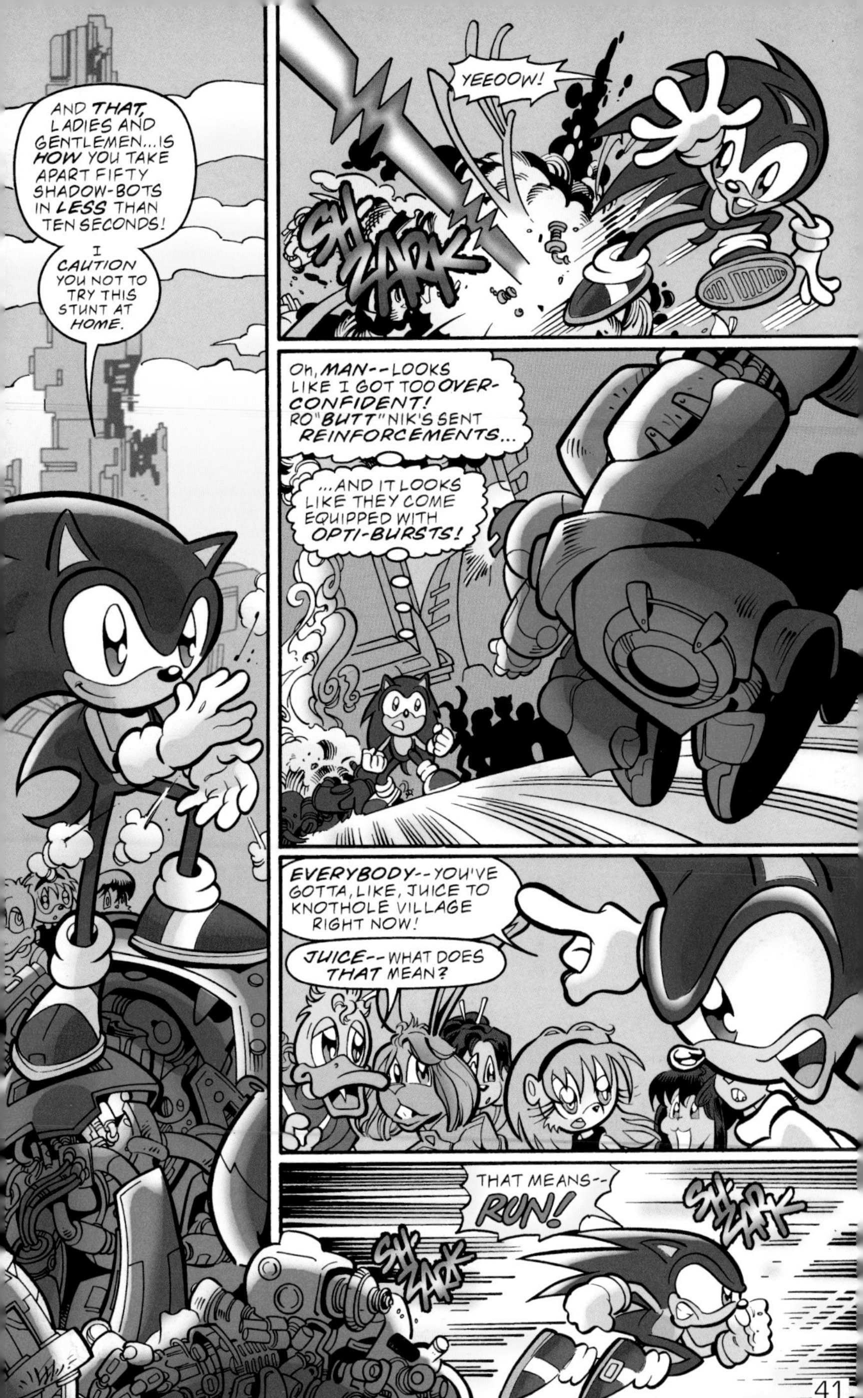
AND THAT, LADIES AND GENTLEMEN... IS HOW YOU TAKE APART FIFTY SHADOW-BOTS IN LESS THAN TEN SECONDS!
I CAUTION YOU NOT TO TRY THIS STUNT AT HOME.
YEEOOW!
SHZAAK
Oh, MAN--LOOKS LIKE I GOT TOO OVER-CONFIDENT! RO"BUTT"NIK'S SENT REINFORCEMENTS...
...AND IT LOOKS LIKE THEY COME EQUIPPED WITH OPTI-BURSTS!
EVERYBODY--YOU'VE GOTTA, LIKE, JUICE TO KNOTHOLE VILLAGE RIGHT NOW!
JUICE--WHAT DOES THAT MEAN?
THAT MEANS--
RUN!
SHZAAK
SHZAAK

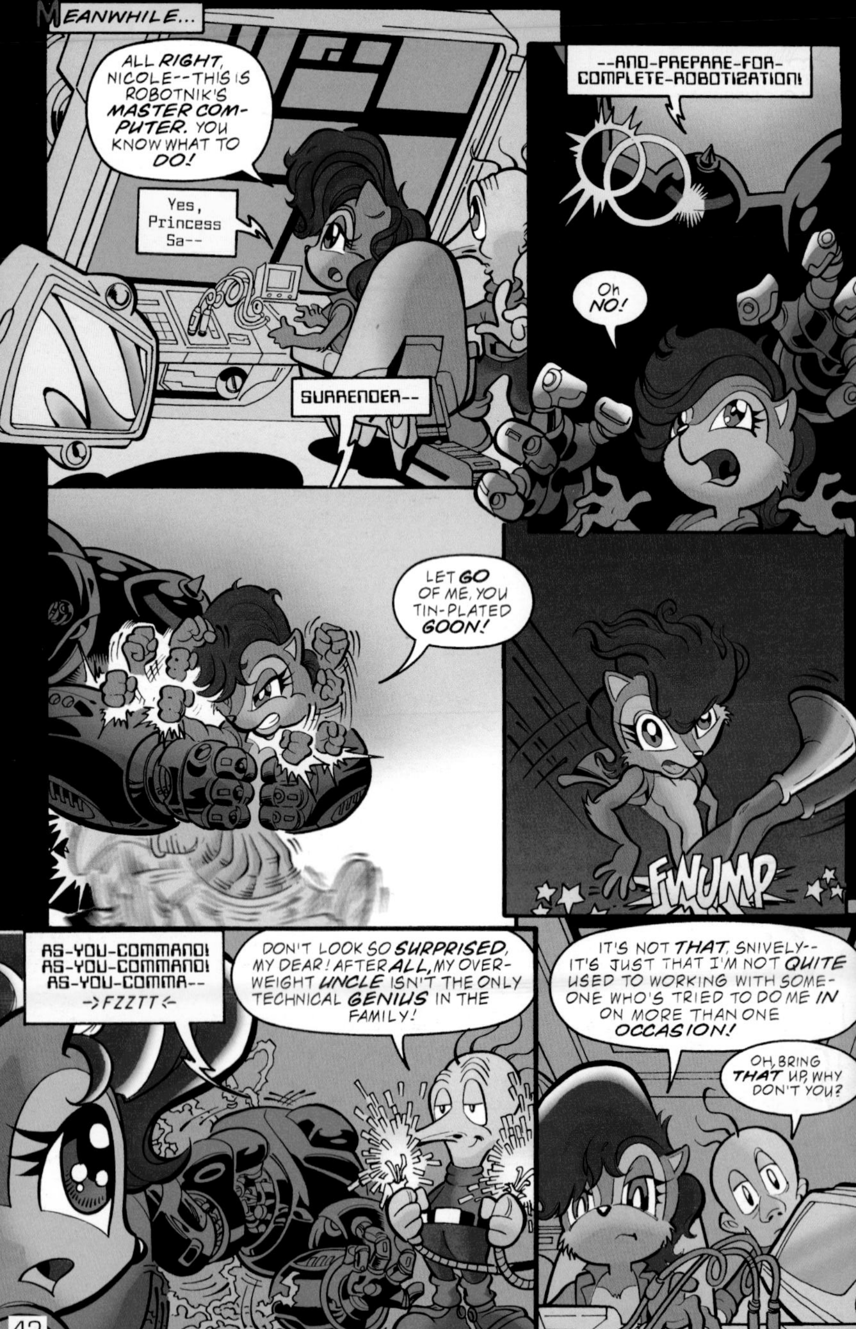
MEANWHILE...
ALL RIGHT, NICOLE--THIS IS ROBOTNIK'S MASTER COMPUTER. YOU KNOW WHAT TO DO!
Yes, Princess Sa--
SURRENDER--
--AND-PREPARE-FOR-COMPLETE-ROBOTIZATION!
Oh NO!
LET GO OF ME, YOU TIN-PLATED GOON!
FWUMP
AS-YOU-COMMAND! AS-YOU-COMMAND! AS-YOU-COMMA--
-> FZZTT <-
DON'T LOOK SO SURPRISED, MY DEAR! AFTER ALL, MY OVER-WEIGHT UNCLE ISN'T THE ONLY TECHNICAL GENIUS IN THE FAMILY!
IT'S NOT THAT, SNIVELY--IT'S JUST THAT I'M NOT QUITE USED TO WORKING WITH SOME-ONE WHO'S TRIED TO DO ME IN ON MORE THAN ONE OCCASION!
OH, BRING THAT UP, WHY DON'T YOU?

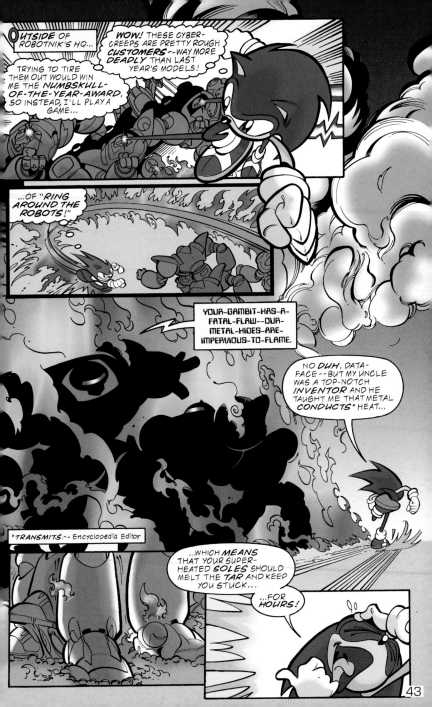

OUTSIDE OF ROBOTNIK'S HQ...

WOW! THESE CYBER-CREEPS ARE PRETTY ROUGH *CUSTOMERS*--WAY MORE *DEADLY* THAN LAST YEAR'S MODELS!

TRYING TO TIRE THEM OUT WOULD WIN ME THE *NUMBSKULL-OF-THE-YEAR-AWARD*, SO INSTEAD, I'LL PLAY A GAME...

...OF "*RING AROUND THE ROBOTS!*"

YOUR-GAMBIT-HAS-A-FATAL-FLAW--OUR-METAL-HIDES-ARE-IMPERVIOUS-TO-FLAME.

NO *DUH*, DATA-FACE--BUT MY UNCLE WAS A TOP-NOTCH *INVENTOR* AND HE TAUGHT ME THAT METAL *CONDUCTS** HEAT...

*TRANSMITS.-- Encyclopedia Editor

...WHICH *MEANS* THAT YOUR SUPER-HEATED *SOLES* SHOULD MELT THE *TAR* AND KEEP YOU STUCK...

...FOR *HOURS!*

43

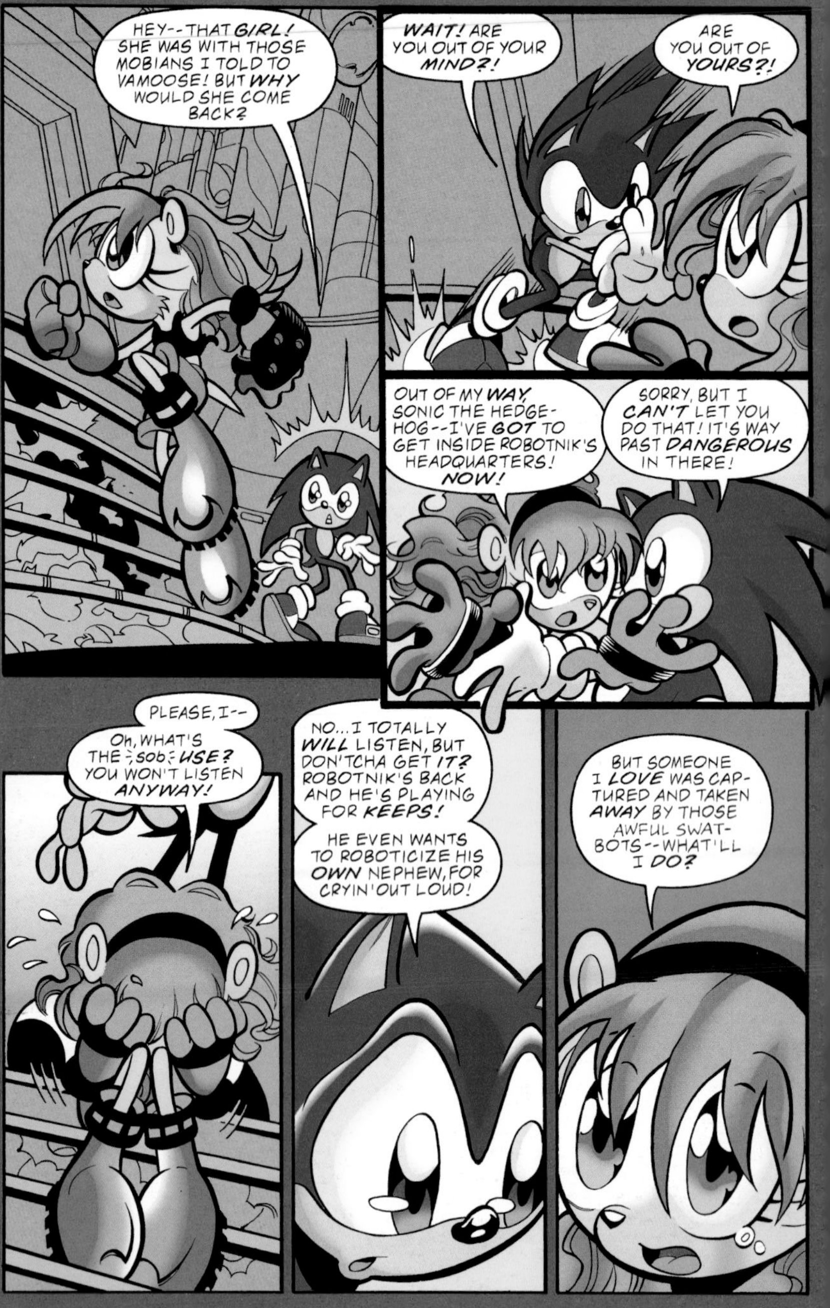
HEY--THAT GIRL! SHE WAS WITH THOSE MOBIANS I TOLD TO VAMOOSE! BUT WHY WOULD SHE COME BACK?
WAIT! ARE YOU OUT OF YOUR MIND?!
ARE YOU OUT OF YOURS?!
OUT OF MY WAY, SONIC THE HEDGE-HOG--I'VE GOT TO GET INSIDE ROBOTNIK'S HEADQUARTERS! NOW!
SORRY, BUT I CAN'T LET YOU DO THAT! IT'S WAY PAST DANGEROUS IN THERE!
PLEASE, I--
Oh, WHAT'S THE -sob- USE? YOU WON'T LISTEN ANYWAY!
NO... I TOTALLY WILL LISTEN, BUT DON'TCHA GET IT? ROBOTNIK'S BACK AND HE'S PLAYING FOR KEEPS!
HE EVEN WANTS TO ROBOTICIZE HIS OWN NEPHEW, FOR CRYIN' OUT LOUD!
BUT SOMEONE I LOVE WAS CAPTURED AND TAKEN AWAY BY THOSE AWFUL SWAT-BOTS--WHAT'LL I DO?

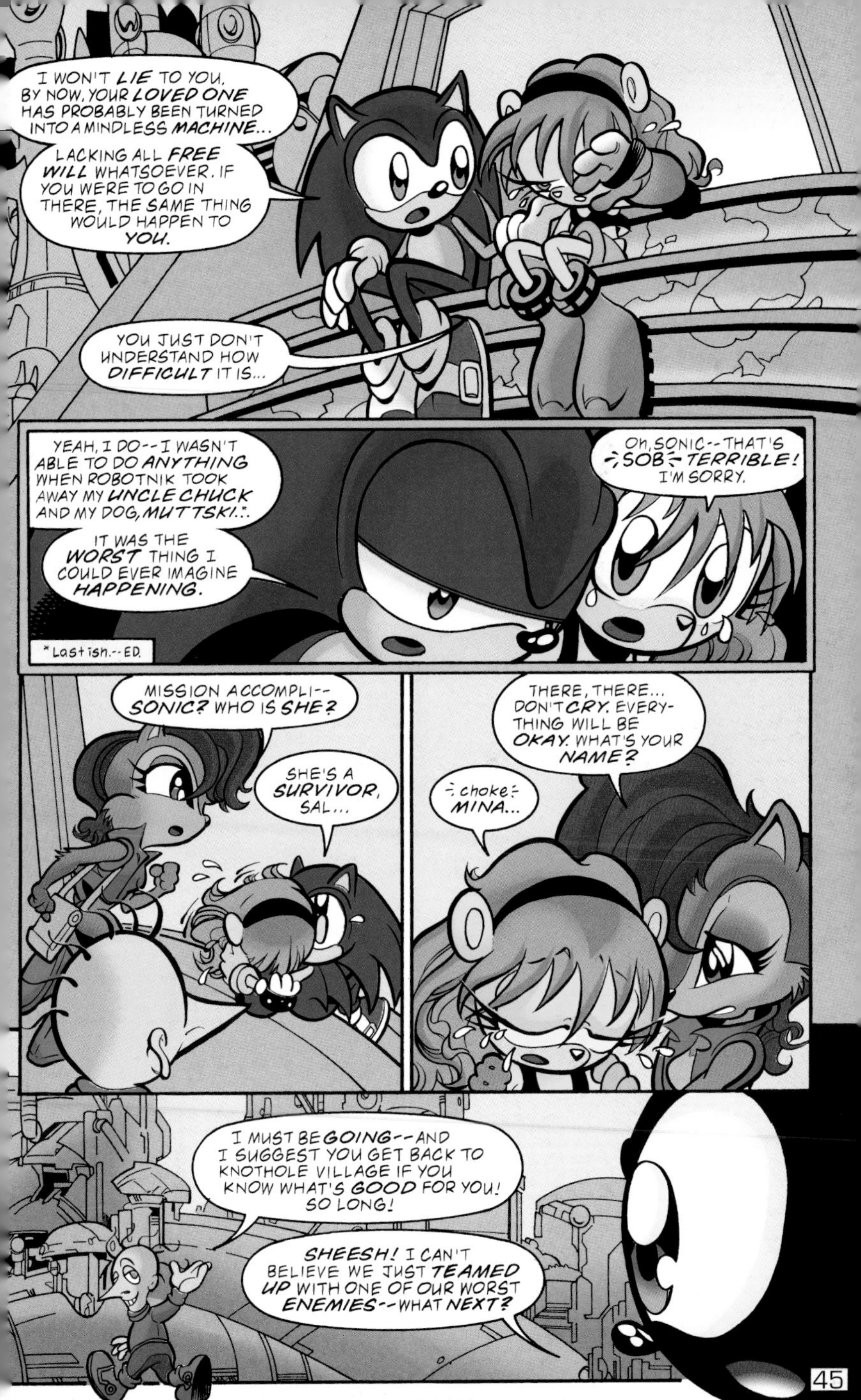
I WON'T LIE TO YOU. BY NOW, YOUR LOVED ONE HAS PROBABLY BEEN TURNED INTO A MINDLESS MACHINE...
LACKING ALL FREE WILL WHATSOEVER. IF YOU WERE TO GO IN THERE, THE SAME THING WOULD HAPPEN TO YOU.
YOU JUST DON'T UNDERSTAND HOW DIFFICULT IT IS...
YEAH, I DO--I WASN'T ABLE TO DO ANYTHING WHEN ROBOTNIK TOOK AWAY MY UNCLE CHUCK AND MY DOG, MUTTSKI..*
IT WAS THE WORST THING I COULD EVER IMAGINE HAPPENING.
OH, SONIC--THAT'S -SOB- TERRIBLE! I'M SORRY.
*Last ish.--ED.
MISSION ACCOMPLI-- SONIC? WHO IS SHE?
SHE'S A SURVIVOR, SAL...
THERE, THERE... DON'T CRY. EVERYTHING WILL BE OKAY. WHAT'S YOUR NAME?
-choke- MINA...
I MUST BE GOING--AND I SUGGEST YOU GET BACK TO KNOTHOLE VILLAGE IF YOU KNOW WHAT'S GOOD FOR YOU! SO LONG!
SHEESH! I CAN'T BELIEVE WE JUST TEAMED UP WITH ONE OF OUR WORST ENEMIES--WHAT NEXT?

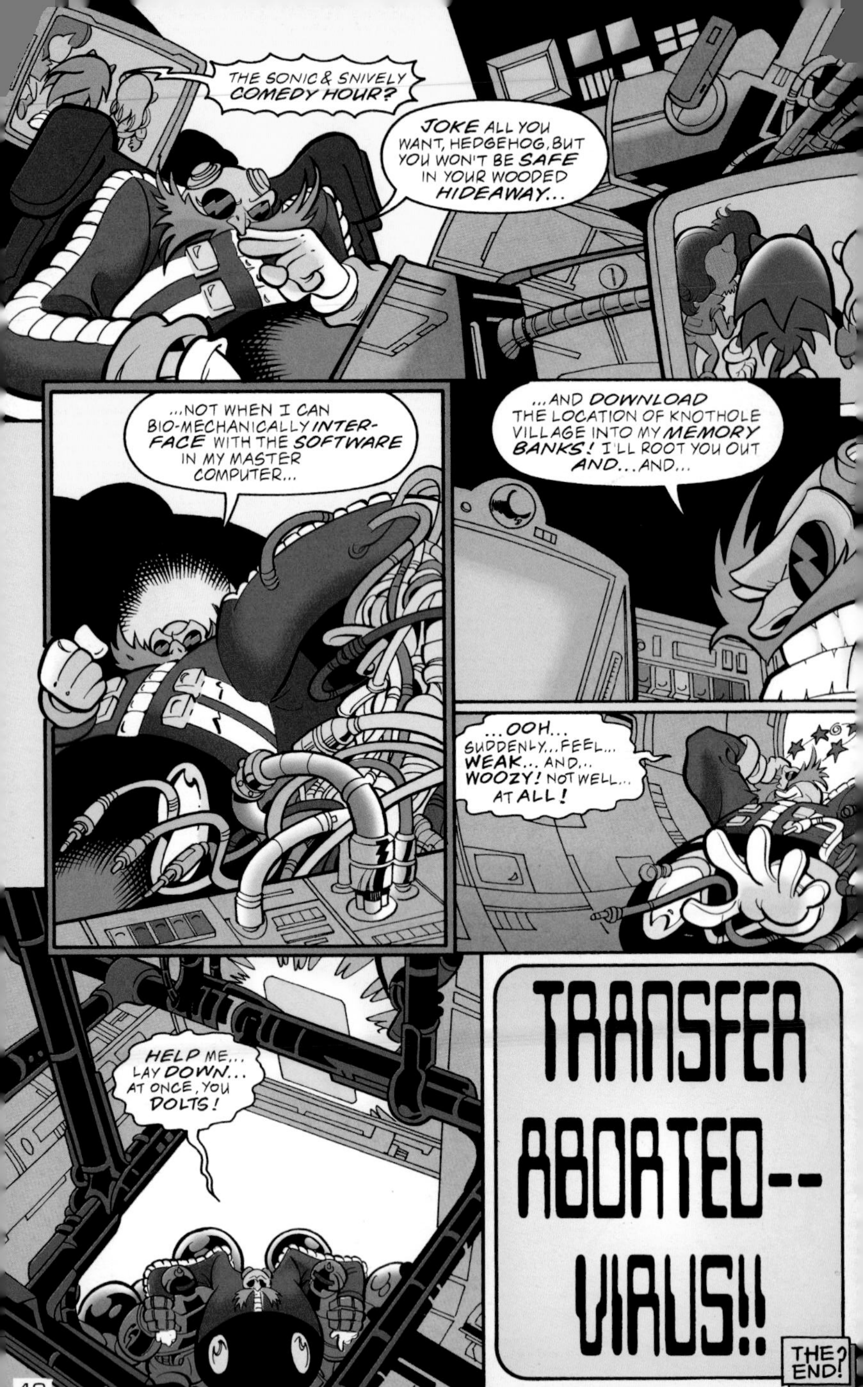
THE SONIC & SNIVELY COMEDY HOUR?
JOKE ALL YOU WANT, HEDGEHOG, BUT YOU WON'T BE SAFE IN YOUR WOODED HIDEAWAY...
...NOT WHEN I CAN BIO-MECHANICALLY INTER-FACE WITH THE SOFTWARE IN MY MASTER COMPUTER...
...AND DOWNLOAD THE LOCATION OF KNOTHOLE VILLAGE INTO MY MEMORY BANKS! I'LL ROOT YOU OUT AND...AND...
...OOH... SUDDENLY...FEEL... WEAK... AND... WOOZY! NOT WELL... AT ALL!
HELP ME... LAY DOWN... AT ONCE, YOU DOLTS!
TRANSFER ABORTED-- VIRUS!!
THE? END!

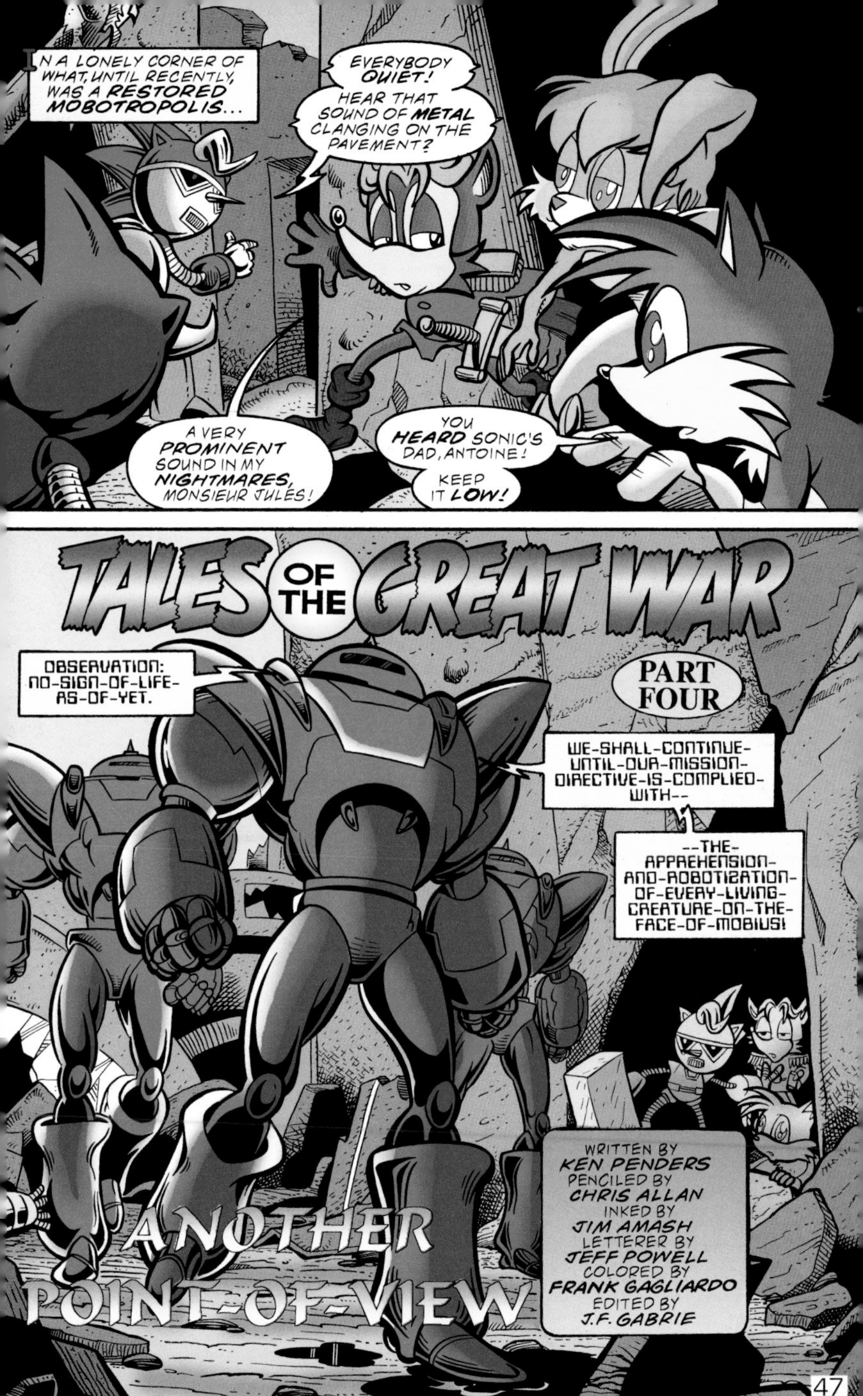
IN A LONELY CORNER OF WHAT, UNTIL RECENTLY, WAS A RESTORED MOBOTROPOLIS...
EVERYBODY QUIET! HEAR THAT SOUND OF METAL CLANGING ON THE PAVEMENT?
A VERY PROMINENT SOUND IN MY NIGHTMARES, MONSIEUR JULÉS!
YOU HEARD SONIC'S DAD, ANTOINE!
KEEP IT LOW!
TALES OF THE GREAT WAR
OBSERVATION: NO-SIGN-OF-LIFE-AS-OF-YET.
PART FOUR
WE-SHALL-CONTINUE-UNTIL-OUR-MISSION-DIRECTIVE-IS-COMPLIED-WITH--
--THE-APPREHENSION-AND-ROBOTIZATION-OF-EVERY-LIVING-CREATURE-ON-THE-FACE-OF-MOBIUS!
ANOTHER POINT-OF-VIEW
WRITTEN BY KEN PENDERS
PENCILED BY CHRIS ALLAN
INKED BY JIM AMASH
LETTERER BY JEFF POWELL
COLORED BY FRANK GAGLIARDO
EDITED BY J.F. GABRIE

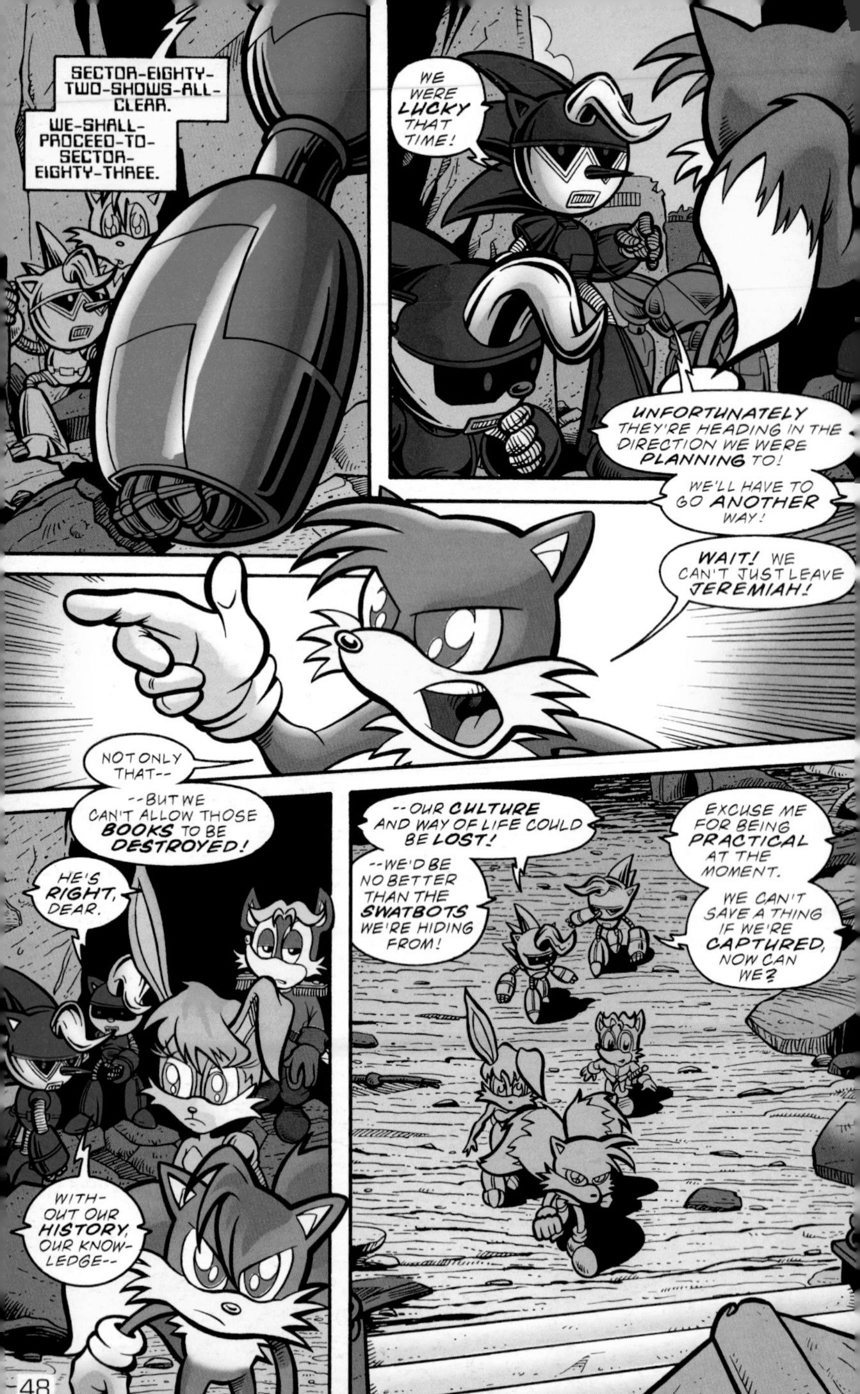
SECTOR-EIGHTY-TWO-SHOWS-ALL-CLEAR.
WE-SHALL-PROCEED-TO-SECTOR-EIGHTY-THREE.
WE WERE LUCKY THAT TIME!
UNFORTUNATELY THEY'RE HEADING IN THE DIRECTION WE WERE PLANNING TO!
WE'LL HAVE TO GO ANOTHER WAY!
WAIT! WE CAN'T JUST LEAVE JEREMIAH!
NOT ONLY THAT--
--BUT WE CAN'T ALLOW THOSE BOOKS TO BE DESTROYED!
HE'S RIGHT, DEAR.
WITH-OUT OUR HISTORY, OUR KNOW-LEDGE--
--OUR CULTURE AND WAY OF LIFE COULD BE LOST!
--WE'D BE NO BETTER THAN THE SWATBOTS WE'RE HIDING FROM!
EXCUSE ME FOR BEING PRACTICAL AT THE MOMENT.
WE CAN'T SAVE A THING IF WE'RE CAPTURED, NOW CAN WE?

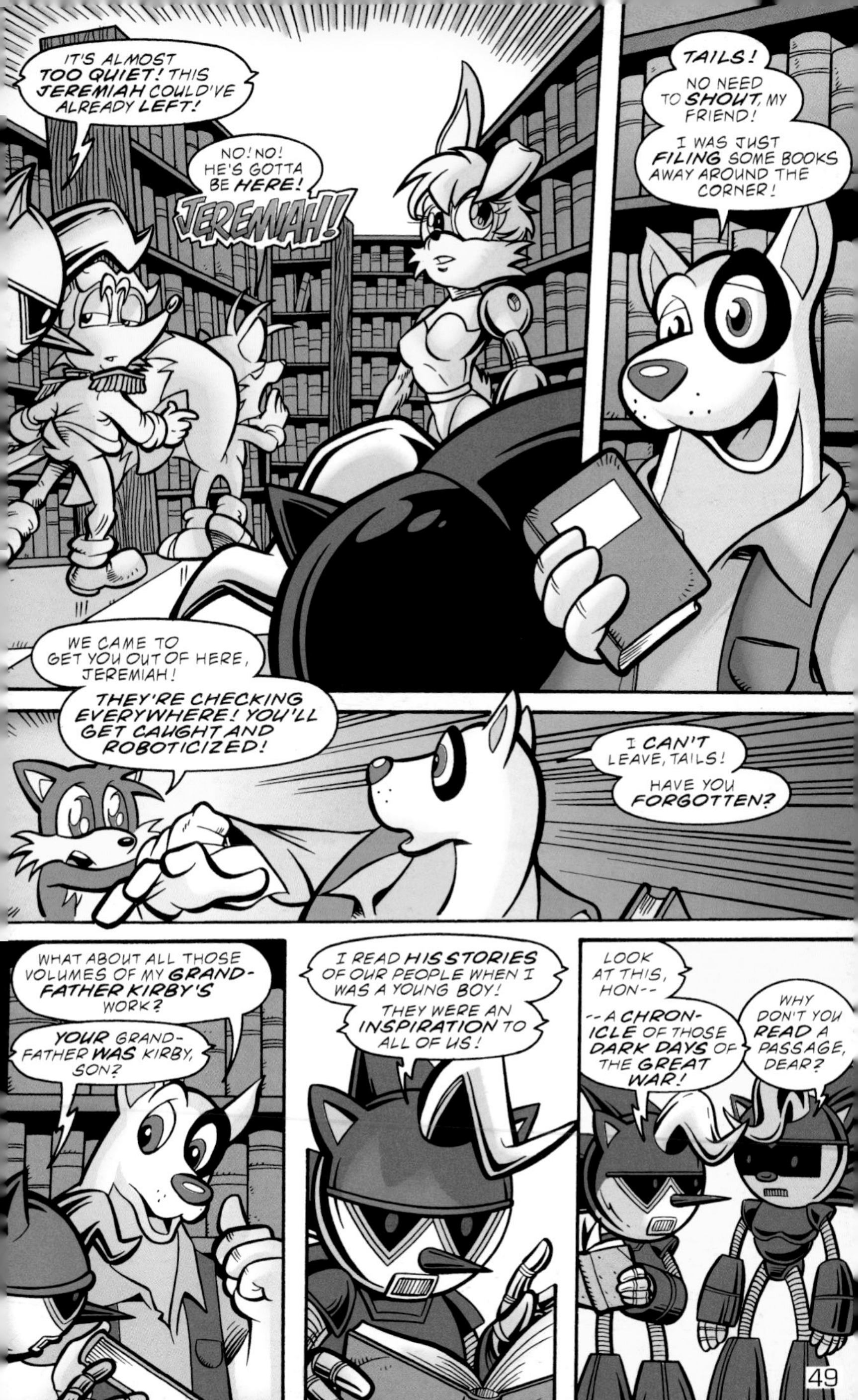
IT'S ALMOST TOO QUIET! THIS JEREMIAH COULD'VE ALREADY LEFT!
NO! NO! HE'S GOTTA BE HERE!
JEREMIAH!
TAILS!
NO NEED TO SHOUT, MY FRIEND!
I WAS JUST FILING SOME BOOKS AWAY AROUND THE CORNER!
WE CAME TO GET YOU OUT OF HERE, JEREMIAH!
THEY'RE CHECKING EVERYWHERE! YOU'LL GET CAUGHT AND ROBOTICIZED!
I CAN'T LEAVE, TAILS!
HAVE YOU FORGOTTEN?
WHAT ABOUT ALL THOSE VOLUMES OF MY GRAND-FATHER KIRBY'S WORK?
YOUR GRAND-FATHER WAS KIRBY, SON?
I READ HIS STORIES OF OUR PEOPLE WHEN I WAS A YOUNG BOY!
THEY WERE AN INSPIRATION TO ALL OF US!
LOOK AT THIS, HON--
--A CHRON-ICLE OF THOSE DARK DAYS OF THE GREAT WAR!
WHY DON'T YOU READ A PASSAGE, DEAR?

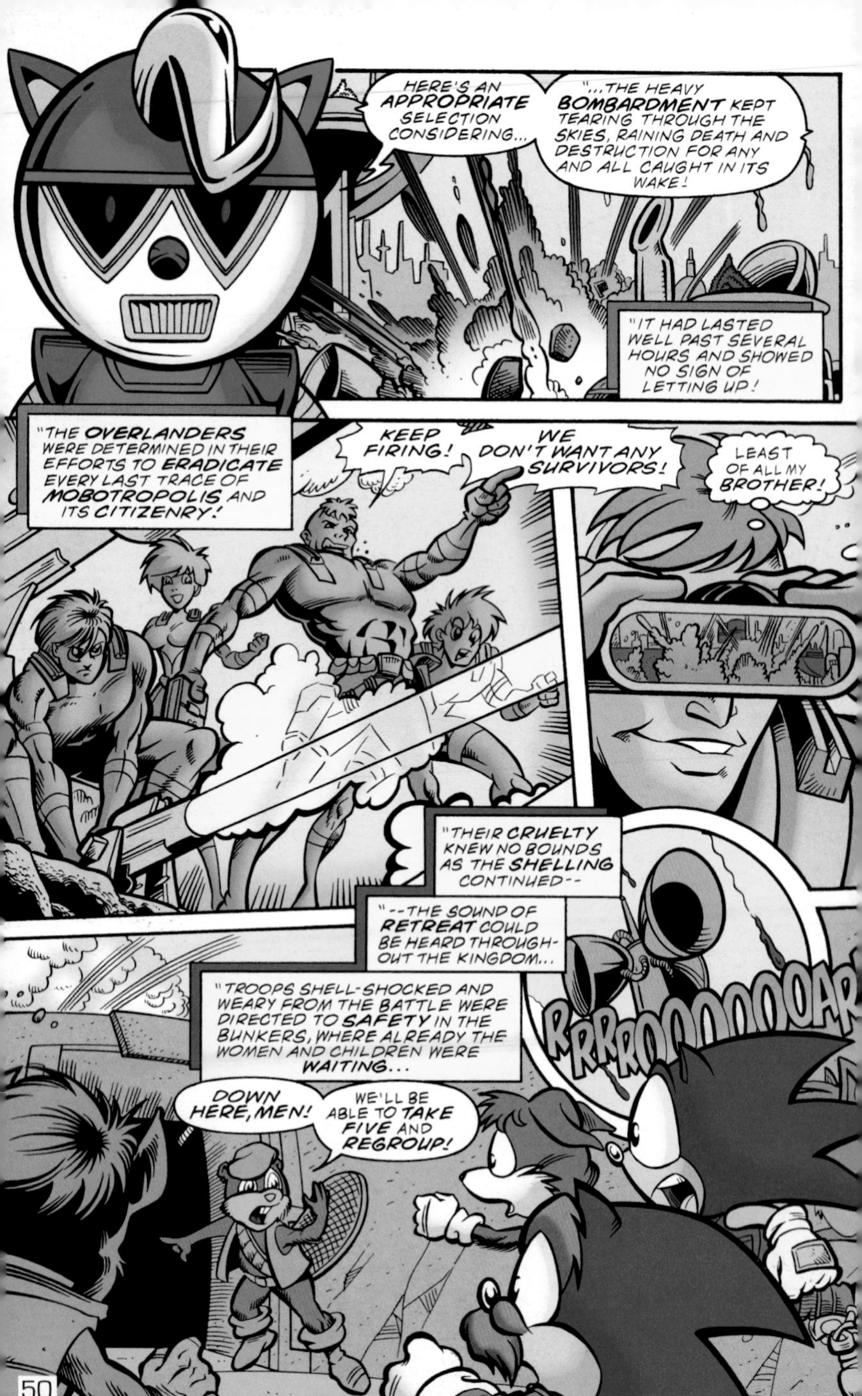

HERE'S AN APPROPRIATE SELECTION CONSIDERING...
"...THE HEAVY BOMBARDMENT KEPT TEARING THROUGH THE SKIES, RAINING DEATH AND DESTRUCTION FOR ANY AND ALL CAUGHT IN ITS WAKE!
"IT HAD LASTED WELL PAST SEVERAL HOURS AND SHOWED NO SIGN OF LETTING UP!
"THE OVERLANDERS WERE DETERMINED IN THEIR EFFORTS TO ERADICATE EVERY LAST TRACE OF MOBOTROPOLIS AND ITS CITIZENRY!
KEEP FIRING!
WE DON'T WANT ANY SURVIVORS!
LEAST OF ALL MY BROTHER!
"THEIR CRUELTY KNEW NO BOUNDS AS THE SHELLING CONTINUED--
"--THE SOUND OF RETREAT COULD BE HEARD THROUGHOUT THE KINGDOM...
"TROOPS SHELL-SHOCKED AND WEARY FROM THE BATTLE WERE DIRECTED TO SAFETY IN THE BUNKERS, WHERE ALREADY THE WOMEN AND CHILDREN WERE WAITING...
RRRROOOOOOOAR
DOWN HERE, MEN!
WE'LL BE ABLE TO TAKE FIVE AND REGROUP!

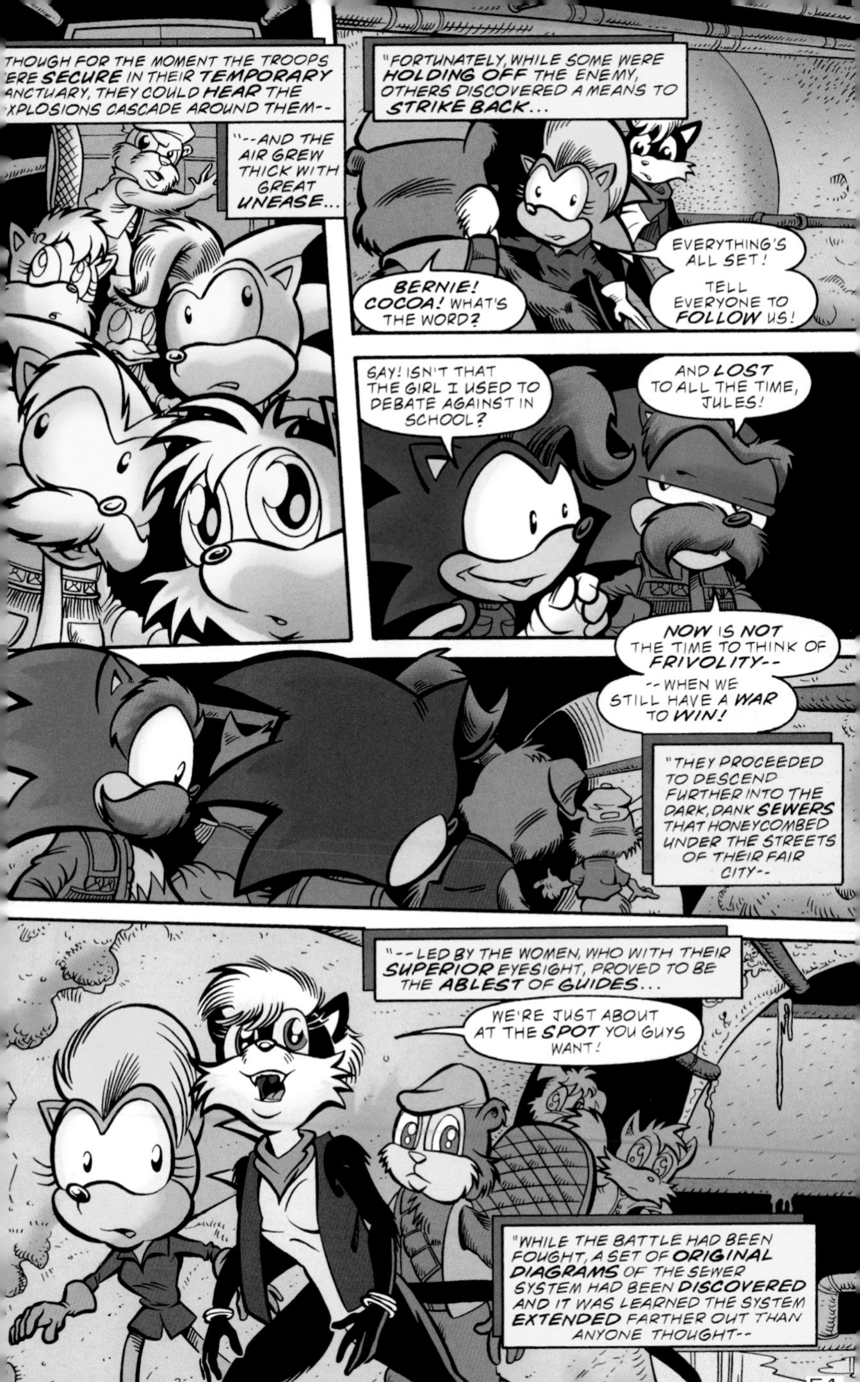

THOUGH FOR THE MOMENT THE TROOPS ERE SECURE IN THEIR TEMPORARY ANCTUARY, THEY COULD HEAR THE XPLOSIONS CASCADE AROUND THEM--
"--AND THE AIR GREW THICK WITH GREAT UNEASE...
"FORTUNATELY, WHILE SOME WERE HOLDING OFF THE ENEMY, OTHERS DISCOVERED A MEANS TO STRIKE BACK...
BERNIE! COCOA! WHAT'S THE WORD?
EVERYTHING'S ALL SET!
TELL EVERYONE TO FOLLOW US!
SAY! ISN'T THAT THE GIRL I USED TO DEBATE AGAINST IN SCHOOL?
AND LOST TO ALL THE TIME, JULES!
NOW IS NOT THE TIME TO THINK OF FRIVOLITY--
--WHEN WE STILL HAVE A WAR TO WIN!
"THEY PROCEEDED TO DESCEND FURTHER INTO THE DARK, DANK SEWERS THAT HONEYCOMBED UNDER THE STREETS OF THEIR FAIR CITY--
"--LED BY THE WOMEN, WHO WITH THEIR SUPERIOR EYESIGHT, PROVED TO BE THE ABLEST OF GUIDES...
WE'RE JUST ABOUT AT THE SPOT YOU GUYS WANT!
"WHILE THE BATTLE HAD BEEN FOUGHT, A SET OF ORIGINAL DIAGRAMS OF THE SEWER SYSTEM HAD BEEN DISCOVERED AND IT WAS LEARNED THE SYSTEM EXTENDED FARTHER OUT THAN ANYONE THOUGHT--

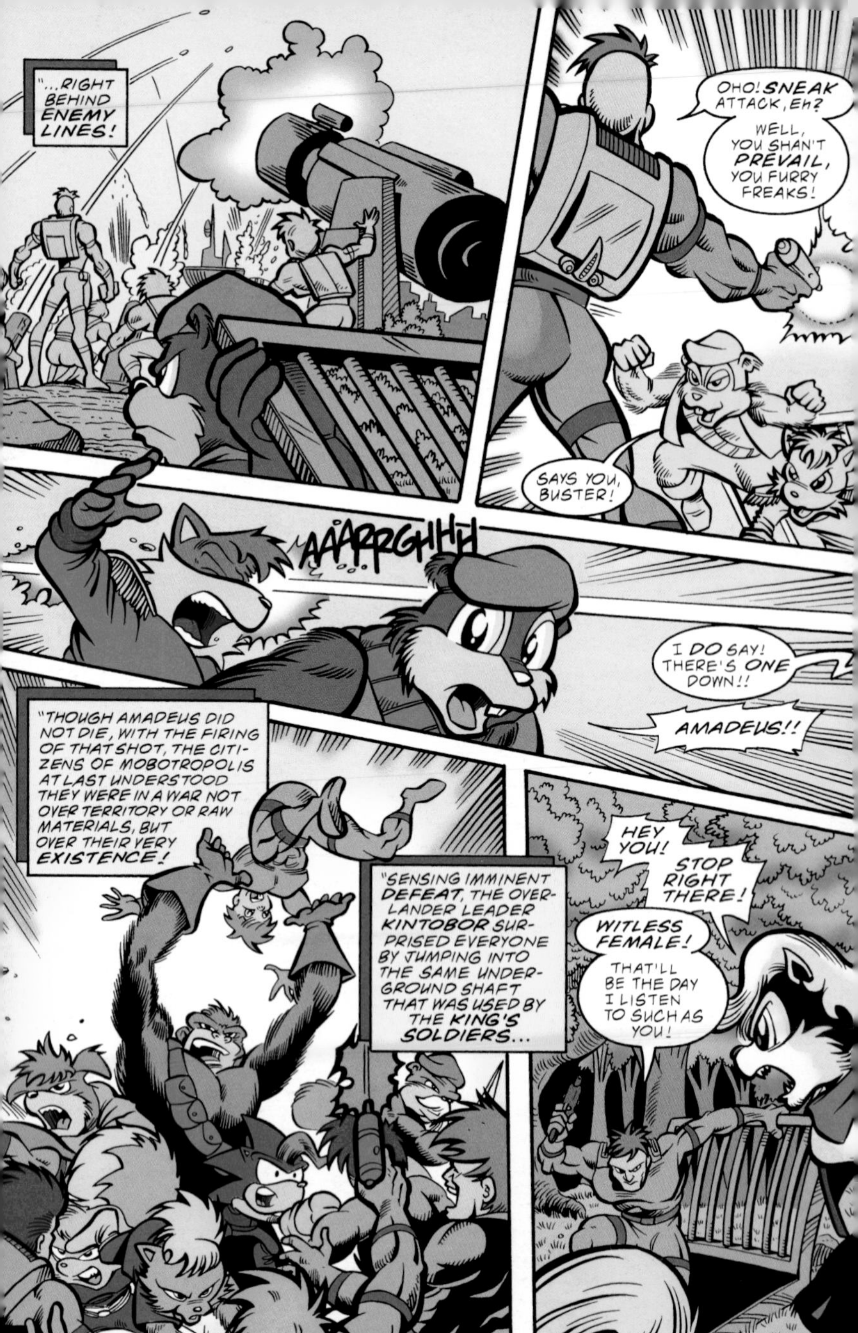

"...RIGHT BEHIND ENEMY LINES!
OHO! SNEAK ATTACK, Eh? WELL, YOU SHAN'T PREVAIL, YOU FURRY FREAKS!
SAYS YOU, BUSTER!
AAARRGHHH
I DO SAY! THERE'S ONE DOWN!!
AMADEUS!!
"THOUGH AMADEUS DID NOT DIE, WITH THE FIRING OF THAT SHOT, THE CITIZENS OF MOBOTROPOLIS AT LAST UNDERSTOOD THEY WERE IN A WAR NOT OVER TERRITORY OR RAW MATERIALS, BUT OVER THEIR VERY EXISTENCE!
"SENSING IMMINENT DEFEAT, THE OVERLANDER LEADER KINTOBOR SURPRISED EVERYONE BY JUMPING INTO THE SAME UNDERGROUND SHAFT THAT WAS USED BY THE KING'S SOLDIERS...
HEY YOU!
STOP RIGHT THERE!
WITLESS FEMALE!
THAT'LL BE THE DAY I LISTEN TO SUCH AS YOU!

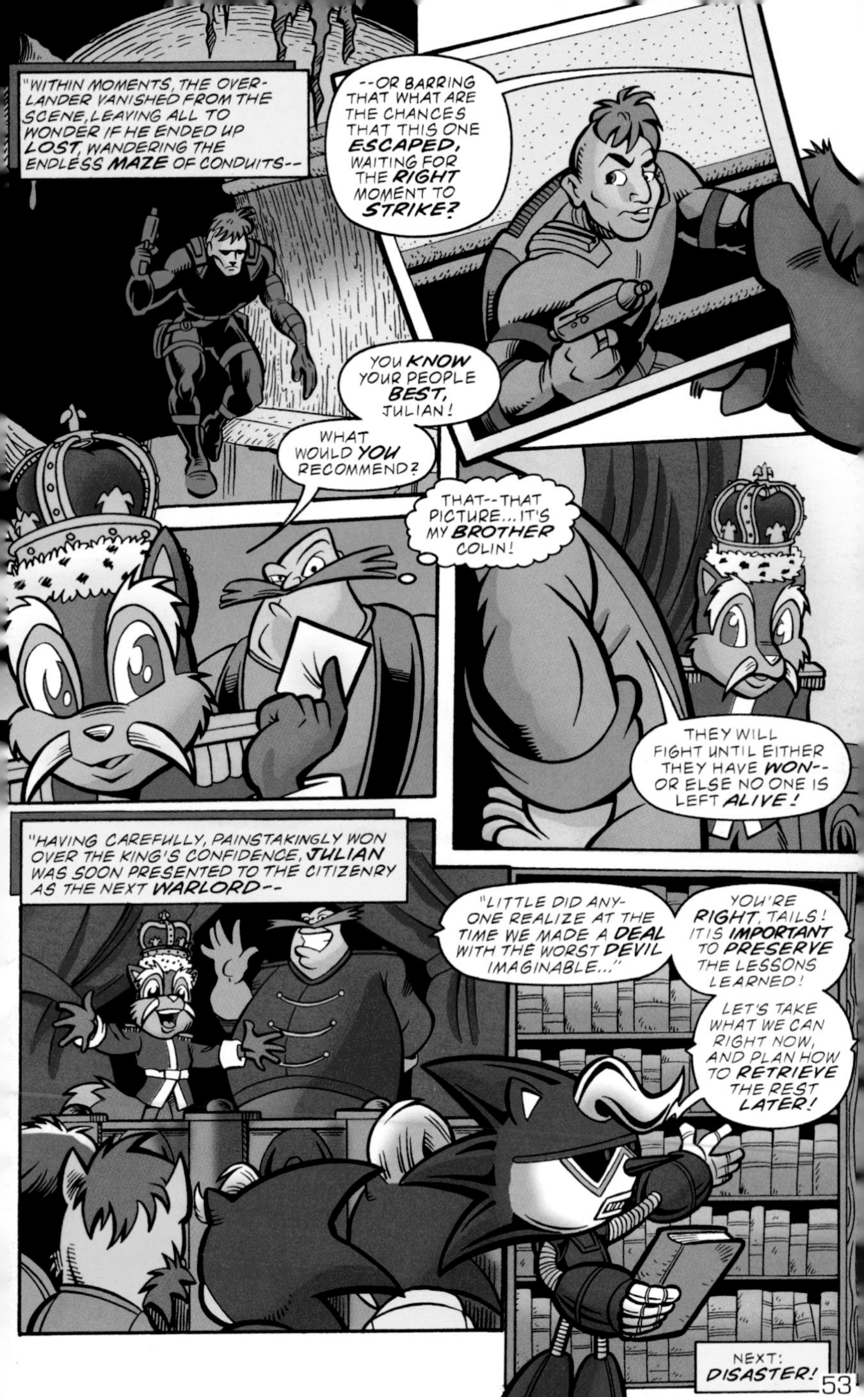
"WITHIN MOMENTS, THE OVER-LANDER VANISHED FROM THE SCENE, LEAVING ALL TO WONDER IF HE ENDED UP LOST, WANDERING THE ENDLESS MAZE OF CONDUITS--
--OR BARRING THAT WHAT ARE THE CHANCES THAT THIS ONE ESCAPED, WAITING FOR THE RIGHT MOMENT TO STRIKE?
YOU KNOW YOUR PEOPLE BEST, JULIAN!
WHAT WOULD YOU RECOMMEND?
THAT--THAT PICTURE... IT'S MY BROTHER COLIN!
THEY WILL FIGHT UNTIL EITHER THEY HAVE WON--OR ELSE NO ONE IS LEFT ALIVE!
"HAVING CAREFULLY, PAINSTAKINGLY WON OVER THE KING'S CONFIDENCE, JULIAN WAS SOON PRESENTED TO THE CITIZENRY AS THE NEXT WARLORD--
"LITTLE DID ANYONE REALIZE AT THE TIME WE MADE A DEAL WITH THE WORST DEVIL IMAGINABLE..."
YOU'RE RIGHT, TAILS! IT IS IMPORTANT TO PRESERVE THE LESSONS LEARNED!
LET'S TAKE WHAT WE CAN RIGHT NOW, AND PLAN HOW TO RETRIEVE THE REST LATER!
NEXT: DISASTER!

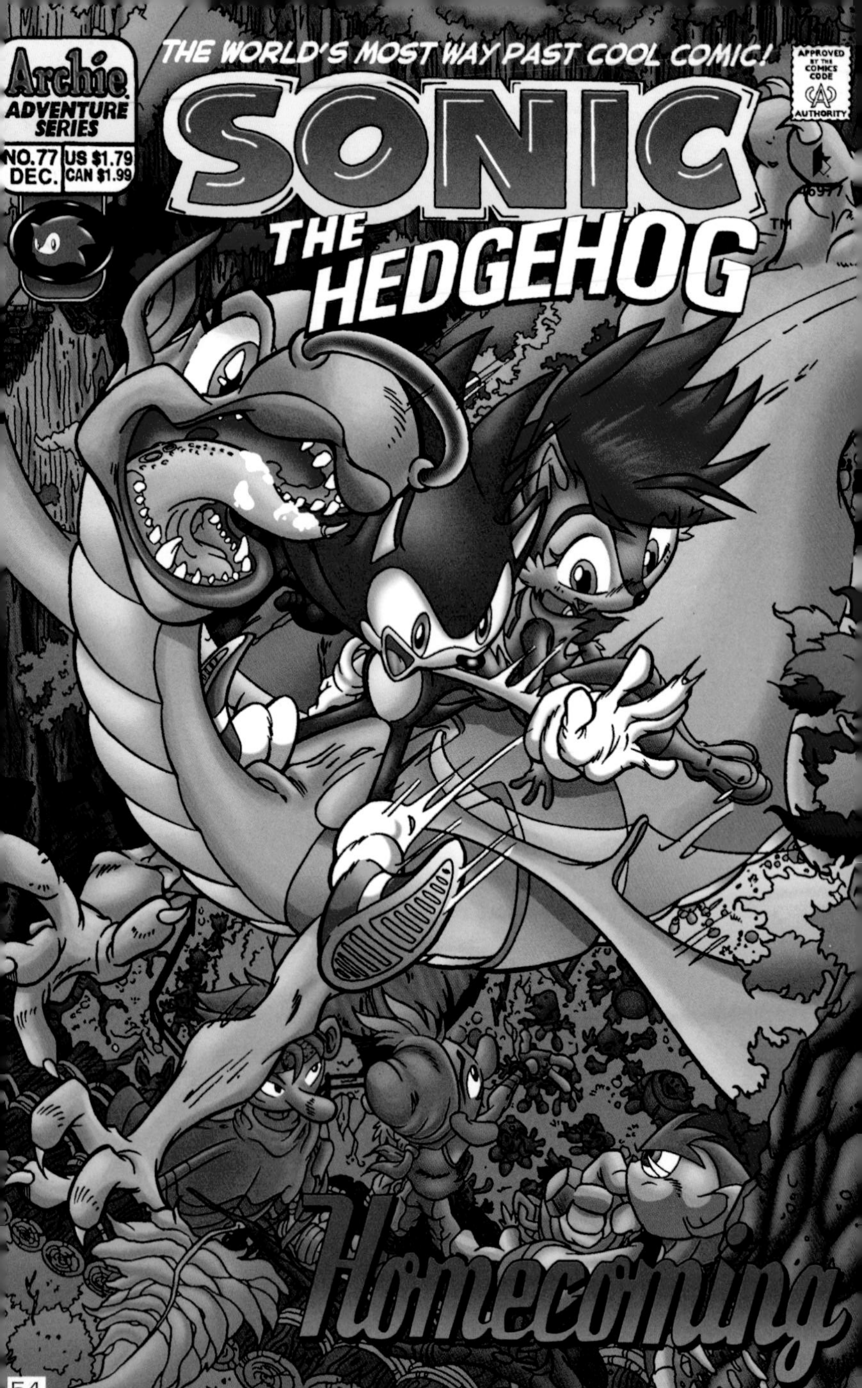
THE WORLD'S MOST WAY PAST COOL COMIC!
Archie ADVENTURE SERIES
NO.77 DEC.
US $1.79 CAN $1.99
APPROVED BY THE COMICS CODE AUTHORITY
SONIC THE HEDGEHOG
Homecoming

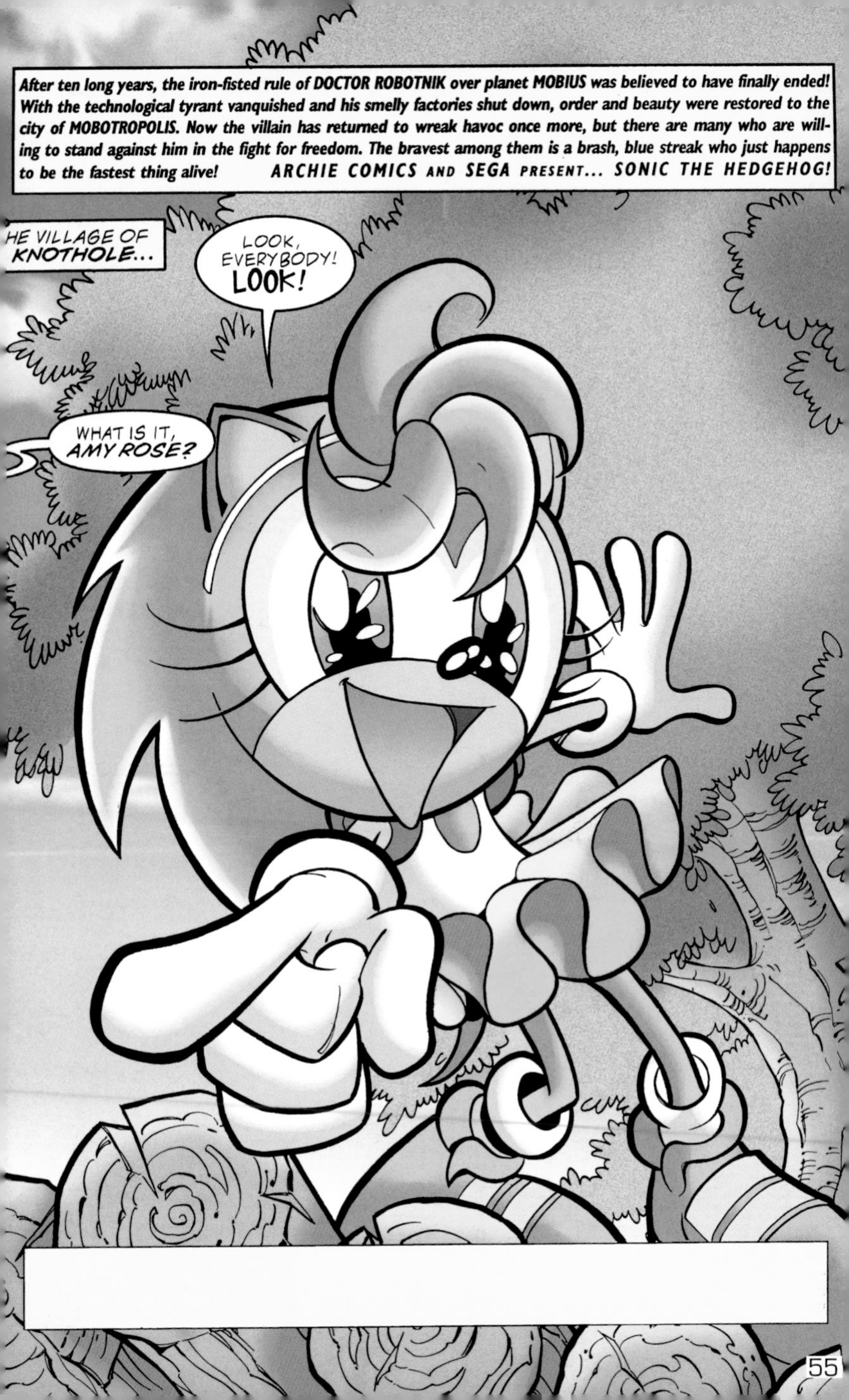

After ten long years, the iron-fisted rule of DOCTOR ROBOTNIK over planet MOBIUS was believed to have finally ended! With the technological tyrant vanquished and his smelly factories shut down, order and beauty were restored to the city of MOBOTROPOLIS. Now the villain has returned to wreak havoc once more, but there are many who are willing to stand against him in the fight for freedom. The bravest among them is a brash, blue streak who just happens to be the fastest thing alive! ARCHIE COMICS AND SEGA PRESENT... SONIC THE HEDGEHOG!
HE VILLAGE OF KNOTHOLE...
LOOK, EVERYBODY! LOOK!
WHAT IS IT, AMY ROSE?

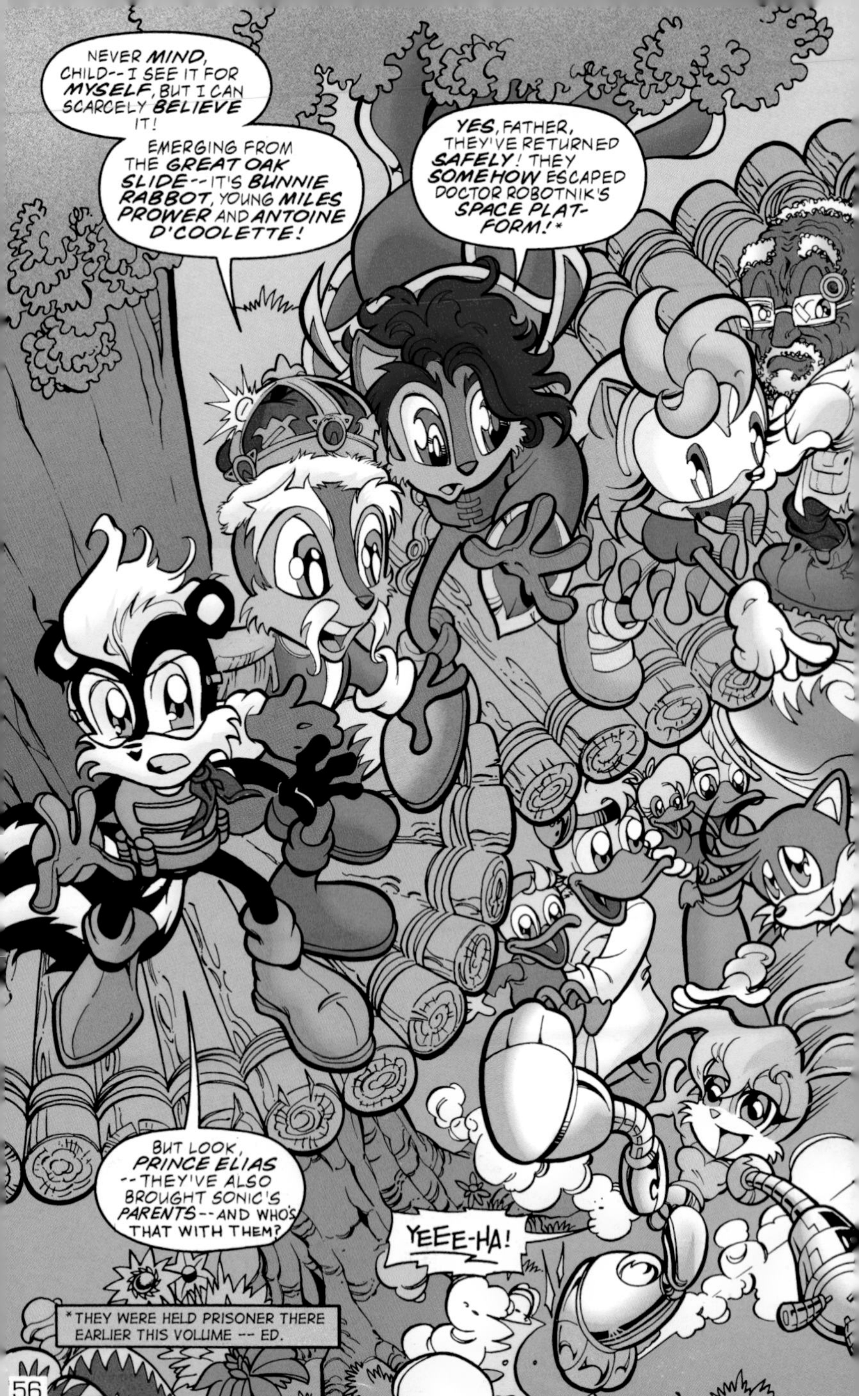
NEVER MIND, CHILD-- I SEE IT FOR MYSELF, BUT I CAN SCARCELY BELIEVE IT!
EMERGING FROM THE GREAT OAK SLIDE-- IT'S BUNNIE RABBOT, YOUNG MILES PROWER AND ANTOINE D'COOLETTE!
YES, FATHER, THEY'VE RETURNED SAFELY! THEY SOMEHOW ESCAPED DOCTOR ROBOTNIK'S SPACE PLAT-FORM!*
BUT LOOK, PRINCE ELIAS --THEY'VE ALSO BROUGHT SONIC'S PARENTS--AND WHO'S THAT WITH THEM?
YEEE-HA!
*THEY WERE HELD PRISONER THERE EARLIER THIS VOLUME -- ED.

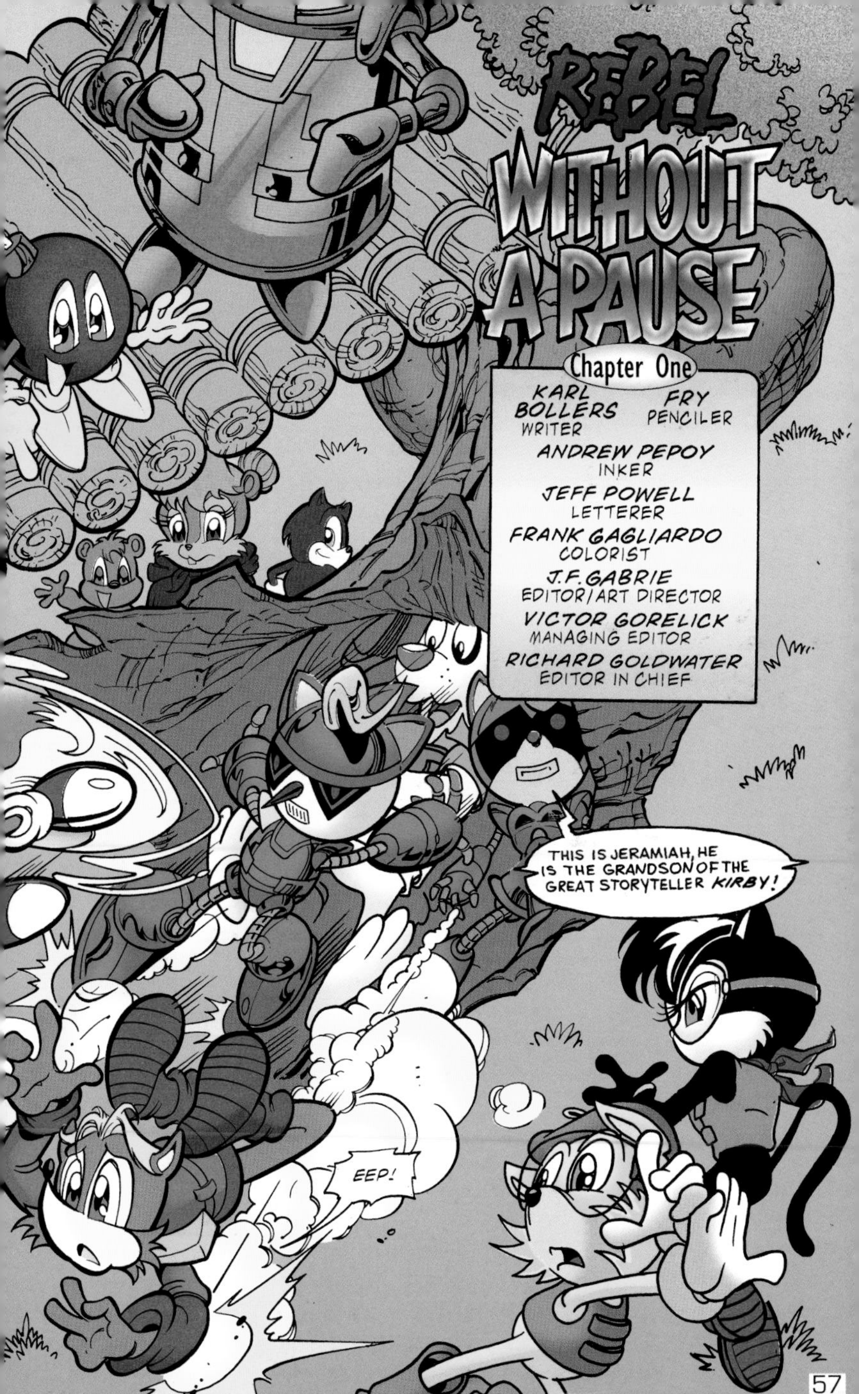
REBEL WITHOUT A PAUSE
Chapter One
KARL BOLLERS WRITER
FRY PENCILER
ANDREW PEPOY INKER
JEFF POWELL LETTERER
FRANK GAGLIARDO COLORIST
J.F. GABRIE EDITOR/ART DIRECTOR
VICTOR GORELICK MANAGING EDITOR
RICHARD GOLDWATER EDITOR IN CHIEF
THIS IS JERAMIAH, HE IS THE GRANDSON OF THE GREAT STORYTELLER KIRBY!
EEP!

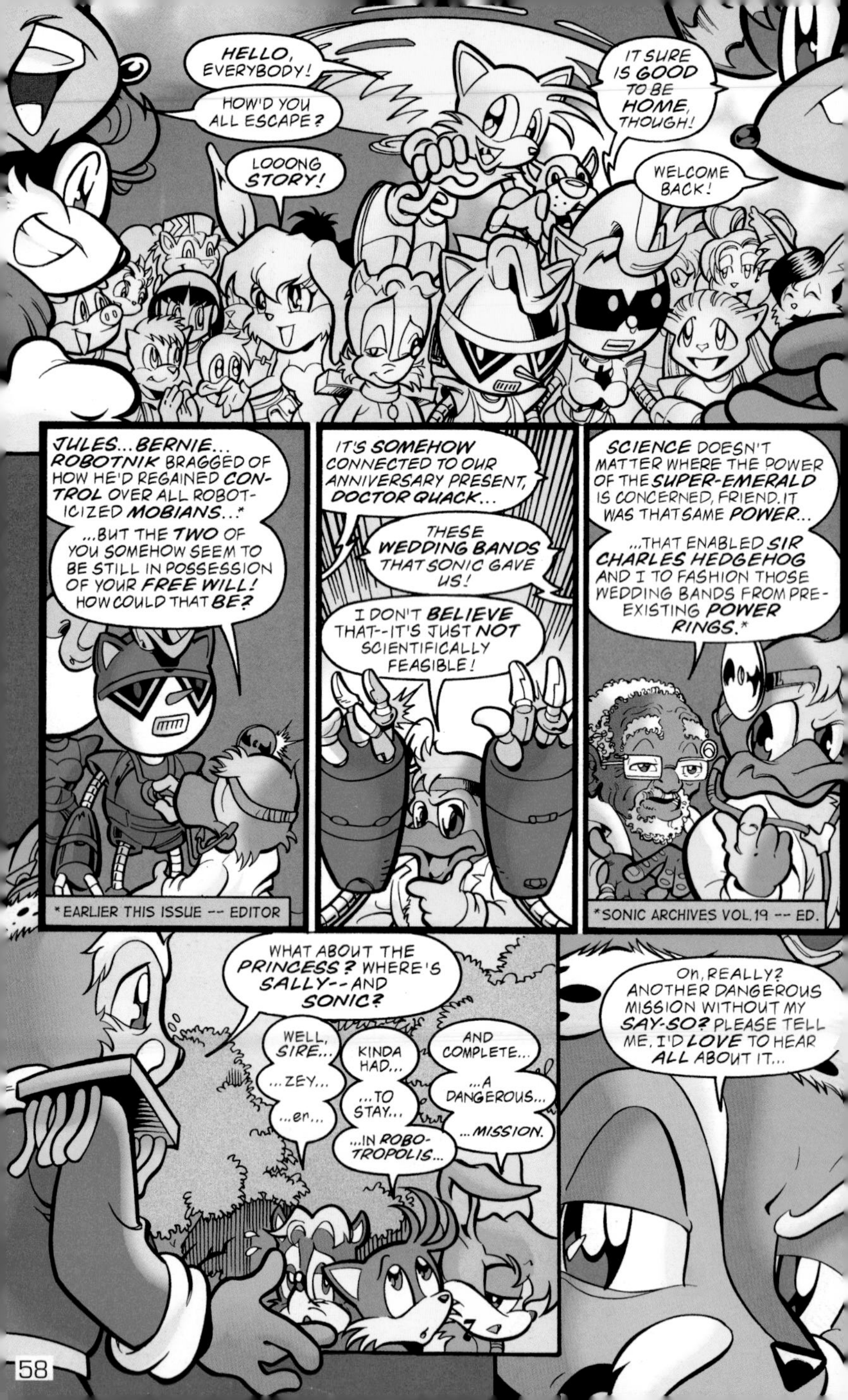
HELLO, EVERYBODY!
HOW'D YOU ALL ESCAPE?
LOOOONG STORY!
IT SURE IS GOOD TO BE HOME, THOUGH!
WELCOME BACK!
JULES... BERNIE... ROBOTNIK BRAGGED OF HOW HE'D REGAINED CONTROL OVER ALL ROBOTICIZED MOBIANS...*
...BUT THE TWO OF YOU SOMEHOW SEEM TO BE STILL IN POSSESSION OF YOUR FREE WILL! HOW COULD THAT BE?
*EARLIER THIS ISSUE -- EDITOR
IT'S SOMEHOW CONNECTED TO OUR ANNIVERSARY PRESENT, DOCTOR QUACK...
THESE WEDDING BANDS THAT SONIC GAVE US!
I DON'T BELIEVE THAT--IT'S JUST NOT SCIENTIFICALLY FEASIBLE!
SCIENCE DOESN'T MATTER WHERE THE POWER OF THE SUPER-EMERALD IS CONCERNED, FRIEND. IT WAS THAT SAME POWER...
...THAT ENABLED SIR CHARLES HEDGEHOG AND I TO FASHION THOSE WEDDING BANDS FROM PRE-EXISTING POWER RINGS.*
*SONIC ARCHIVES VOL. 19 -- ED.
WHAT ABOUT THE PRINCESS? WHERE'S SALLY--AND SONIC?
WELL, SIRE...
...ZEY...
...er...
KINDA HAD...
...TO STAY...
...IN ROBOTROPOLIS...
AND COMPLETE...
...A DANGEROUS...
...MISSION.
OH, REALLY? ANOTHER DANGEROUS MISSION WITHOUT MY SAY-SO? PLEASE TELL ME. I'D LOVE TO HEAR ALL ABOUT IT...

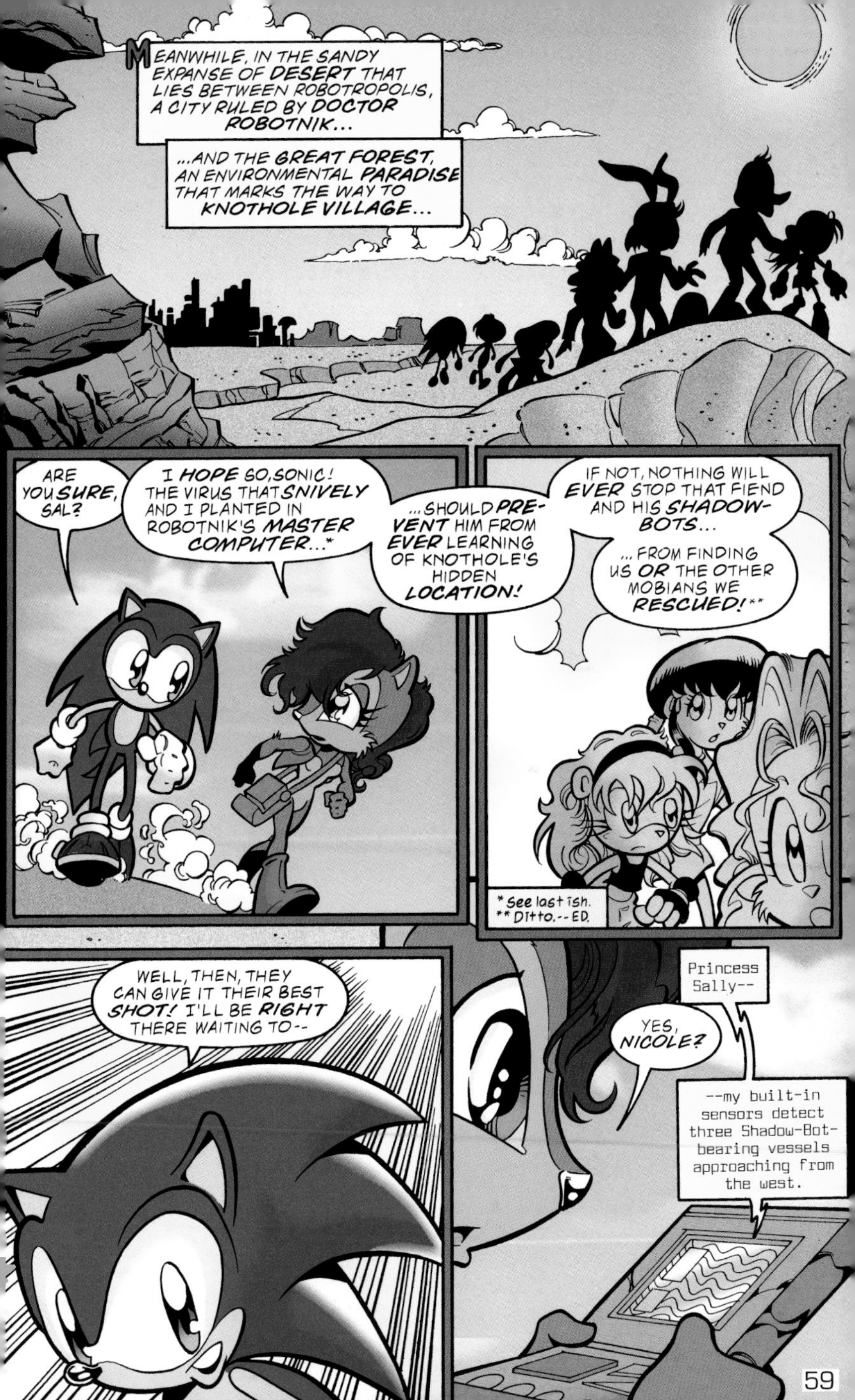
MEANWHILE, IN THE SANDY EXPANSE OF DESERT THAT LIES BETWEEN ROBOTROPOLIS, A CITY RULED BY DOCTOR ROBOTNIK...
...AND THE GREAT FOREST, AN ENVIRONMENTAL PARADISE THAT MARKS THE WAY TO KNOTHOLE VILLAGE...
ARE YOU SURE, SAL?
I HOPE SO, SONIC! THE VIRUS THAT SNIVELY AND I PLANTED IN ROBOTNIK'S MASTER COMPUTER...*
...SHOULD PREVENT HIM FROM EVER LEARNING OF KNOTHOLE'S HIDDEN LOCATION!
IF NOT, NOTHING WILL EVER STOP THAT FIEND AND HIS SHADOW-BOTS...
...FROM FINDING US OR THE OTHER MOBIANS WE RESCUED!**
*See last ish.
**Ditto.--ED.
WELL, THEN, THEY CAN GIVE IT THEIR BEST SHOT! I'LL BE RIGHT THERE WAITING TO--
Princess Sally--
YES, NICOLE?
--my built-in sensors detect three Shadow-Bot-bearing vessels approaching from the west.

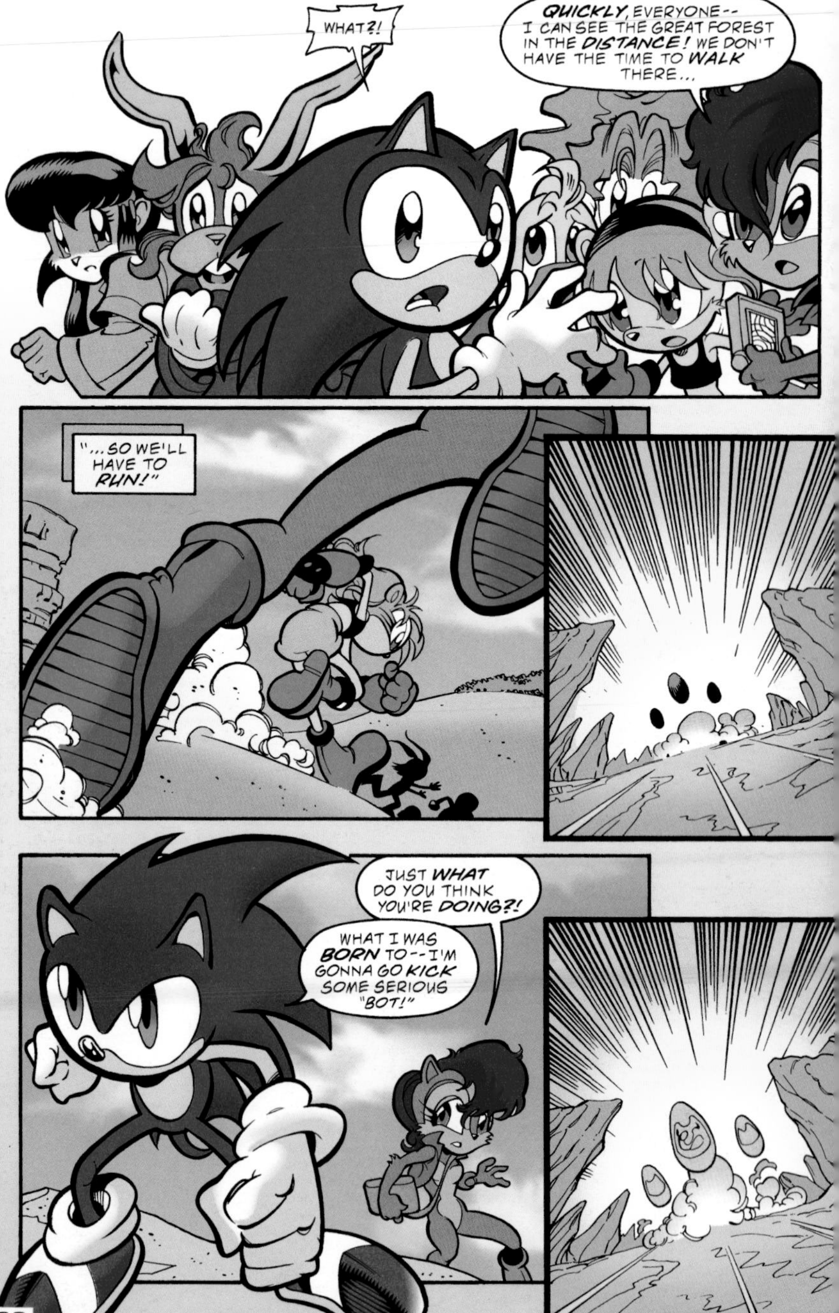
WHAT?!
QUICKLY, EVERYONE-- I CAN SEE THE GREAT FOREST IN THE DISTANCE! WE DON'T HAVE THE TIME TO WALK THERE...
"...SO WE'LL HAVE TO RUN!"
JUST WHAT DO YOU THINK YOU'RE DOING?!
WHAT I WAS BORN TO--I'M GONNA GO KICK SOME SERIOUS "BOT!"

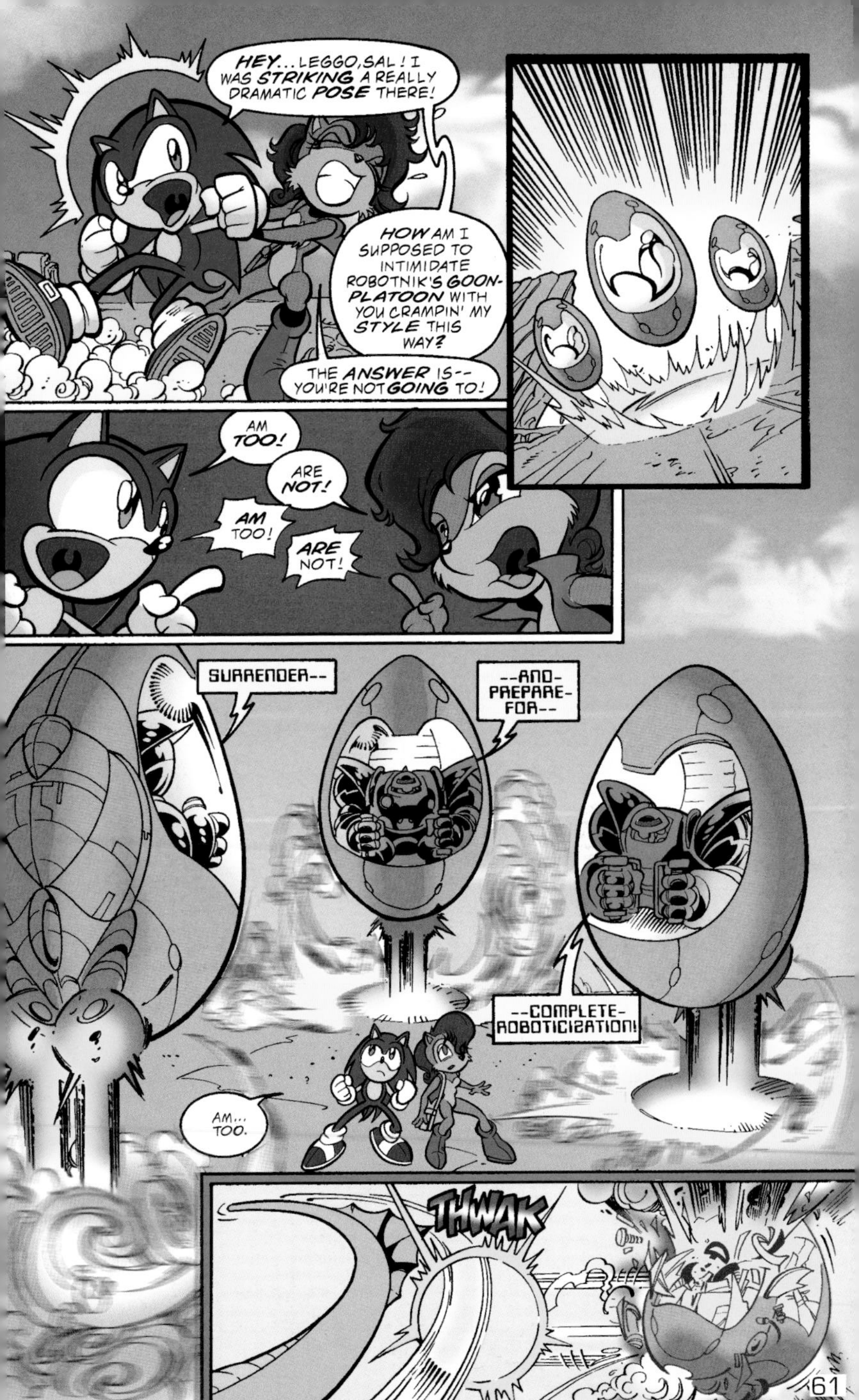
HEY...LEGGO, SAL! I WAS STRIKING A REALLY DRAMATIC POSE THERE!
HOW AM I SUPPOSED TO INTIMIDATE ROBOTNIK'S GOON-PLATOON WITH YOU CRAMPIN' MY STYLE THIS WAY?
THE ANSWER IS--YOU'RE NOT GOING TO!
AM TOO!
ARE NOT!
AM TOO!
ARE NOT!
SURRENDER--
--AND-PREPARE-FOR--
--COMPLETE-ROBOTICIZATION!
AM... TOO.
THWAK

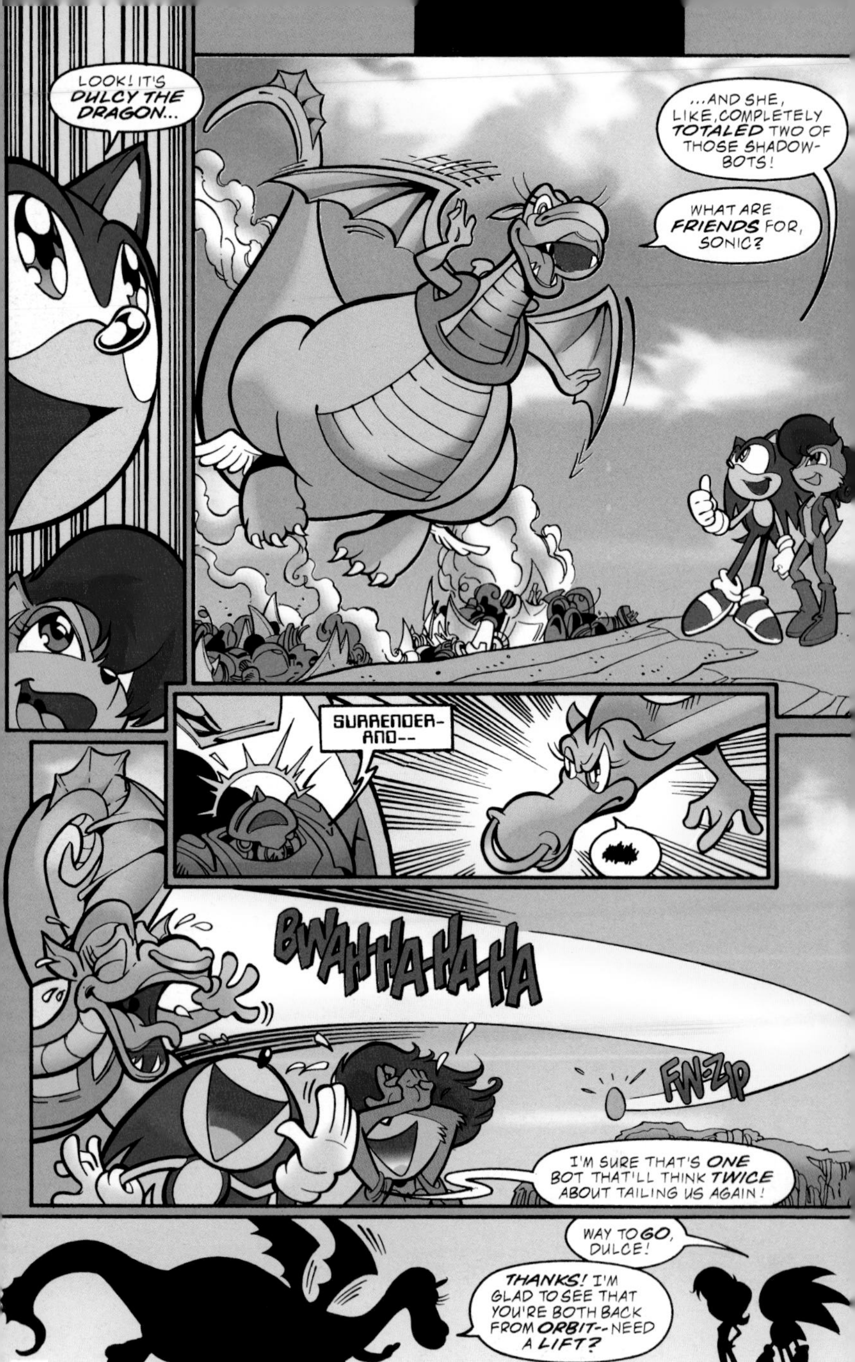

LOOK! IT'S DULCY THE DRAGON...
...AND SHE, LIKE, COMPLETELY TOTALED TWO OF THOSE SHADOW-BOTS!
WHAT ARE FRIENDS FOR, SONIC?
SURRENDER-AND--
BWAH-HA-HA-HA-HA
FWZIP
I'M SURE THAT'S ONE BOT THAT'LL THINK TWICE ABOUT TAILING US AGAIN!
WAY TO GO, DULCE!
THANKS! I'M GLAD TO SEE THAT YOU'RE BOTH BACK FROM ORBIT--NEED A LIFT?

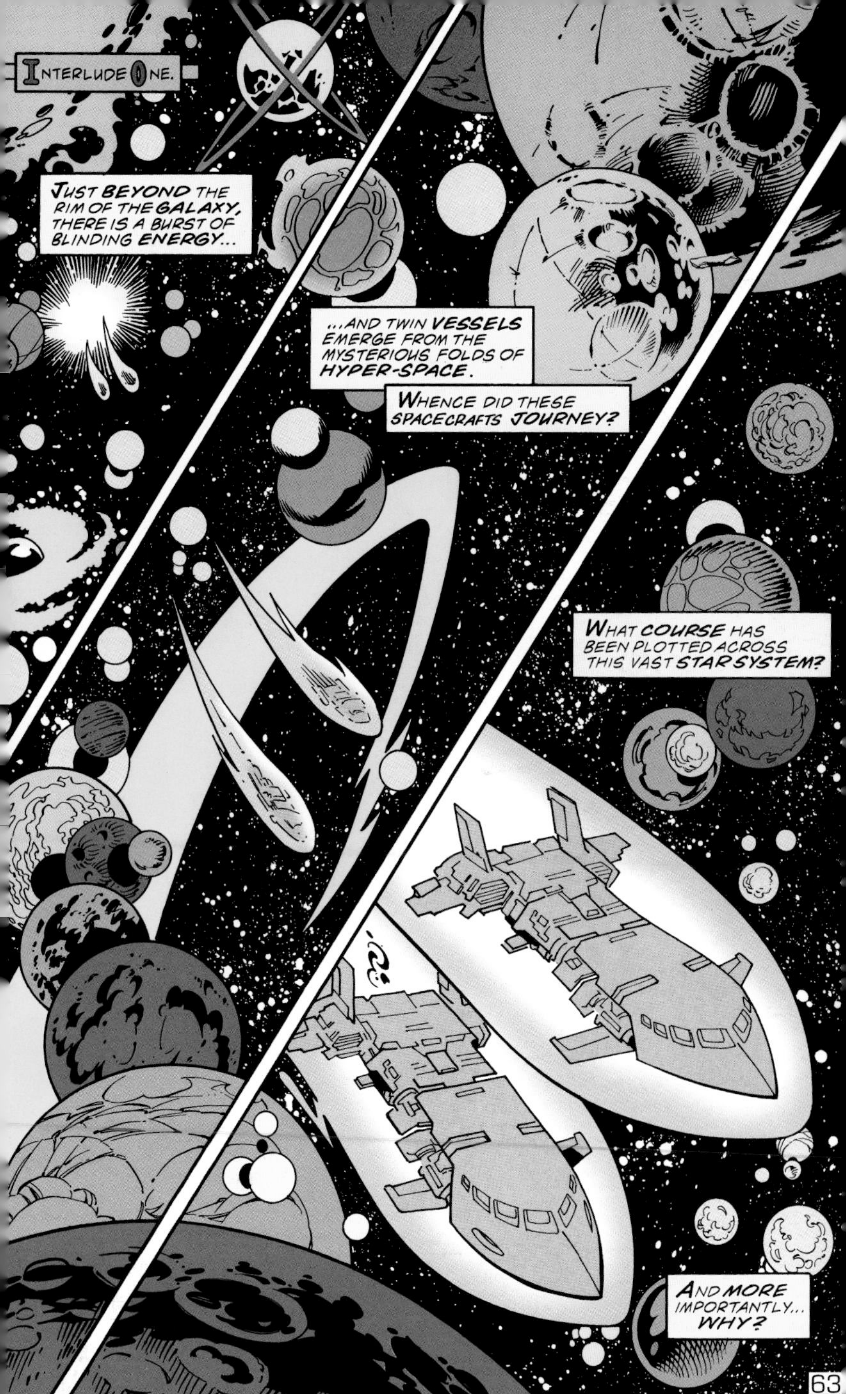
INTERLUDE ONE.
JUST BEYOND THE RIM OF THE GALAXY, THERE IS A BURST OF BLINDING ENERGY...
...AND TWIN VESSELS EMERGE FROM THE MYSTERIOUS FOLDS OF HYPER-SPACE.
WHENCE DID THESE SPACECRAFTS JOURNEY?
WHAT COURSE HAS BEEN PLOTTED ACROSS THIS VAST STAR SYSTEM?
AND MORE IMPORTANTLY... WHY?

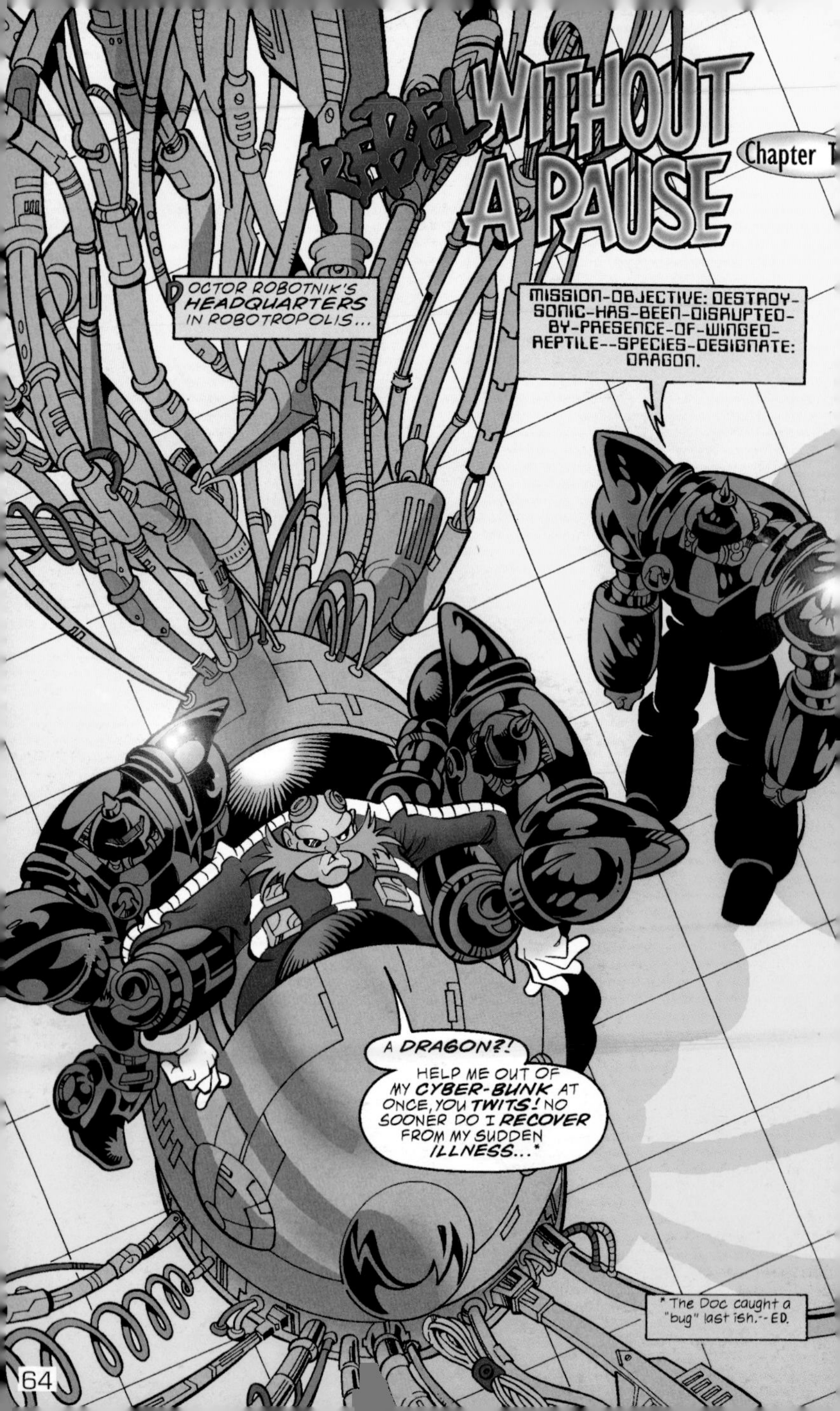
REBEL WITHOUT A PAUSE
Chapter T
DOCTOR ROBOTNIK'S HEADQUARTERS IN ROBOTROPOLIS...
MISSION-OBJECTIVE: DESTROY-SONIC-HAS-BEEN-DISRUPTED-BY-PRESENCE-OF-WINGED-REPTILE--SPECIES-DESIGNATE: DRAGON.
A DRAGON?!
HELP ME OUT OF MY CYBER-BUNK AT ONCE, YOU TWITS! NO SOONER DO I RECOVER FROM MY SUDDEN ILLNESS...*
*The Doc caught a "bug" last ish.--ED.

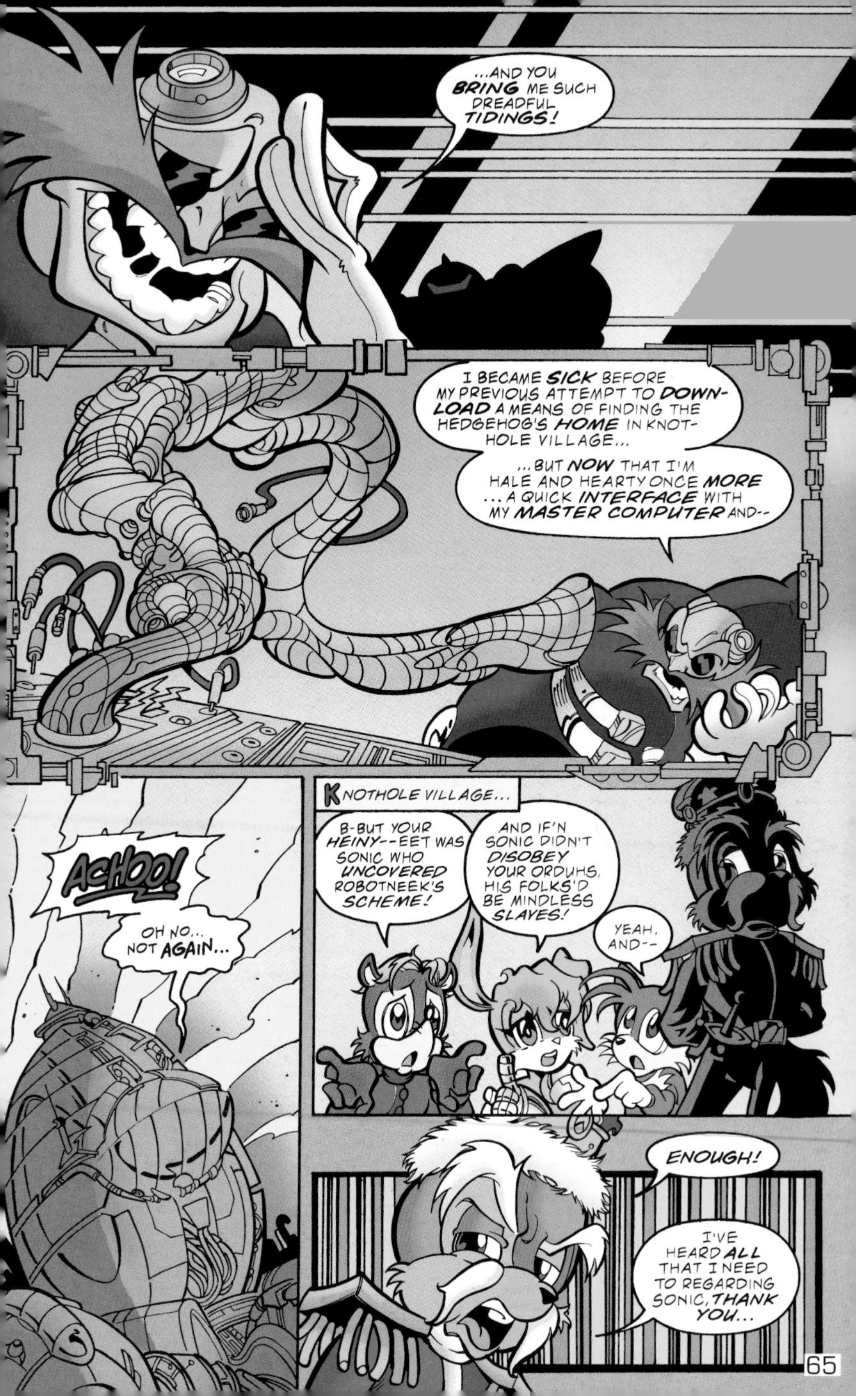
...AND YOU BRING ME SUCH DREADFUL TIDINGS!
I BECAME SICK BEFORE MY PREVIOUS ATTEMPT TO DOWNLOAD A MEANS OF FINDING THE HEDGEHOG'S HOME IN KNOTHOLE VILLAGE...
...BUT NOW THAT I'M HALE AND HEARTY ONCE MORE ...A QUICK INTERFACE WITH MY MASTER COMPUTER AND--
ACHOO!
OH NO... NOT AGAIN...
KNOTHOLE VILLAGE...
B-BUT YOUR HEINY--EET WAS SONIC WHO UNCOVERED ROBOTNEEK'S SCHEME!
AND IF'N SONIC DIDN'T DISOBEY YOUR ORDUHS, HIS FOLKS'D BE MINDLESS SLAVES!
YEAH, AND--
ENOUGH!
I'VE HEARD ALL THAT I NEED TO REGARDING SONIC, THANK YOU...

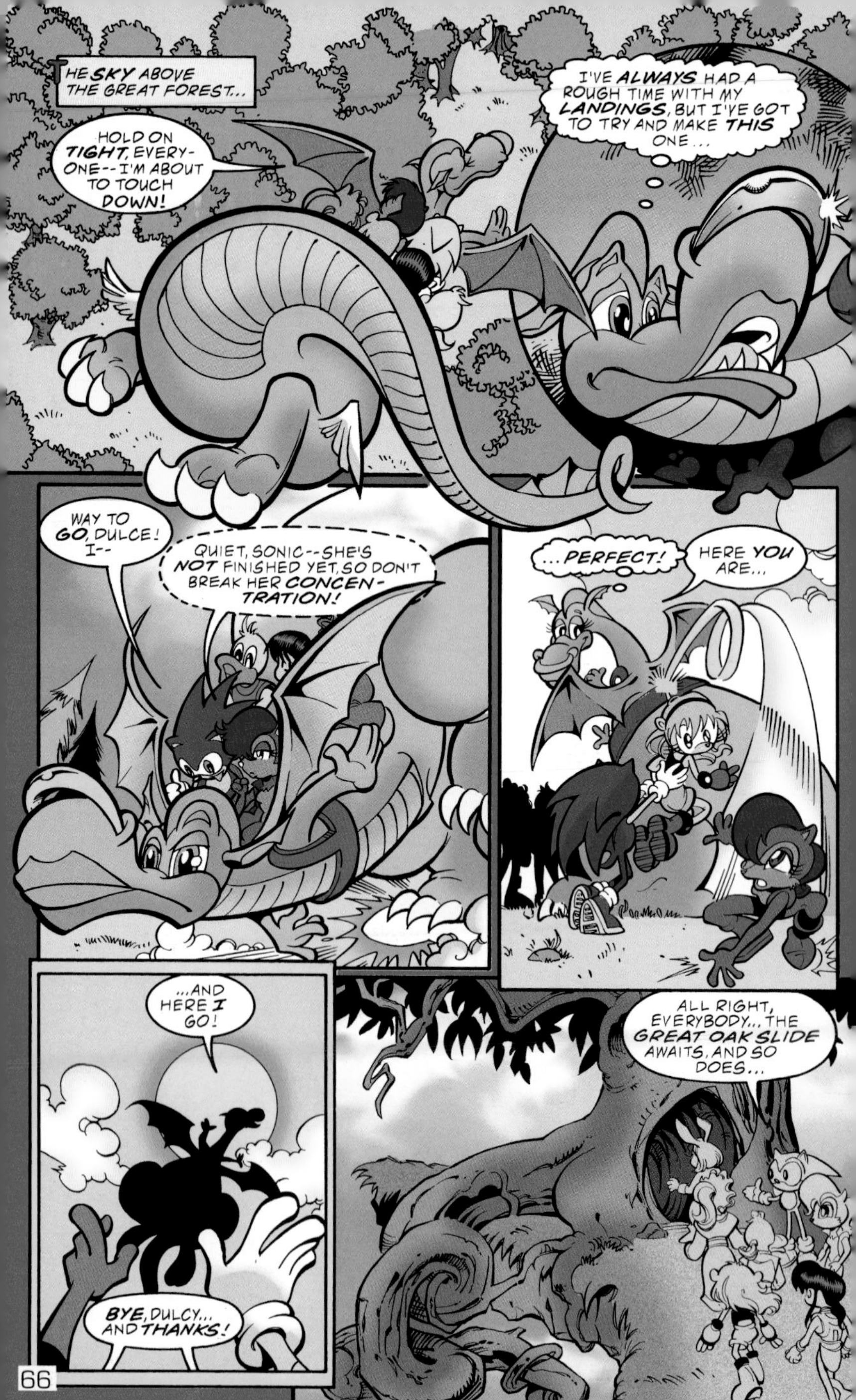
THE SKY ABOVE THE GREAT FOREST...
HOLD ON TIGHT, EVERY-ONE--I'M ABOUT TO TOUCH DOWN!
I'VE ALWAYS HAD A ROUGH TIME WITH MY LANDINGS, BUT I'VE GOT TO TRY AND MAKE THIS ONE...
WAY TO GO, DULCE! I--
QUIET, SONIC--SHE'S NOT FINISHED YET, SO DON'T BREAK HER CONCEN-TRATION!
...PERFECT!
HERE YOU ARE...
...AND HERE I GO!
BYE, DULCY... AND THANKS!
ALL RIGHT, EVERYBODY... THE GREAT OAK SLIDE AWAITS, AND SO DOES...

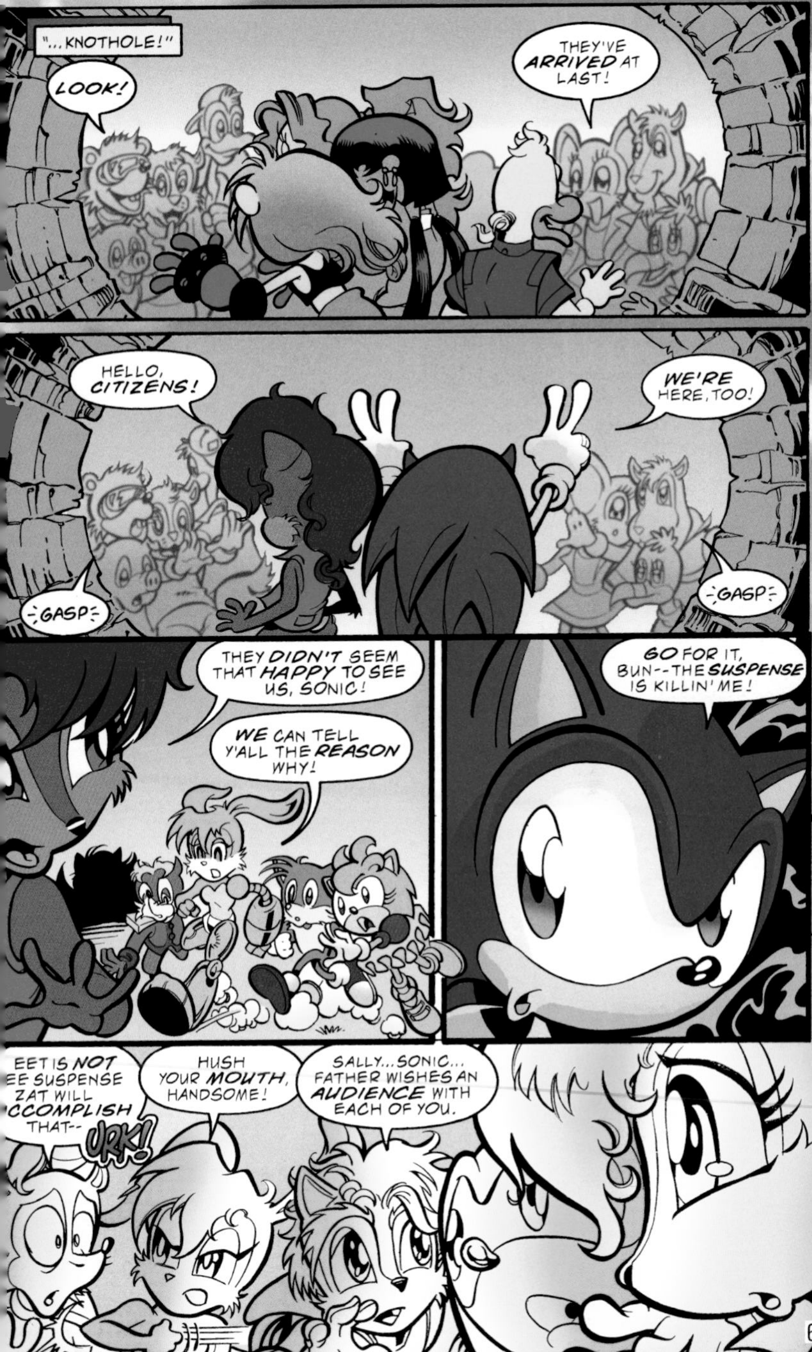
"...KNOTHOLE!"
LOOK!
THEY'VE ARRIVED AT LAST!
HELLO, CITIZENS!
WE'RE HERE, TOO!
-GASP-
-GASP-
THEY DIDN'T SEEM THAT HAPPY TO SEE US, SONIC!
WE CAN TELL Y'ALL THE REASON WHY!
GO FOR IT, BUN--THE SUSPENSE IS KILLIN' ME!
EET IS NOT EE SUSPENSE ZAT WILL CCOMPLISH THAT--
URK!
HUSH YOUR MOUTH, HANDSOME!
SALLY...SONIC... FATHER WISHES AN AUDIENCE WITH EACH OF YOU.

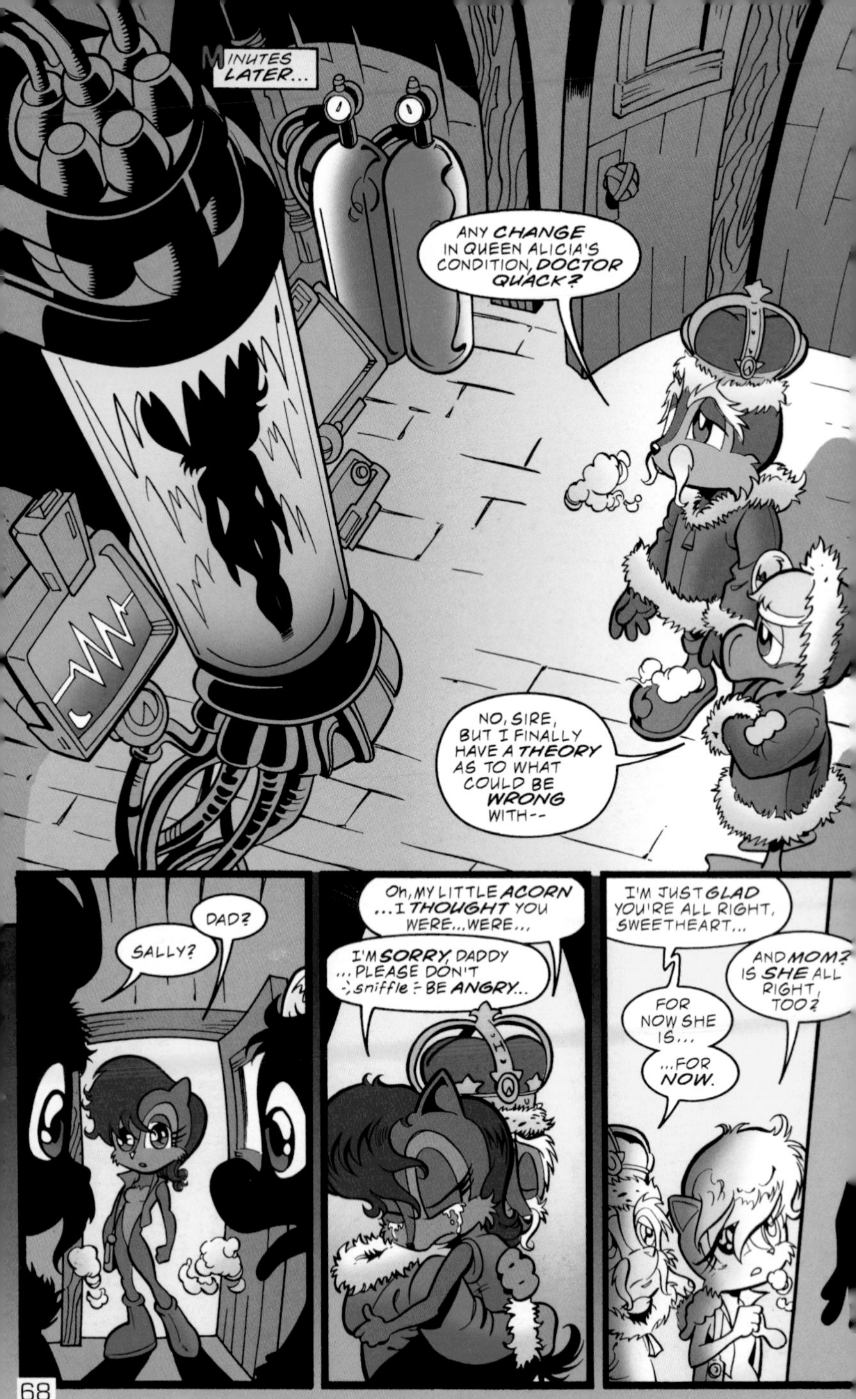

MINUTES LATER...
ANY CHANGE IN QUEEN ALICIA'S CONDITION, DOCTOR QUACK?
NO, SIRE, BUT I FINALLY HAVE A THEORY AS TO WHAT COULD BE WRONG WITH--
DAD?
SALLY?
Oh, MY LITTLE ACORN ...I THOUGHT YOU WERE...WERE...
I'M SORRY, DADDY ... PLEASE DON'T -; sniffle ;- BE ANGRY...
I'M JUST GLAD YOU'RE ALL RIGHT, SWEETHEART...
AND MOM? IS SHE ALL RIGHT, TOO?
FOR NOW SHE IS...
...FOR NOW.

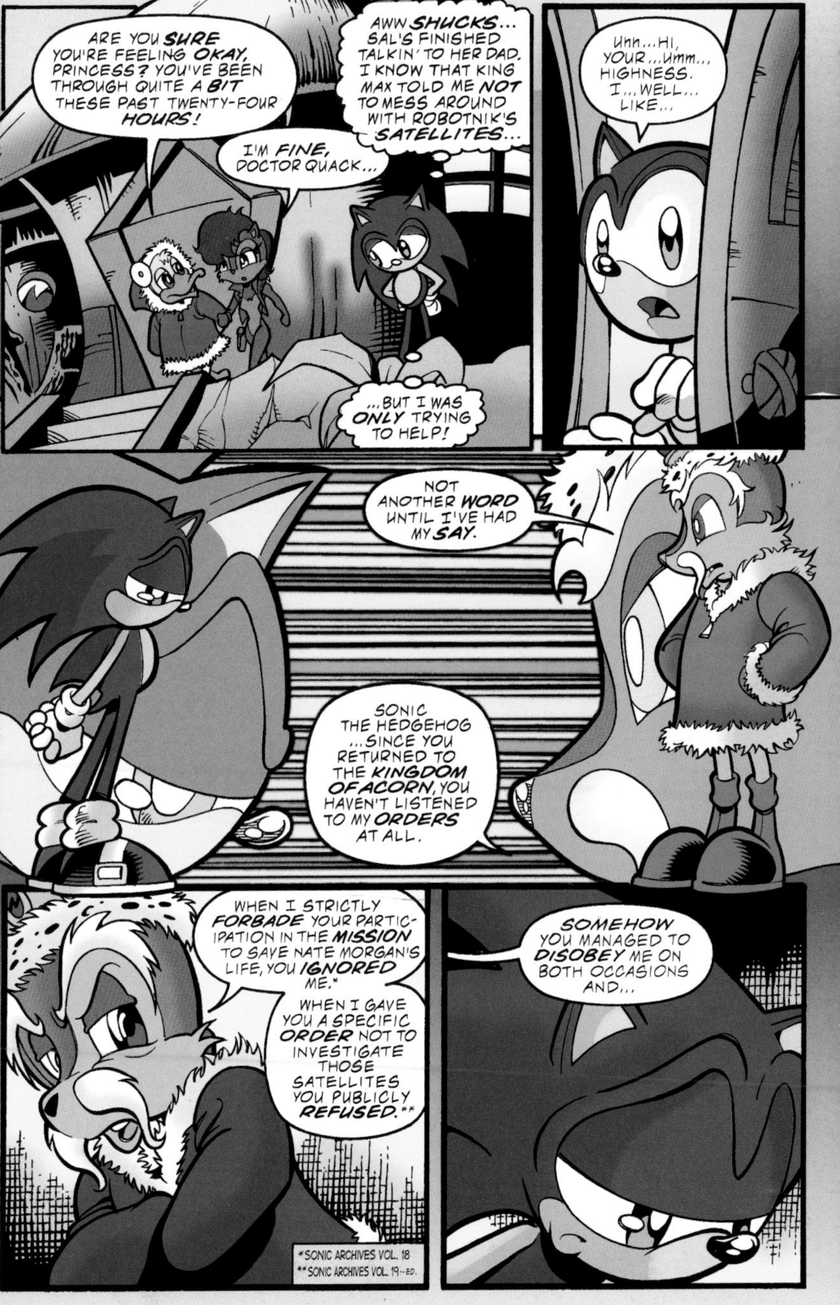
ARE YOU SURE YOU'RE FEELING OKAY, PRINCESS? YOU'VE BEEN THROUGH QUITE A BIT THESE PAST TWENTY-FOUR HOURS!
I'M FINE, DOCTOR QUACK...
AWW SHUCKS... SAL'S FINISHED TALKIN' TO HER DAD. I KNOW THAT KING MAX TOLD ME NOT TO MESS AROUND WITH ROBOTNIK'S SATELLITES...
...BUT I WAS ONLY TRYING TO HELP!
Unn...HI, YOUR...Umm... HIGHNESS. I...WELL... LIKE...
NOT ANOTHER WORD UNTIL I'VE HAD MY SAY.
SONIC THE HEDGEHOG ...SINCE YOU RETURNED TO THE KINGDOM OF ACORN, YOU HAVEN'T LISTENED TO MY ORDERS AT ALL.
WHEN I STRICTLY FORBADE YOUR PARTIC-IPATION IN THE MISSION TO SAVE NATE MORGAN'S LIFE, YOU IGNORED ME.*
WHEN I GAVE YOU A SPECIFIC ORDER NOT TO INVESTIGATE THOSE SATELLITES YOU PUBLICLY REFUSED.**
*SONIC ARCHIVES VOL. 18
**SONIC ARCHIVES VOL. 19--ED.
SOMEHOW YOU MANAGED TO DISOBEY ME ON BOTH OCCASIONS AND...

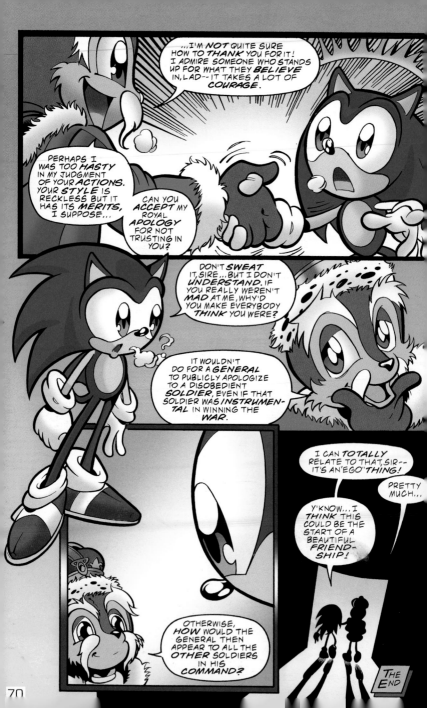

...I'm *NOT* quite sure how to *THANK* you for it! I admire someone who stands up for what they *BELIEVE* in, lad-- it takes a lot of *COURAGE*.

PERHAPS I was too *HASTY* in my judgment of your *ACTIONS*. Your *STYLE* is *RECKLESS* but it has its *MERITS*, I suppose...

CAN YOU *ACCEPT* MY ROYAL *APOLOGY* for not trusting in you?

DON'T *SWEAT* it, sire...but I don't *UNDERSTAND*. If you really weren't *MAD* at me, why'd you make everybody *THINK* you were?

IT WOULDN'T do for a *GENERAL* to publicly apologize to a disobedient *SOLDIER*, even if that soldier was *INSTRUMENTAL* in winning the *WAR*.

I CAN *TOTALLY* relate to that, sir-- it's an "EGO" thing!

PRETTY MUCH...

Y'KNOW...I *THINK* this could be the start of a beautiful *FRIEND-SHIP*!

OTHERWISE, *HOW* would the general then appear to all the *OTHER* soldiers in his *COMMAND*?

THE END

70

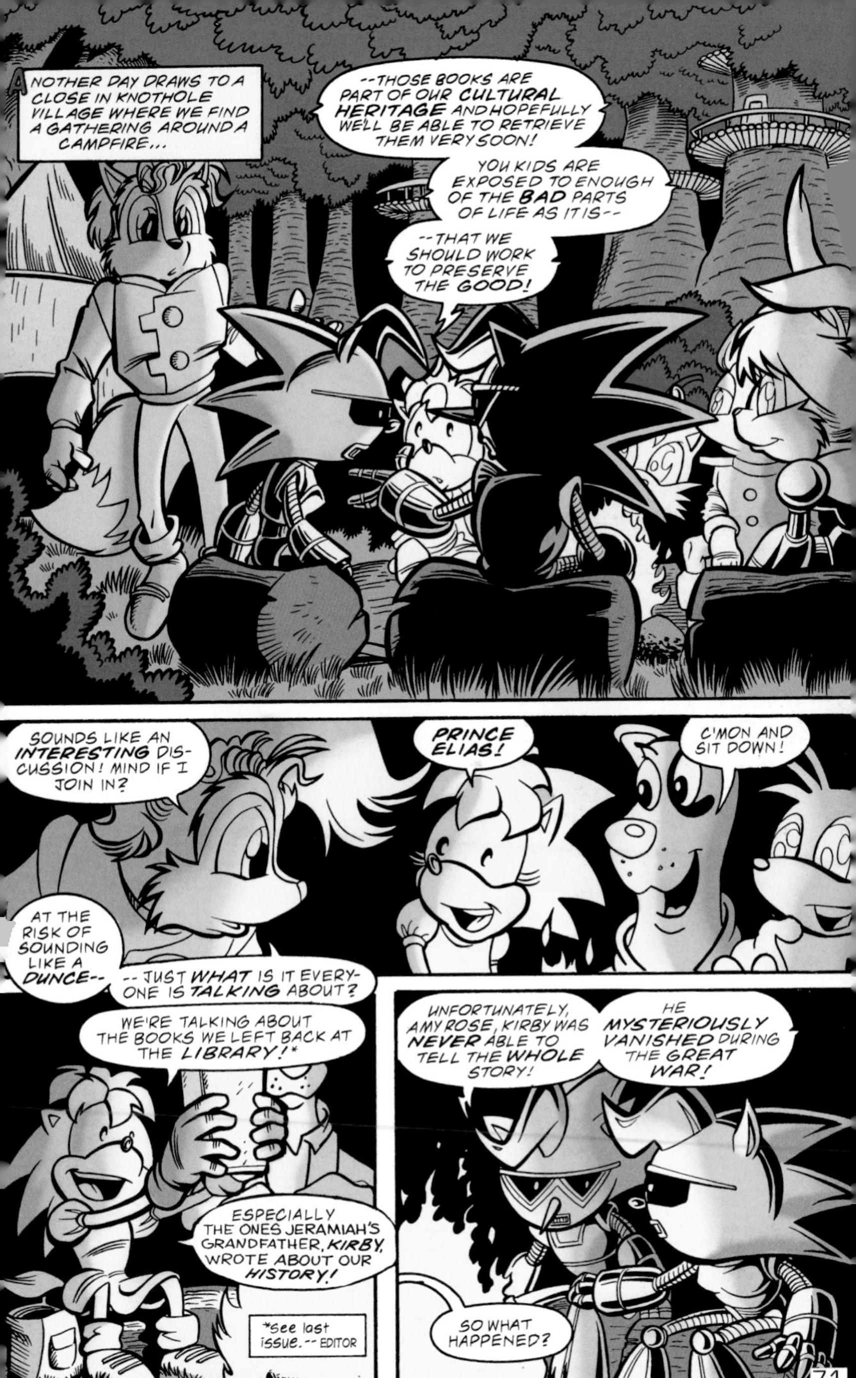
ANOTHER DAY DRAWS TO A CLOSE IN KNOTHOLE VILLAGE WHERE WE FIND A GATHERING AROUND A CAMPFIRE...
--THOSE BOOKS ARE PART OF OUR CULTURAL HERITAGE AND HOPEFULLY WE'LL BE ABLE TO RETRIEVE THEM VERY SOON!
YOU KIDS ARE EXPOSED TO ENOUGH OF THE BAD PARTS OF LIFE AS IT IS--
--THAT WE SHOULD WORK TO PRESERVE THE GOOD!
SOUNDS LIKE AN INTERESTING DISCUSSION! MIND IF I JOIN IN?
PRINCE ELIAS!
C'MON AND SIT DOWN!
AT THE RISK OF SOUNDING LIKE A DUNCE--
--JUST WHAT IS IT EVERYONE IS TALKING ABOUT?
WE'RE TALKING ABOUT THE BOOKS WE LEFT BACK AT THE LIBRARY!*
ESPECIALLY THE ONES JERAMIAH'S GRANDFATHER, KIRBY, WROTE ABOUT OUR HISTORY!
*See last issue. --EDITOR
UNFORTUNATELY, AMY ROSE, KIRBY WAS NEVER ABLE TO TELL THE WHOLE STORY!
HE MYSTERIOUSLY VANISHED DURING THE GREAT WAR!
SO WHAT HAPPENED?

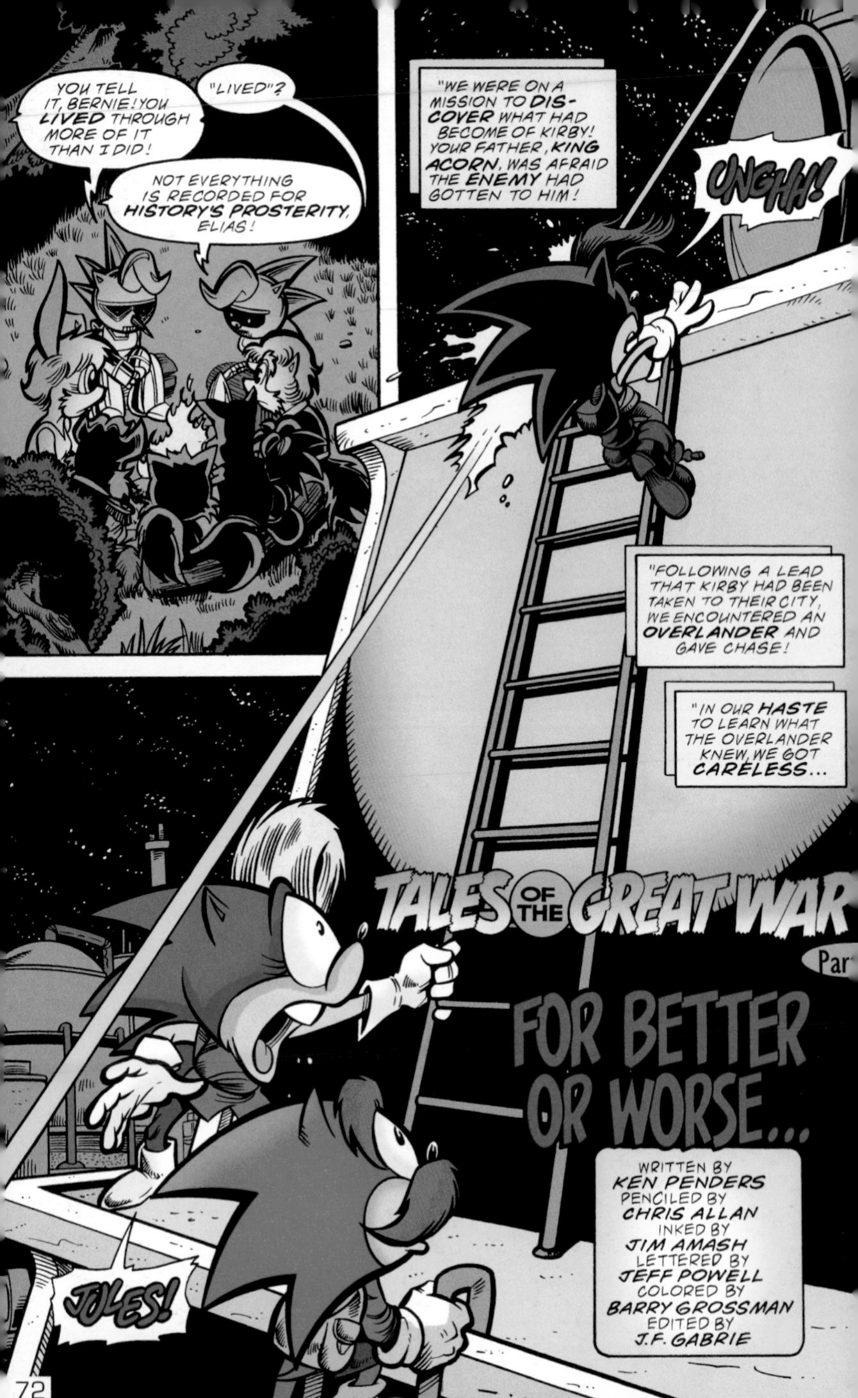
YOU TELL IT, BERNIE! YOU LIVED THROUGH MORE OF IT THAN I DID!
"LIVED"?
NOT EVERYTHING IS RECORDED FOR HISTORY'S PROSTERITY, ELIAS!
"WE WERE ON A MISSION TO DIS-COVER WHAT HAD BECOME OF KIRBY! YOUR FATHER, KING ACORN, WAS AFRAID THE ENEMY HAD GOTTEN TO HIM!
UNGHH!
"FOLLOWING A LEAD THAT KIRBY HAD BEEN TAKEN TO THEIR CITY, WE ENCOUNTERED AN OVERLANDER AND GAVE CHASE!
"IN OUR HASTE TO LEARN WHAT THE OVERLANDER KNEW, WE GOT CARELESS...
TALES OF THE GREAT WAR
Par
FOR BETTER OR WORSE...
WRITTEN BY KEN PENDERS
PENCILED BY CHRIS ALLAN
INKED BY JIM AMASH
LETTERED BY JEFF POWELL
COLORED BY BARRY GROSSMAN
EDITED BY J.F. GABRIE
JULES!

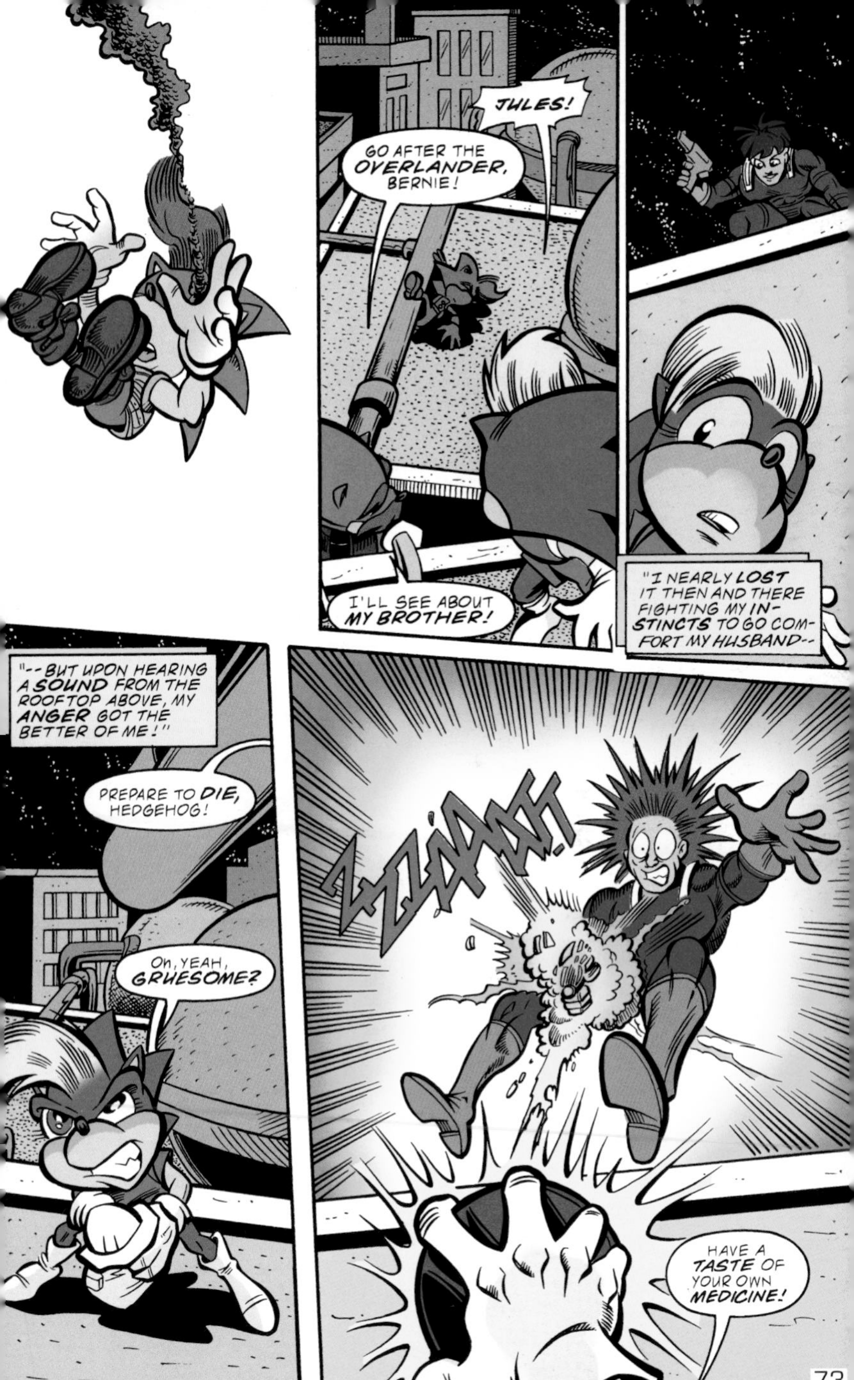
JULES!
GO AFTER THE OVERLANDER, BERNIE!
I'LL SEE ABOUT MY BROTHER!
"I NEARLY LOST IT THEN AND THERE FIGHTING MY IN-STINCTS TO GO COM-FORT MY HUSBAND--
"--BUT UPON HEARING A SOUND FROM THE ROOFTOP ABOVE, MY ANGER GOT THE BETTER OF ME!"
PREPARE TO DIE, HEDGEHOG!
OH, YEAH, GRUESOME?
ZZZAPPT!
HAVE A TASTE OF YOUR OWN MEDICINE!

"EVEN THOUGH I HAD **LOST** OTHER RELATIVES AND FRIENDS DURING THE WAR, **NOTHING** SEEMED AS **PERSONAL** AS EVERYTHING DID AT THAT MOMENT.

"MY **RAGE** LASTED ONLY A MOMENT AS MY **PRIMARY** CONCERN FOCUSED BACK UPON MY **HUSBAND**...

HE'S STILL BREATHING **BUT** WE NEED SOMETHING TO **STOP** THE BLEEDING!

I HAVE A **MEDI-KIT** IN MY BACK-PACK!

WHILE YOU BANDAGE JULES--

--I'LL GET A **STRETCHER** READY FOR US TO **CARRY** HIM!

I'VE GOT JULES **STABILIZED,** BERNIE, BUT HE'S GOING TO NEED A **LOT** MORE THAN WHAT I CAN **DO!**

I'M JUST ABOUT SET, CHARLES!

THERE! LET'S GET JULES ON AND **AWAY** FROM HERE!

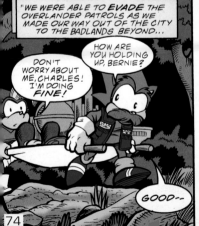

"WE WERE ABLE TO **EVADE** THE OVERLANDER PATROLS AS WE MADE OUR WAY OUT OF THE CITY TO THE BADLANDS BEYOND...

HOW ARE YOU HOLDING UP, BERNIE?

DON'T WORRY ABOUT ME, CHARLES! I'M DOING **FINE!**

GOOD--

--CAUSE THERE'S A **SIGHT** FOR SORE EYES!

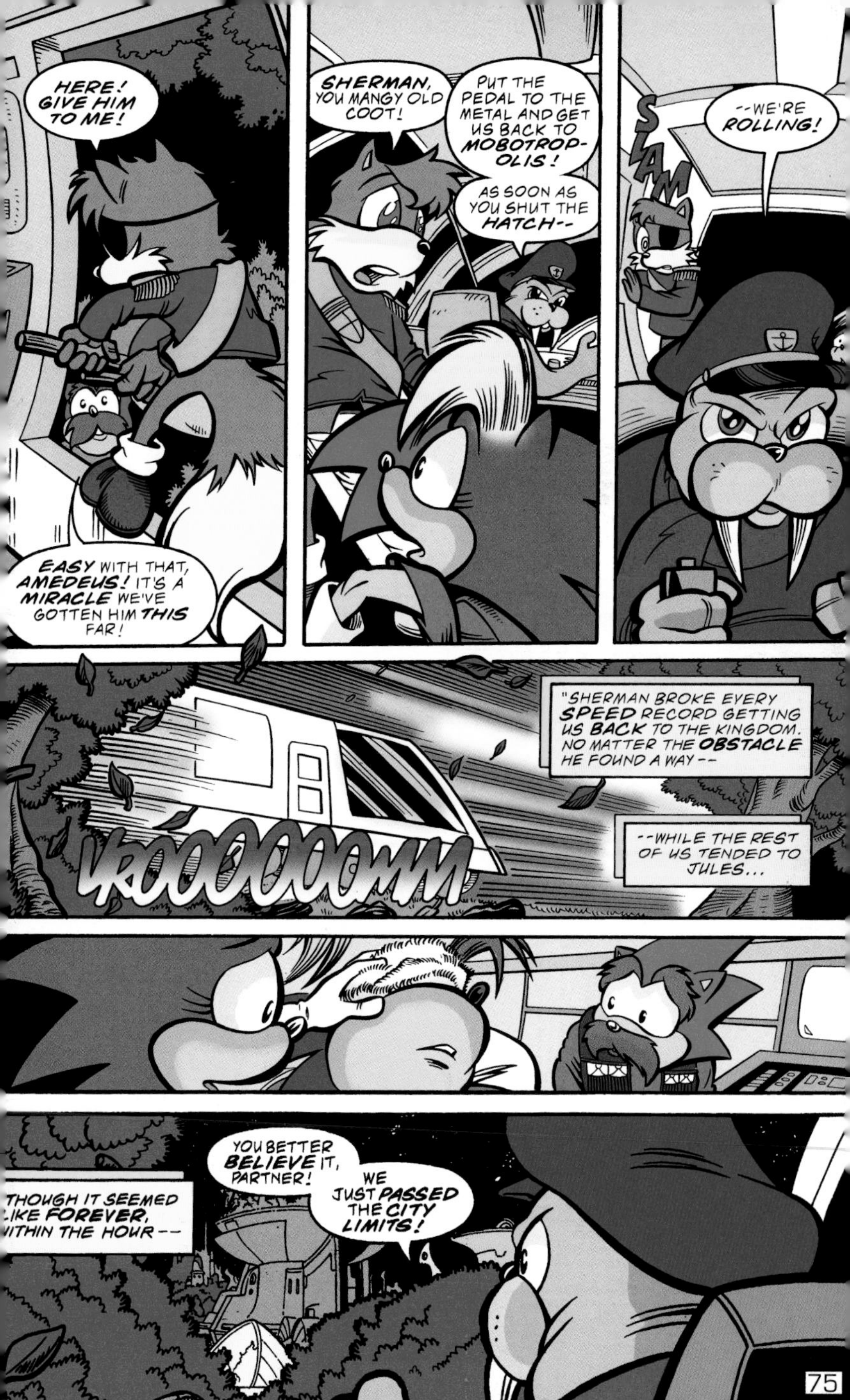
HERE! GIVE HIM TO ME!
EASY WITH THAT, AMEDEUS! IT'S A MIRACLE WE'VE GOTTEN HIM THIS FAR!
SHERMAN, YOU MANGY OLD COOT!
PUT THE PEDAL TO THE METAL AND GET US BACK TO MOBOTROPOLIS!
AS SOON AS YOU SHUT THE HATCH--
SLAM
--WE'RE ROLLING!
"SHERMAN BROKE EVERY SPEED RECORD GETTING US BACK TO THE KINGDOM. NO MATTER THE OBSTACLE HE FOUND A WAY--
VROOOOOOMM
--WHILE THE REST OF US TENDED TO JULES...
THOUGH IT SEEMED LIKE FOREVER, WITHIN THE HOUR--
YOU BETTER BELIEVE IT, PARTNER!
WE JUST PASSED THE CITY LIMITS!

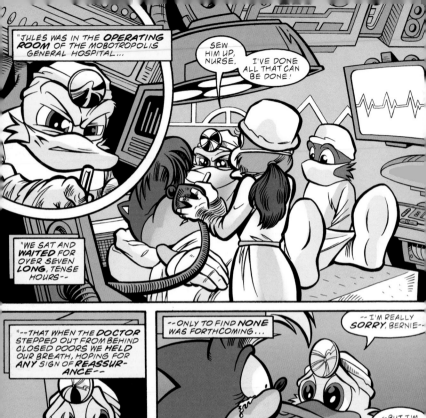

"JULES WAS IN THE **OPERATING ROOM** OF THE MOBOTROPOLIS GENERAL HOSPITAL..."

SEW HIM UP, NURSE.

I'VE DONE ALL THAT CAN BE DONE!

"WE SAT AND **WAITED** FOR OVER SEVEN **LONG,** TENSE HOURS--"

"--THAT WHEN THE **DOCTOR** STEPPED OUT FROM BEHIND CLOSED DOORS WE HELD OUR BREATH, HOPING FOR **ANY** SIGN OF **REASSURANCE**--"

--ONLY TO FIND **NONE** WAS FORTHCOMING...

--I'M REALLY **SORRY,** BERNIE.

--BUT I'M AFRAID THERE'S LITTLE **HOPE!**

"FIGURING JULES HAD NOTHING LEFT TO LOSE, **CHARLES** STEPPED FORWARD WITH A **DESPERATE** PLEA..."

IF THERE'S ABSOLUTELY, POSITIVELY **NOTHING** ELSE YOU CAN DO FOR MY BROTHER--

--WOULD YOU CONSIDER AN **ALTERNATIVE?**

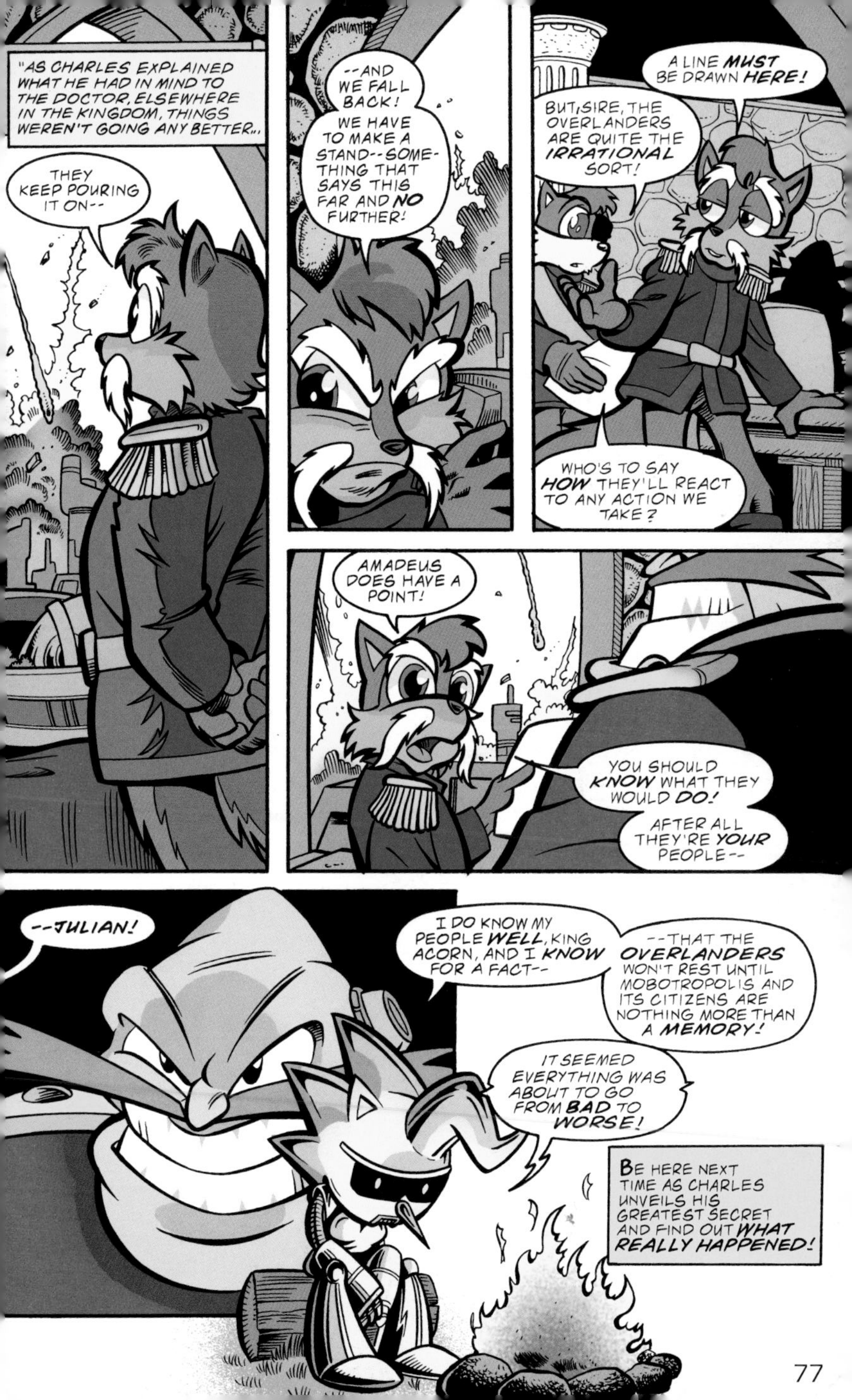
"AS CHARLES EXPLAINED WHAT HE HAD IN MIND TO THE DOCTOR, ELSEWHERE IN THE KINGDOM, THINGS WEREN'T GOING ANY BETTER...
THEY KEEP POURING IT ON--
--AND WE FALL BACK!
WE HAVE TO MAKE A STAND--SOMETHING THAT SAYS THIS FAR AND NO FURTHER!
A LINE MUST BE DRAWN HERE!
BUT, SIRE, THE OVERLANDERS ARE QUITE THE IRRATIONAL SORT!
WHO'S TO SAY HOW THEY'LL REACT TO ANY ACTION WE TAKE?
AMADEUS DOES HAVE A POINT!
YOU SHOULD KNOW WHAT THEY WOULD DO!
AFTER ALL THEY'RE YOUR PEOPLE--
--JULIAN!
I DO KNOW MY PEOPLE WELL, KING ACORN, AND I KNOW FOR A FACT--
--THAT THE OVERLANDERS WON'T REST UNTIL MOBOTROPOLIS AND ITS CITIZENS ARE NOTHING MORE THAN A MEMORY!
IT SEEMED EVERYTHING WAS ABOUT TO GO FROM BAD TO WORSE!
BE HERE NEXT TIME AS CHARLES UNVEILS HIS GREATEST SECRET AND FIND OUT WHAT REALLY HAPPENED!

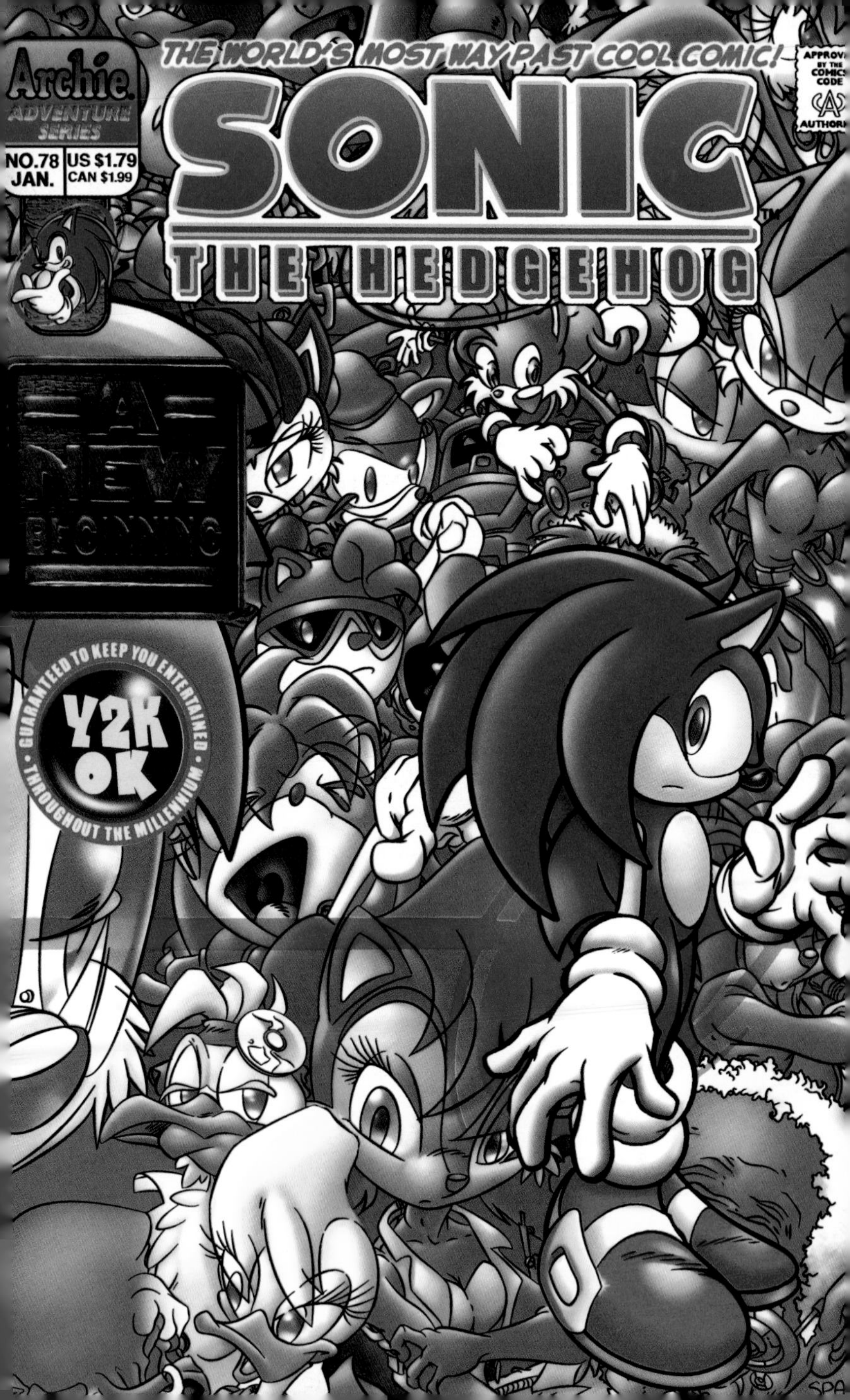
Archie
ADVENTURE SERIES
NO.78 JAN.
US $1.79
CAN $1.99
THE WORLD'S MOST WAY PAST COOL COMIC!
SONIC
THE HEDGEHOG
APPROV
BY THE COMICS CODE
AUTHOR
A NEW BEGINNING
GUARANTEED TO KEEP YOU ENTERTAINED
Y2K OK
THROUGHOUT THE MILLENNIUM

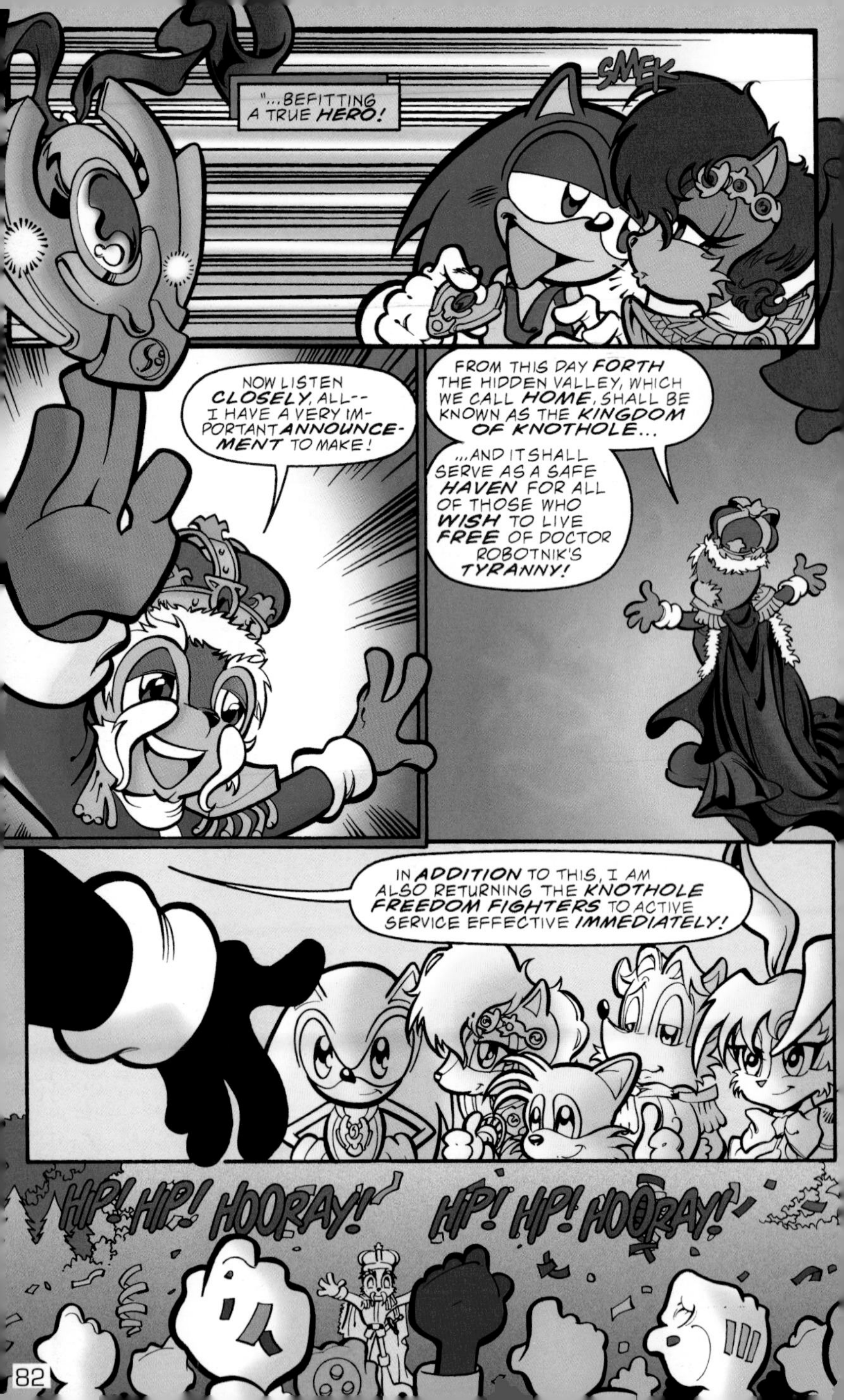
"...BEFITTING A TRUE HERO!
SMEK
NOW LISTEN CLOSELY, ALL-- I HAVE A VERY IMPORTANT ANNOUNCEMENT TO MAKE!
FROM THIS DAY FORTH THE HIDDEN VALLEY, WHICH WE CALL HOME, SHALL BE KNOWN AS THE KINGDOM OF KNOTHOLE...
...AND IT SHALL SERVE AS A SAFE HAVEN FOR ALL OF THOSE WHO WISH TO LIVE FREE OF DOCTOR ROBOTNIK'S TYRANNY!
IN ADDITION TO THIS, I AM ALSO RETURNING THE KNOTHOLE FREEDOM FIGHTERS TO ACTIVE SERVICE EFFECTIVE IMMEDIATELY!
HIP! HIP! HOORAY!
HIP! HIP! HOORAY!

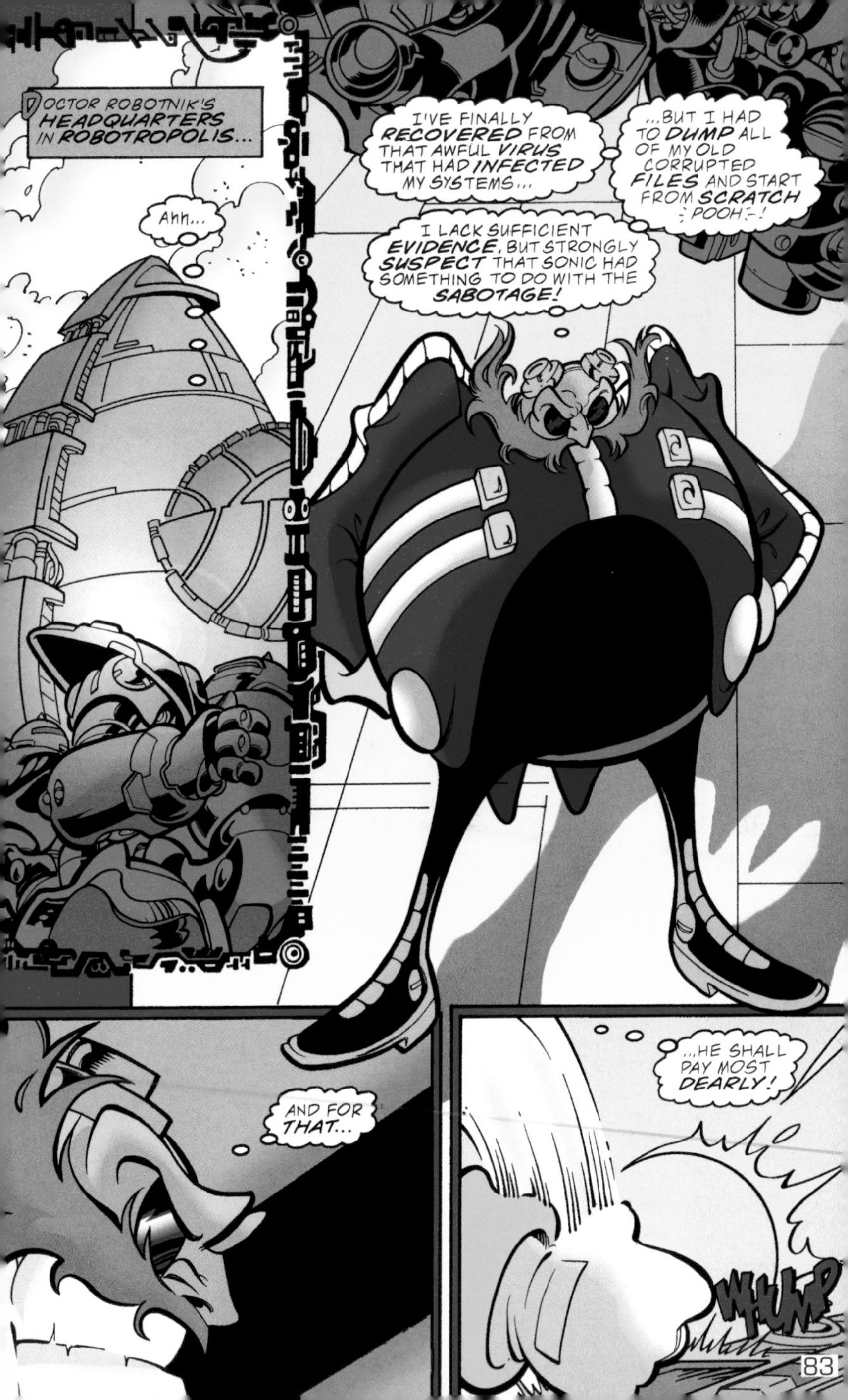
DOCTOR ROBOTNIK'S HEADQUARTERS IN ROBOTROPOLIS...
Ahh...
I'VE FINALLY RECOVERED FROM THAT AWFUL VIRUS THAT HAD INFECTED MY SYSTEMS...
...BUT I HAD TO DUMP ALL OF MY OLD CORRUPTED FILES AND START FROM SCRATCH -POOH-!
I LACK SUFFICIENT EVIDENCE, BUT STRONGLY SUSPECT THAT SONIC HAD SOMETHING TO DO WITH THE SABOTAGE!
AND FOR THAT...
...HE SHALL PAY MOST DEARLY!
WHUMP

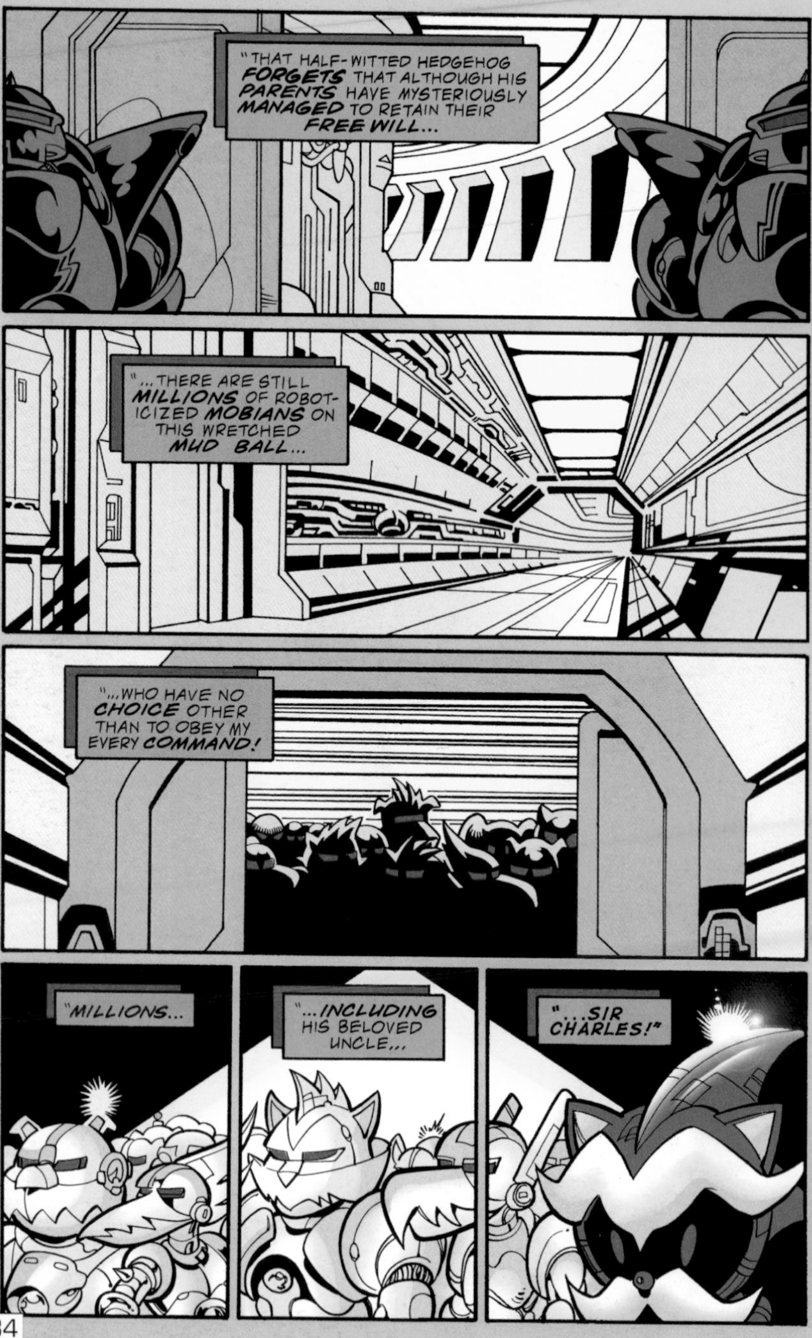
"THAT HALF-WITTED HEDGEHOG FORGETS THAT ALTHOUGH HIS PARENTS HAVE MYSTERIOUSLY MANAGED TO RETAIN THEIR FREE WILL...
"...THERE ARE STILL MILLIONS OF ROBOTICIZED MOBIANS ON THIS WRETCHED MUD BALL...
"...WHO HAVE NO CHOICE OTHER THAN TO OBEY MY EVERY COMMAND!
"MILLIONS...
"...INCLUDING HIS BELOVED UNCLE...
"...SIR CHARLES!"

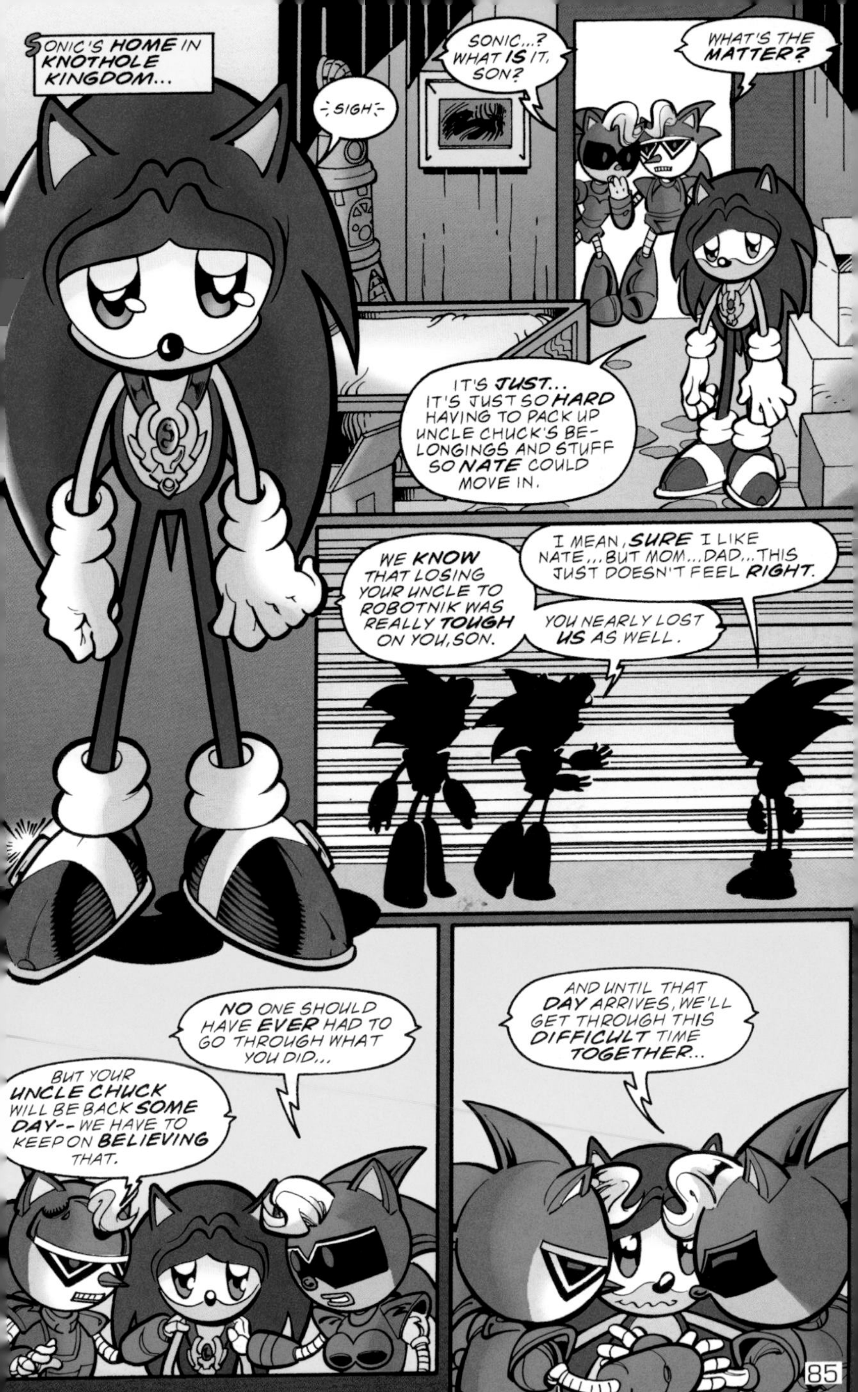
SONIC'S HOME IN KNOTHOLE KINGDOM...
-; SIGH ;-
SONIC...? WHAT IS IT, SON?
WHAT'S THE MATTER?
IT'S JUST... IT'S JUST SO HARD HAVING TO PACK UP UNCLE CHUCK'S BE-LONGINGS AND STUFF SO NATE COULD MOVE IN.
I MEAN, SURE I LIKE NATE... BUT MOM... DAD... THIS JUST DOESN'T FEEL RIGHT.
WE KNOW THAT LOSING YOUR UNCLE TO ROBOTNIK WAS REALLY TOUGH ON YOU, SON.
YOU NEARLY LOST US AS WELL.
NO ONE SHOULD HAVE EVER HAD TO GO THROUGH WHAT YOU DID...
BUT YOUR UNCLE CHUCK WILL BE BACK SOME DAY-- WE HAVE TO KEEP ON BELIEVING THAT.
AND UNTIL THAT DAY ARRIVES, WE'LL GET THROUGH THIS DIFFICULT TIME TOGETHER...

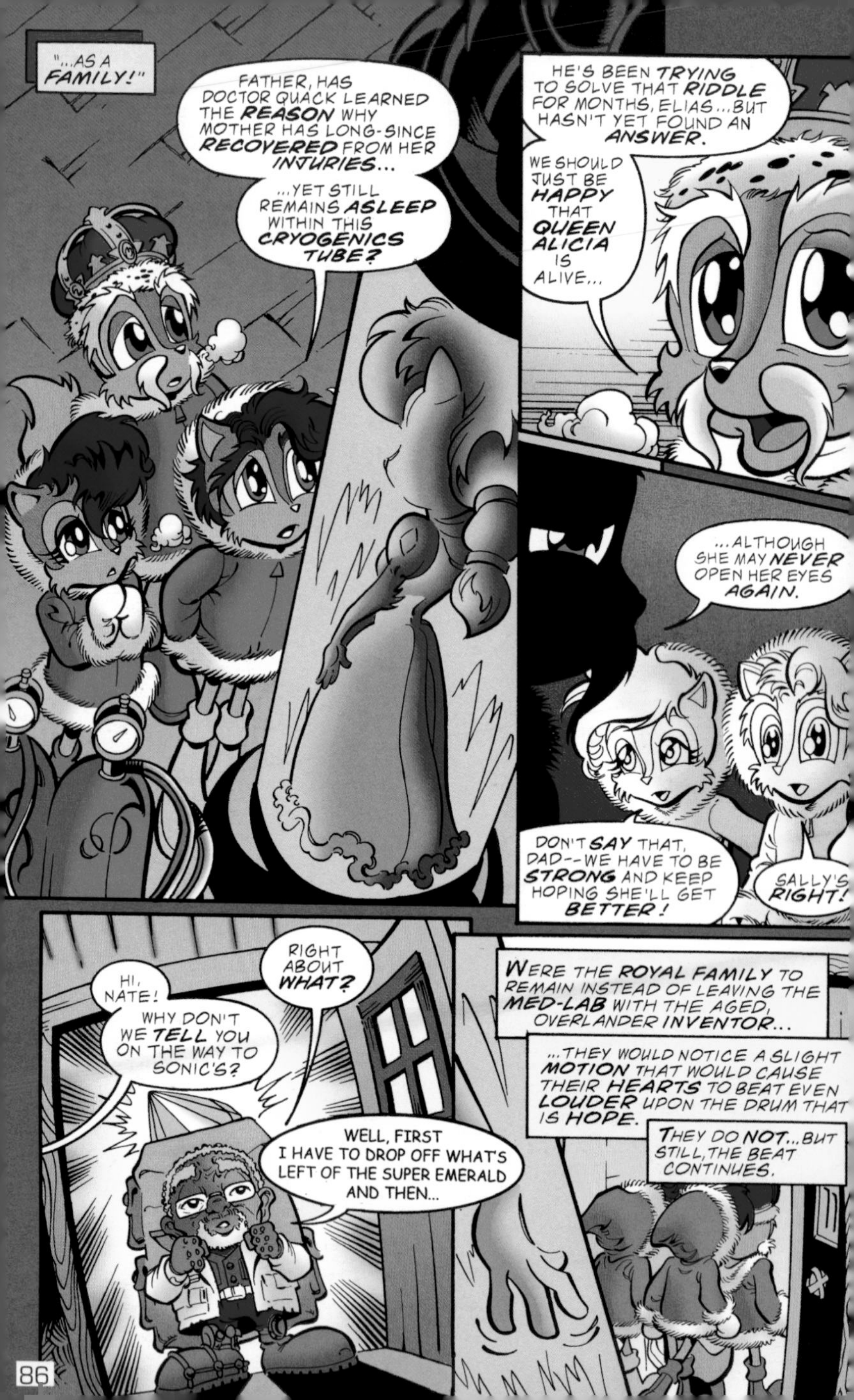
"...AS A FAMILY!"
FATHER, HAS DOCTOR QUACK LEARNED THE REASON WHY MOTHER HAS LONG-SINCE RECOVERED FROM HER INJURIES...
...YET STILL REMAINS ASLEEP WITHIN THIS CRYOGENICS TUBE?
HE'S BEEN TRYING TO SOLVE THAT RIDDLE FOR MONTHS, ELIAS...BUT HASN'T YET FOUND AN ANSWER.
WE SHOULD JUST BE HAPPY THAT QUEEN ALICIA IS ALIVE...
...ALTHOUGH SHE MAY NEVER OPEN HER EYES AGAIN.
DON'T SAY THAT, DAD--WE HAVE TO BE STRONG AND KEEP HOPING SHE'LL GET BETTER!
SALLY'S RIGHT!
HI, NATE!
RIGHT ABOUT WHAT?
WHY DON'T WE TELL YOU ON THE WAY TO SONIC'S?
WELL, FIRST I HAVE TO DROP OFF WHAT'S LEFT OF THE SUPER EMERALD AND THEN...
WERE THE ROYAL FAMILY TO REMAIN INSTEAD OF LEAVING THE MED-LAB WITH THE AGED, OVERLANDER INVENTOR...
...THEY WOULD NOTICE A SLIGHT MOTION THAT WOULD CAUSE THEIR HEARTS TO BEAT EVEN LOUDER UPON THE DRUM THAT IS HOPE.
THEY DO NOT...BUT STILL, THE BEAT CONTINUES.

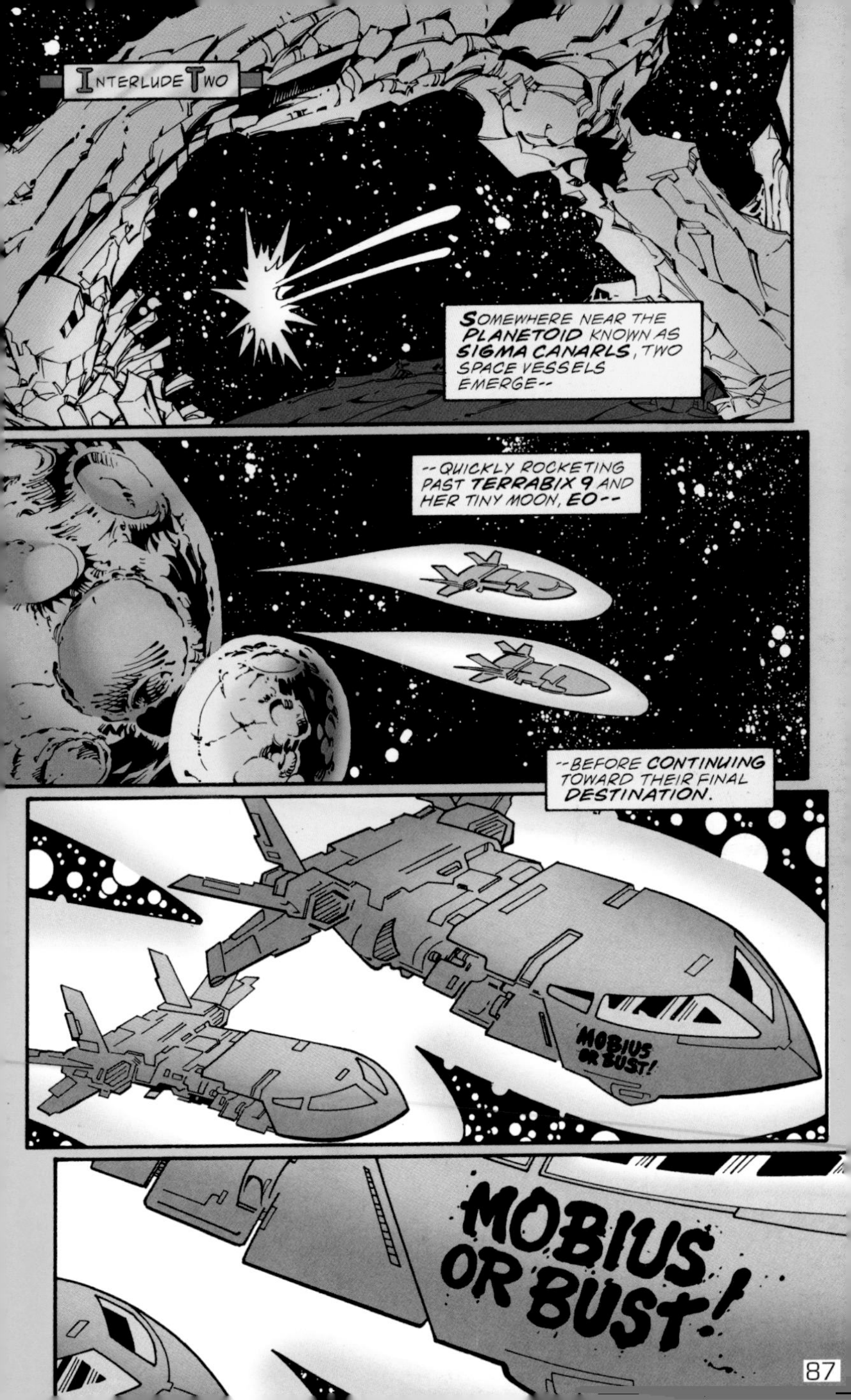
INTERLUDE TWO
SOMEWHERE NEAR THE PLANETOID KNOWN AS SIGMA CANARLS, TWO SPACE VESSELS EMERGE--
--QUICKLY ROCKETING PAST TERRABIX 9 AND HER TINY MOON, EO--
--BEFORE CONTINUING TOWARD THEIR FINAL DESTINATION.
MOBIUS OR BUST!
MOBIUS OR BUST!

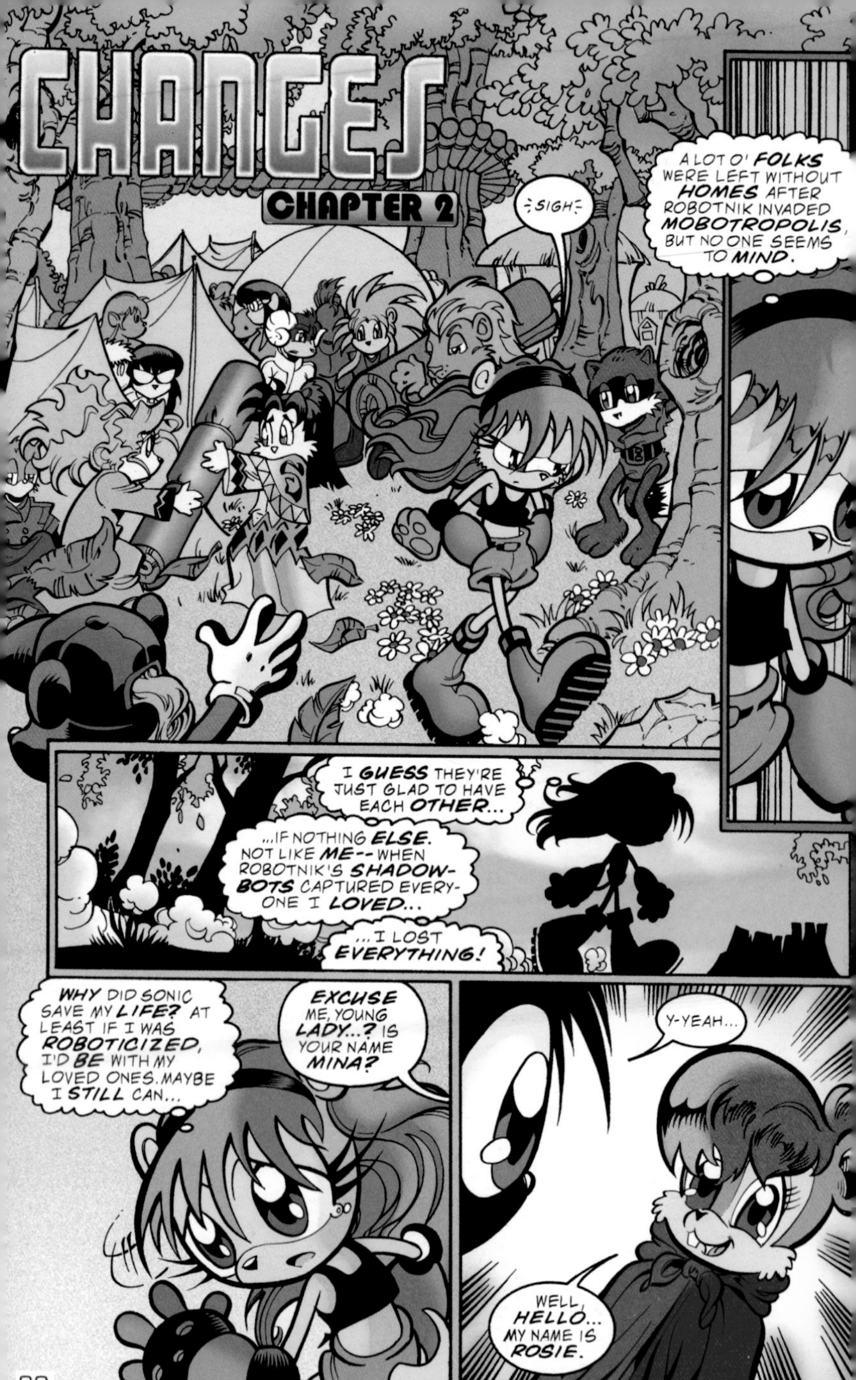
CHANGES
CHAPTER 2
-SIGH-
A LOT O' FOLKS WERE LEFT WITHOUT HOMES AFTER ROBOTNIK INVADED MOBOTROPOLIS, BUT NO ONE SEEMS TO MIND.
I GUESS THEY'RE JUST GLAD TO HAVE EACH OTHER...
...IF NOTHING ELSE. NOT LIKE ME--WHEN ROBOTNIK'S SHADOW-BOTS CAPTURED EVERY-ONE I LOVED...
...I LOST EVERYTHING!
WHY DID SONIC SAVE MY LIFE? AT LEAST IF I WAS ROBOTICIZED, I'D BE WITH MY LOVED ONES. MAYBE I STILL CAN...
EXCUSE ME, YOUNG LADY...? IS YOUR NAME MINA?
Y-YEAH...
WELL, HELLO... MY NAME IS ROSIE.

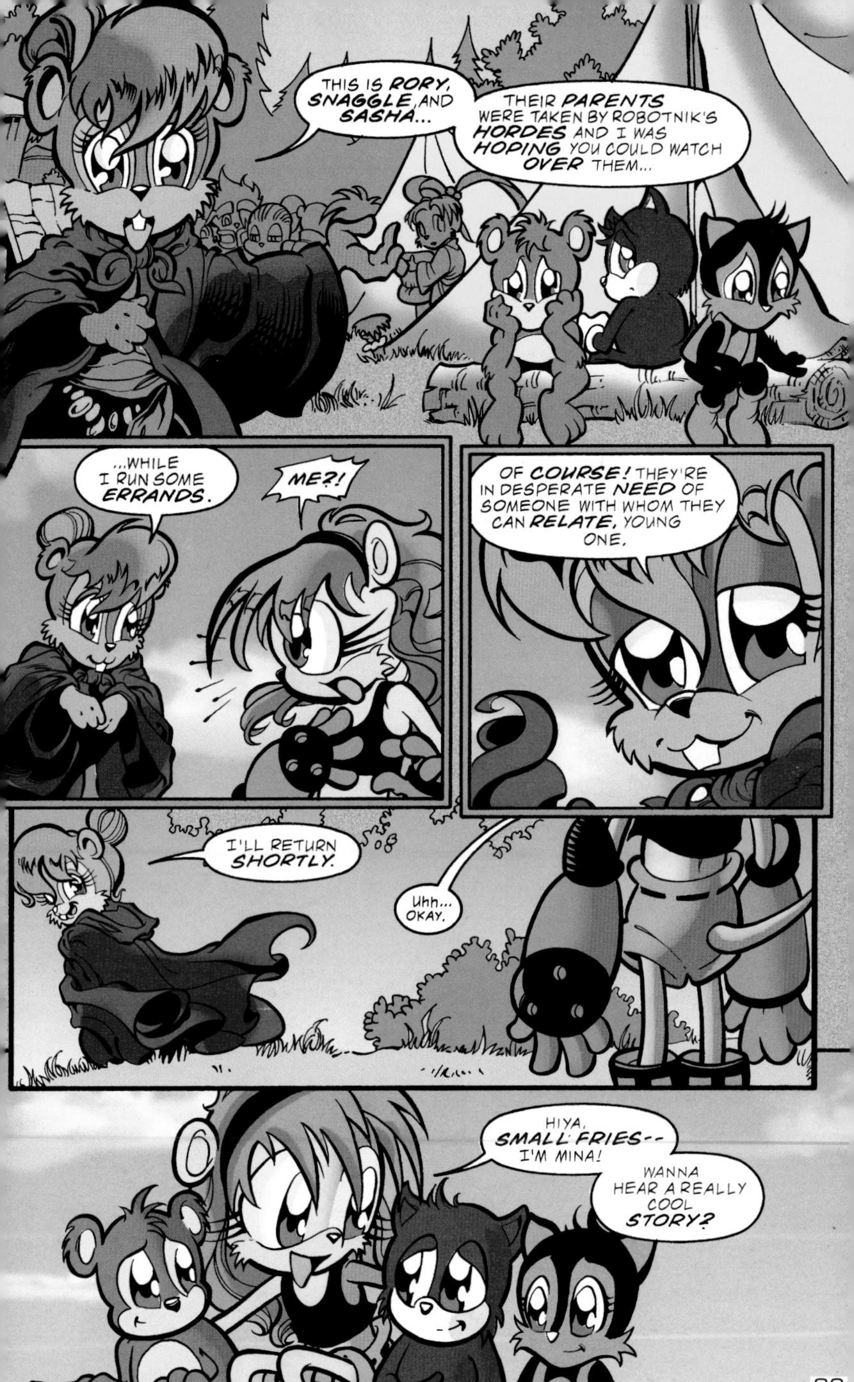

THIS IS RORY, SNAGGLE, AND SASHA...
THEIR PARENTS WERE TAKEN BY ROBOTNIK'S HORDES AND I WAS HOPING YOU COULD WATCH OVER THEM...
...WHILE I RUN SOME ERRANDS.
ME?!
OF COURSE! THEY'RE IN DESPERATE NEED OF SOMEONE WITH WHOM THEY CAN RELATE, YOUNG ONE.
I'LL RETURN SHORTLY.
Uhh... OKAY.
HIYA, SMALL FRIES-- I'M MINA!
WANNA HEAR A REALLY COOL STORY?

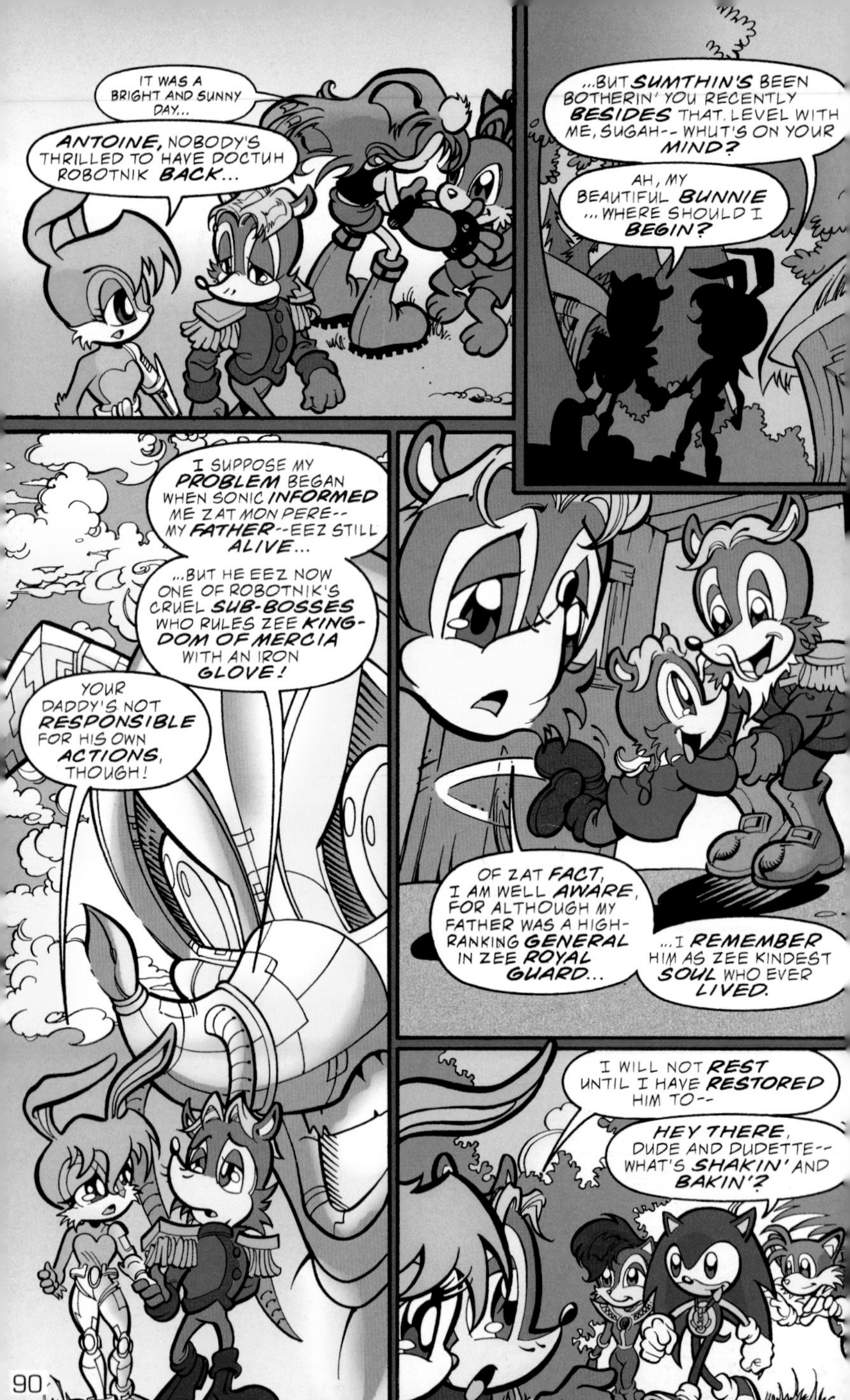

IT WAS A BRIGHT AND SUNNY DAY...
ANTOINE, NOBODY'S THRILLED TO HAVE DOCTUH ROBOTNIK BACK...
...BUT SUMTHIN'S BEEN BOTHERIN' YOU RECENTLY BESIDES THAT. LEVEL WITH ME, SUGAH-- WHUT'S ON YOUR MIND?
AH, MY BEAUTIFUL BUNNIE ...WHERE SHOULD I BEGIN?
I SUPPOSE MY PROBLEM BEGAN WHEN SONIC INFORMED ME ZAT MON PERE-- MY FATHER--EEZ STILL ALIVE...
...BUT HE EEZ NOW ONE OF ROBOTNIK'S CRUEL SUB-BOSSES WHO RULES ZEE KINGDOM OF MERCIA WITH AN IRON GLOVE!
YOUR DADDY'S NOT RESPONSIBLE FOR HIS OWN ACTIONS, THOUGH!
OF ZAT FACT, I AM WELL AWARE, FOR ALTHOUGH MY FATHER WAS A HIGH-RANKING GENERAL IN ZEE ROYAL GUARD...
...I REMEMBER HIM AS ZEE KINDEST SOUL WHO EVER LIVED.
I WILL NOT REST UNTIL I HAVE RESTORED HIM TO--
HEY THERE, DUDE AND DUDETTE-- WHAT'S SHAKIN' AND BAKIN'?

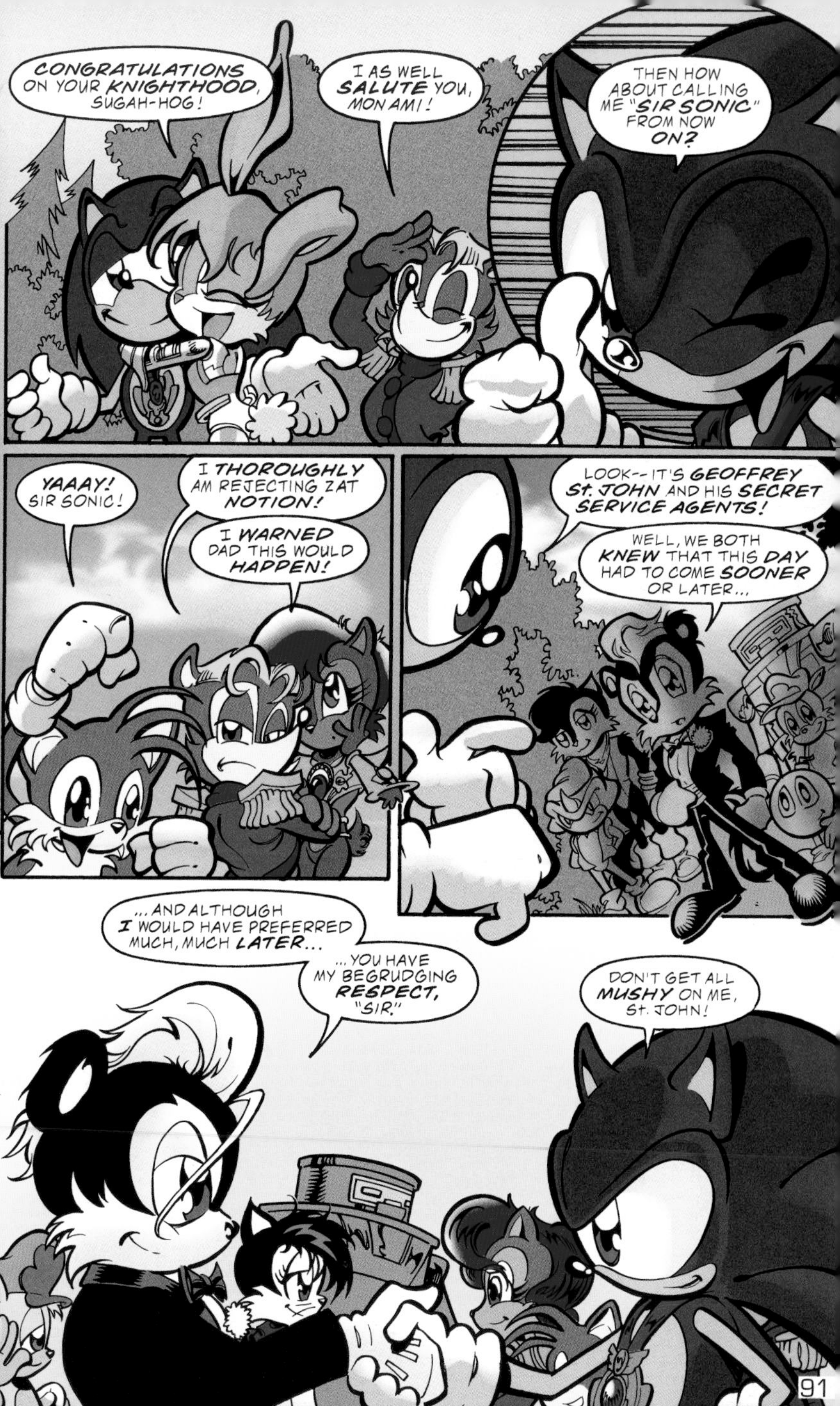
CONGRATULATIONS ON YOUR KNIGHTHOOD, SUGAH-HOG!
I AS WELL SALUTE YOU, MON AMI!
THEN HOW ABOUT CALLING ME "SIR SONIC" FROM NOW ON?
YAAAY! SIR SONIC!
I THOROUGHLY AM REJECTING ZAT NOTION!
I WARNED DAD THIS WOULD HAPPEN!
LOOK-- IT'S GEOFFREY St. JOHN AND HIS SECRET SERVICE AGENTS!
WELL, WE BOTH KNEW THAT THIS DAY HAD TO COME SOONER OR LATER...
...AND ALTHOUGH I WOULD HAVE PREFERRED MUCH, MUCH LATER...
...YOU HAVE MY BEGRUDGING RESPECT, "SIR."
DON'T GET ALL MUSHY ON ME, St. JOHN!

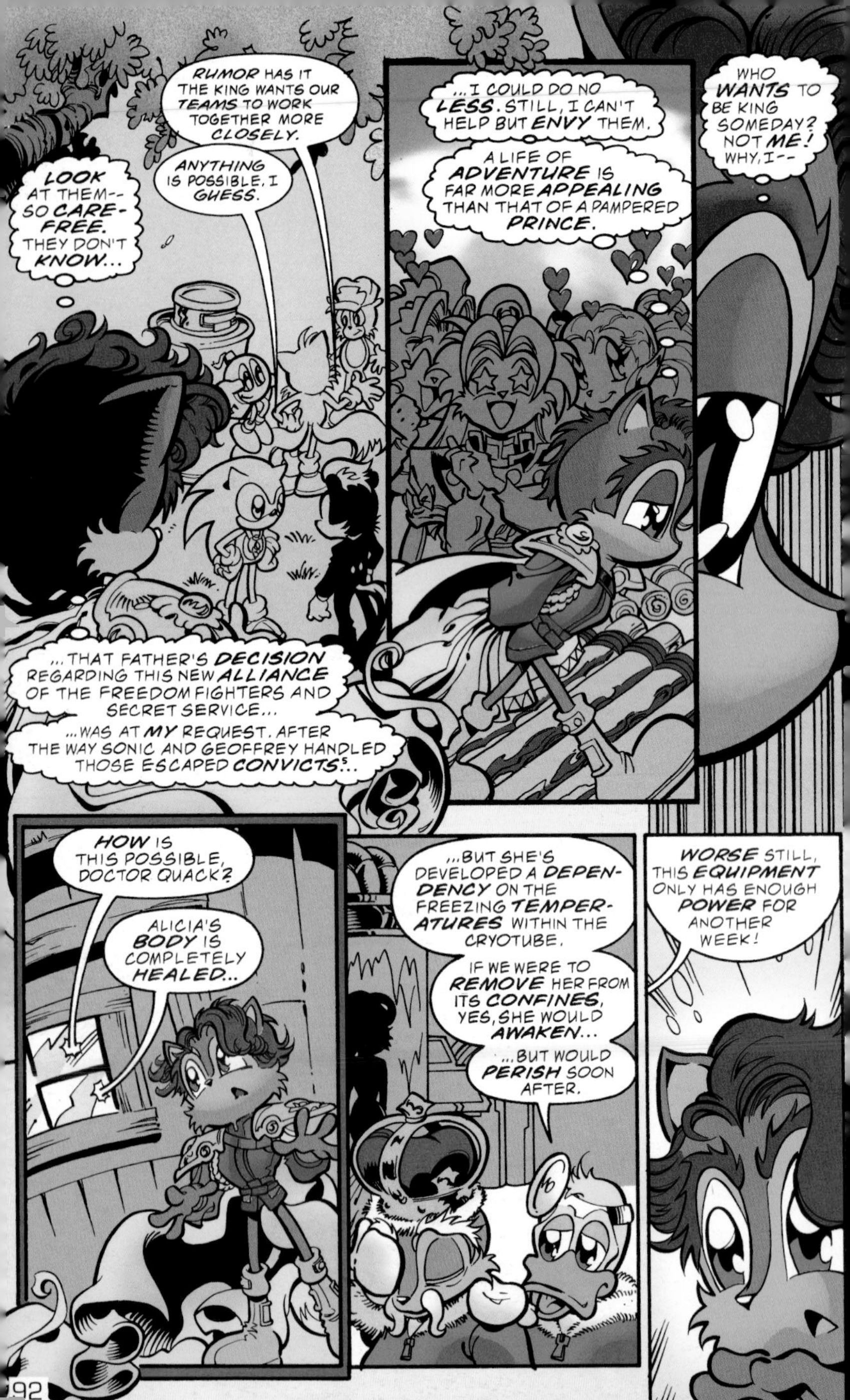

LOOK AT THEM--SO CAREFREE. THEY DON'T KNOW...
RUMOR HAS IT THE KING WANTS OUR TEAMS TO WORK TOGETHER MORE CLOSELY.
ANYTHING IS POSSIBLE, I GUESS.
...I COULD DO NO LESS. STILL, I CAN'T HELP BUT ENVY THEM.
A LIFE OF ADVENTURE IS FAR MORE APPEALING THAN THAT OF A PAMPERED PRINCE.
WHO WANTS TO BE KING SOMEDAY? NOT ME! WHY, I--
...THAT FATHER'S DECISION REGARDING THIS NEW ALLIANCE OF THE FREEDOM FIGHTERS AND SECRET SERVICE...
...WAS AT MY REQUEST. AFTER THE WAY SONIC AND GEOFFREY HANDLED THOSE ESCAPED CONVICTS[5]...
HOW IS THIS POSSIBLE, DOCTOR QUACK?
ALICIA'S BODY IS COMPLETELY HEALED...
...BUT SHE'S DEVELOPED A DEPENDENCY ON THE FREEZING TEMPERATURES WITHIN THE CRYOTUBE.
IF WE WERE TO REMOVE HER FROM ITS CONFINES, YES, SHE WOULD AWAKEN...
...BUT WOULD PERISH SOON AFTER.
WORSE STILL, THIS EQUIPMENT ONLY HAS ENOUGH POWER FOR ANOTHER WEEK!

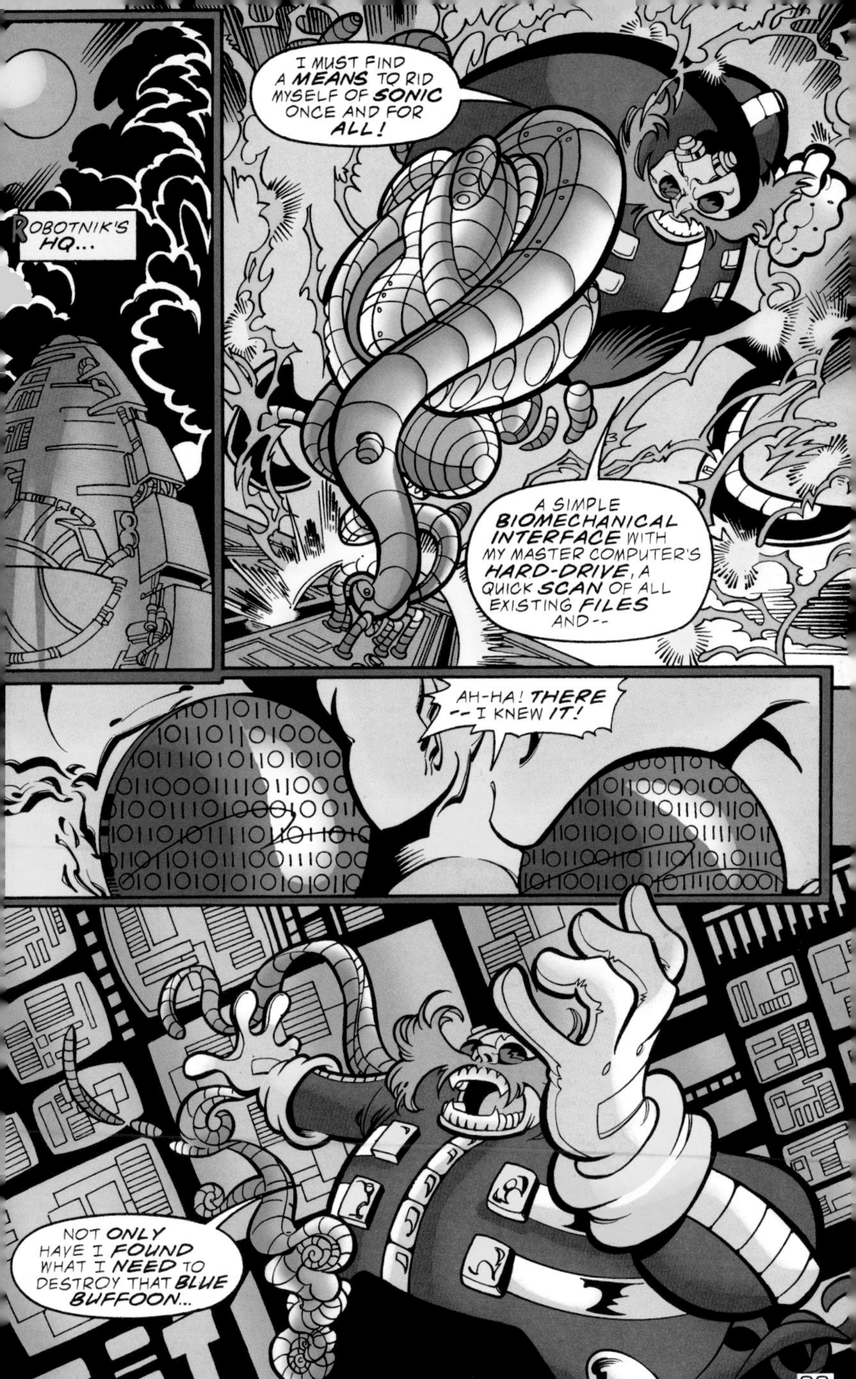
ROBOTNIK'S HQ...
I MUST FIND A MEANS TO RID MYSELF OF SONIC ONCE AND FOR ALL!
A SIMPLE BIOMECHANICAL INTERFACE WITH MY MASTER COMPUTER'S HARD-DRIVE, A QUICK SCAN OF ALL EXISTING FILES AND--
AH-HA! THERE -- I KNEW IT!
NOT ONLY HAVE I FOUND WHAT I NEED TO DESTROY THAT BLUE BUFFOON...

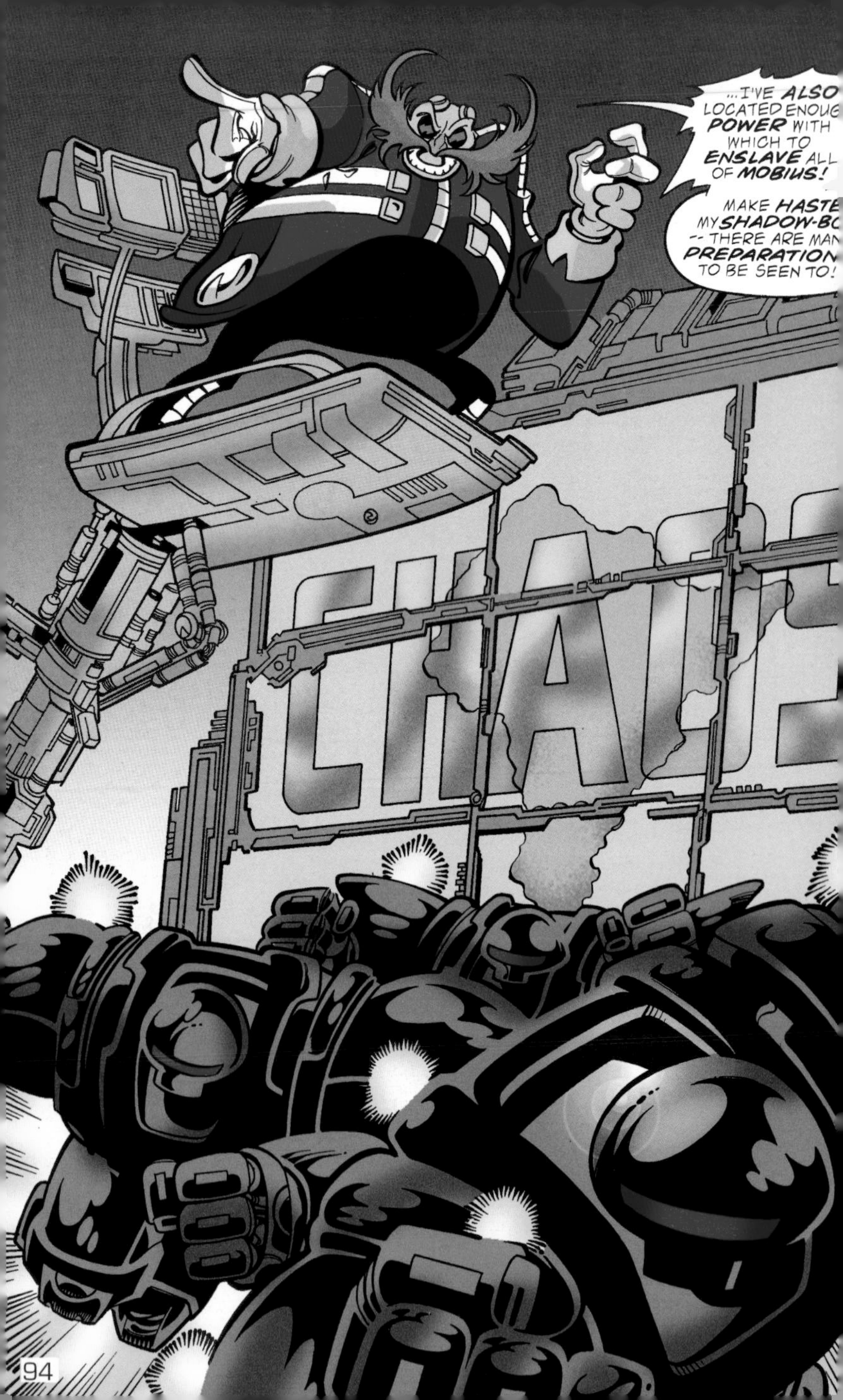
...I'VE ALSO LOCATED ENOUG POWER WITH WHICH TO ENSLAVE ALL OF MOBIUS!
MAKE HASTE MY SHADOW-BO -- THERE ARE MAN PREPARATION TO BE SEEN TO!

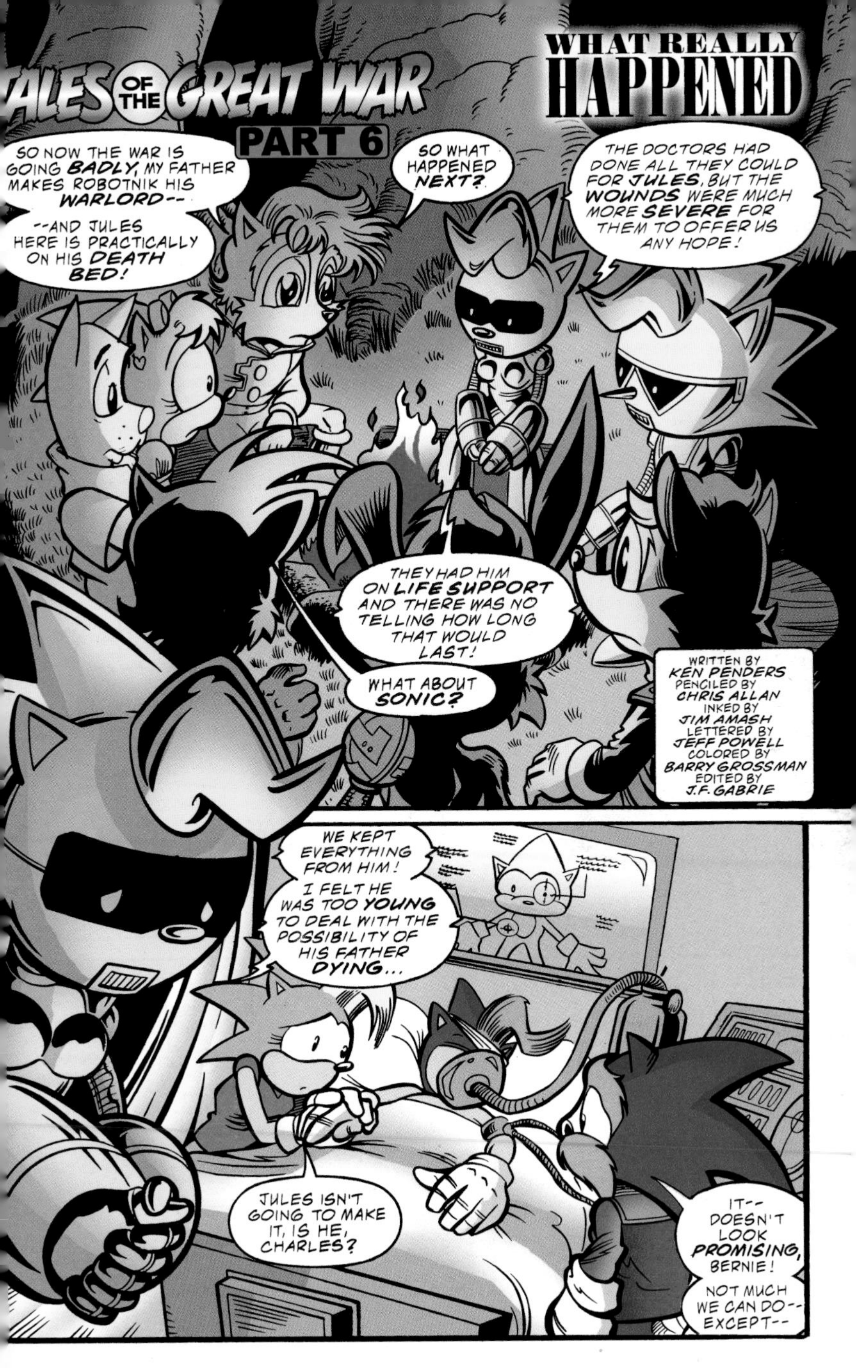
TALES OF THE GREAT WAR
PART 6
WHAT REALLY HAPPENED
SO NOW THE WAR IS GOING BADLY, MY FATHER MAKES ROBOTNIK HIS WARLORD--
--AND JULES HERE IS PRACTICALLY ON HIS DEATH BED!
SO WHAT HAPPENED NEXT?
THE DOCTORS HAD DONE ALL THEY COULD FOR JULES, BUT THE WOUNDS WERE MUCH MORE SEVERE FOR THEM TO OFFER US ANY HOPE!
THEY HAD HIM ON LIFE SUPPORT AND THERE WAS NO TELLING HOW LONG THAT WOULD LAST!
WHAT ABOUT SONIC?
WRITTEN BY KEN PENDERS PENCILED BY CHRIS ALLAN INKED BY JIM AMASH LETTERED BY JEFF POWELL COLORED BY BARRY GROSSMAN EDITED BY J.F. GABRIE
WE KEPT EVERYTHING FROM HIM!
I FELT HE WAS TOO YOUNG TO DEAL WITH THE POSSIBILITY OF HIS FATHER DYING...
JULES ISN'T GOING TO MAKE IT, IS HE, CHARLES?
IT-- DOESN'T LOOK PROMISING, BERNIE!
NOT MUCH WE CAN DO-- EXCEPT--

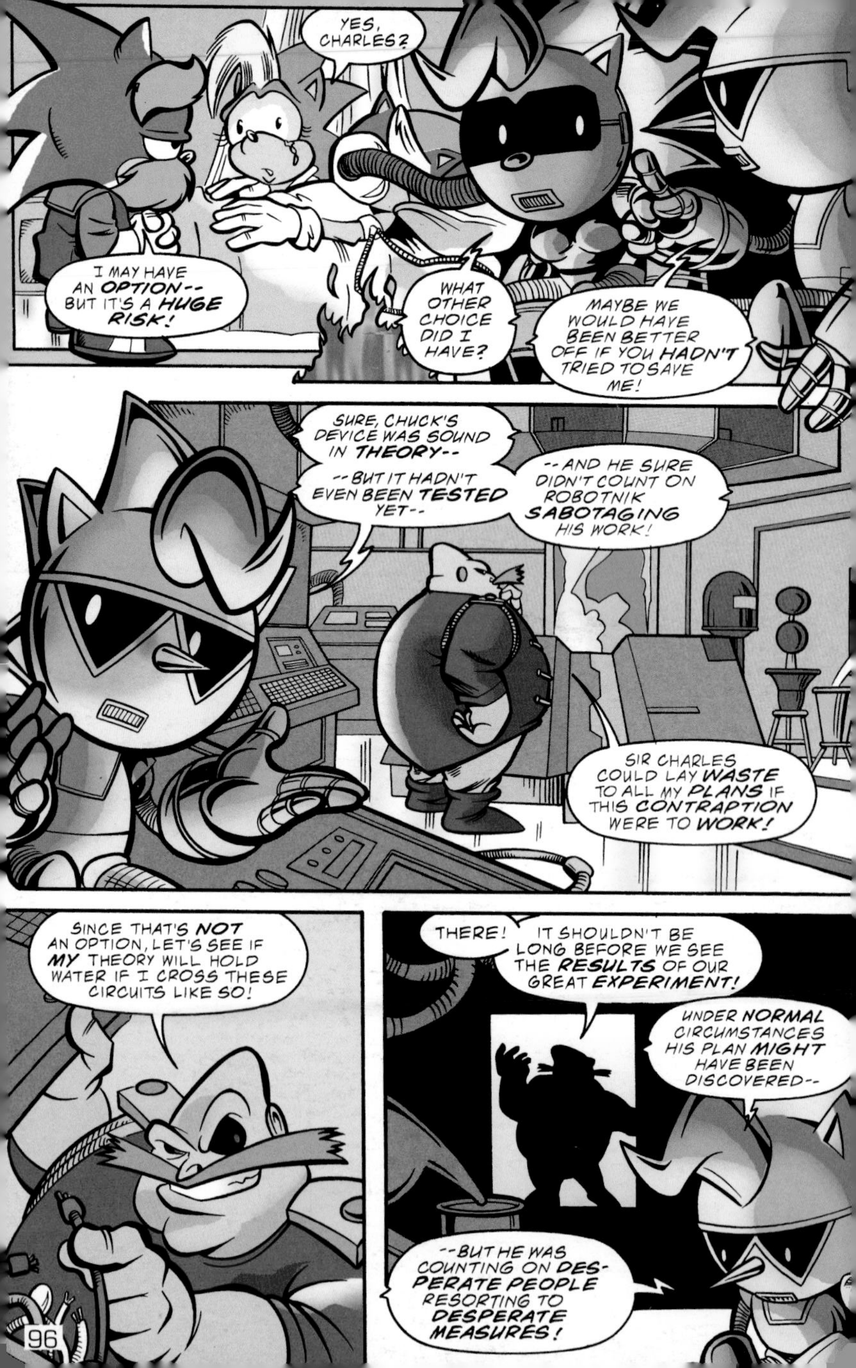
YES, CHARLES?
I MAY HAVE AN OPTION-- BUT IT'S A HUGE RISK!
WHAT OTHER CHOICE DID I HAVE?
MAYBE WE WOULD HAVE BEEN BETTER OFF IF YOU HADN'T TRIED TO SAVE ME!
SURE, CHUCK'S DEVICE WAS SOUND IN THEORY--
--BUT IT HADN'T EVEN BEEN TESTED YET--
--AND HE SURE DIDN'T COUNT ON ROBOTNIK SABOTAGING HIS WORK!
SIR CHARLES COULD LAY WASTE TO ALL MY PLANS IF THIS CONTRAPTION WERE TO WORK!
SINCE THAT'S NOT AN OPTION, LET'S SEE IF MY THEORY WILL HOLD WATER IF I CROSS THESE CIRCUITS LIKE SO!
THERE!
IT SHOULDN'T BE LONG BEFORE WE SEE THE RESULTS OF OUR GREAT EXPERIMENT!
UNDER NORMAL CIRCUMSTANCES HIS PLAN MIGHT HAVE BEEN DISCOVERED--
--BUT HE WAS COUNTING ON DESPERATE PEOPLE RESORTING TO DESPERATE MEASURES!

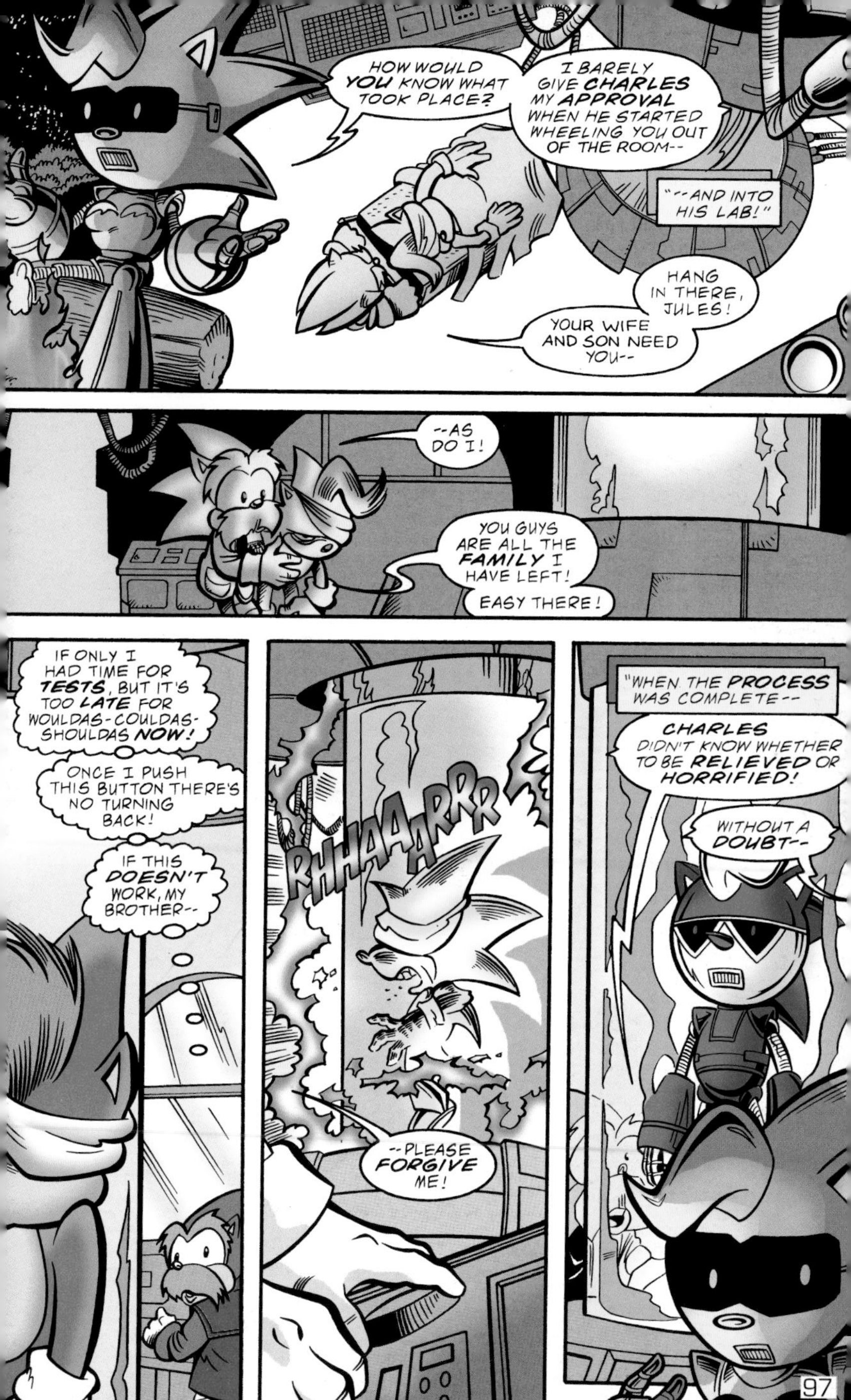
HOW WOULD YOU KNOW WHAT TOOK PLACE?
I BARELY GIVE CHARLES MY APPROVAL WHEN HE STARTED WHEELING YOU OUT OF THE ROOM--
"--AND INTO HIS LAB!"
HANG IN THERE, JULES!
YOUR WIFE AND SON NEED YOU--
--AS DO I!
YOU GUYS ARE ALL THE FAMILY I HAVE LEFT!
EASY THERE!
IF ONLY I HAD TIME FOR TESTS, BUT IT'S TOO LATE FOR WOULDAS-COULDAS-SHOULDAS NOW!
ONCE I PUSH THIS BUTTON THERE'S NO TURNING BACK!
IF THIS DOESN'T WORK, MY BROTHER--
RHHAAARRR
--PLEASE FORGIVE ME!
"WHEN THE PROCESS WAS COMPLETE--
CHARLES DIDN'T KNOW WHETHER TO BE RELIEVED OR HORRIFIED!
WITHOUT A DOUBT--

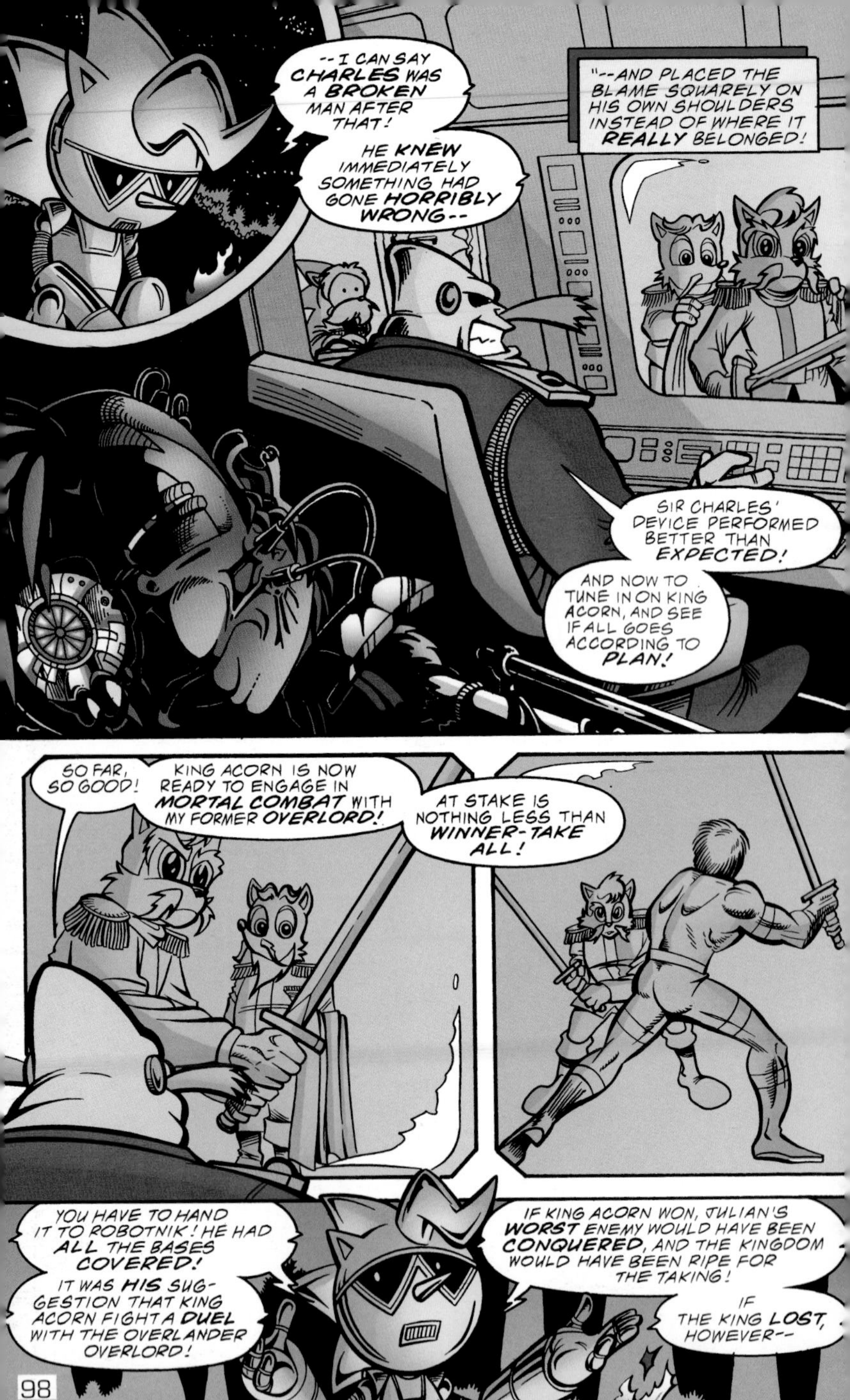
--I CAN SAY CHARLES WAS A BROKEN MAN AFTER THAT!
HE KNEW IMMEDIATELY SOMETHING HAD GONE HORRIBLY WRONG--
"--AND PLACED THE BLAME SQUARELY ON HIS OWN SHOULDERS INSTEAD OF WHERE IT REALLY BELONGED!
SIR CHARLES' DEVICE PERFORMED BETTER THAN EXPECTED!
AND NOW TO TUNE IN ON KING ACORN, AND SEE IF ALL GOES ACCORDING TO PLAN!
SO FAR, SO GOOD!
KING ACORN IS NOW READY TO ENGAGE IN MORTAL COMBAT WITH MY FORMER OVERLORD!
AT STAKE IS NOTHING LESS THAN WINNER-TAKE ALL!
YOU HAVE TO HAND IT TO ROBOTNIK! HE HAD ALL THE BASES COVERED!
IT WAS HIS SUGGESTION THAT KING ACORN FIGHT A DUEL WITH THE OVERLANDER OVERLORD!
IF KING ACORN WON, JULIAN'S WORST ENEMY WOULD HAVE BEEN CONQUERED, AND THE KINGDOM WOULD HAVE BEEN RIPE FOR THE TAKING!
IF THE KING LOST, HOWEVER--

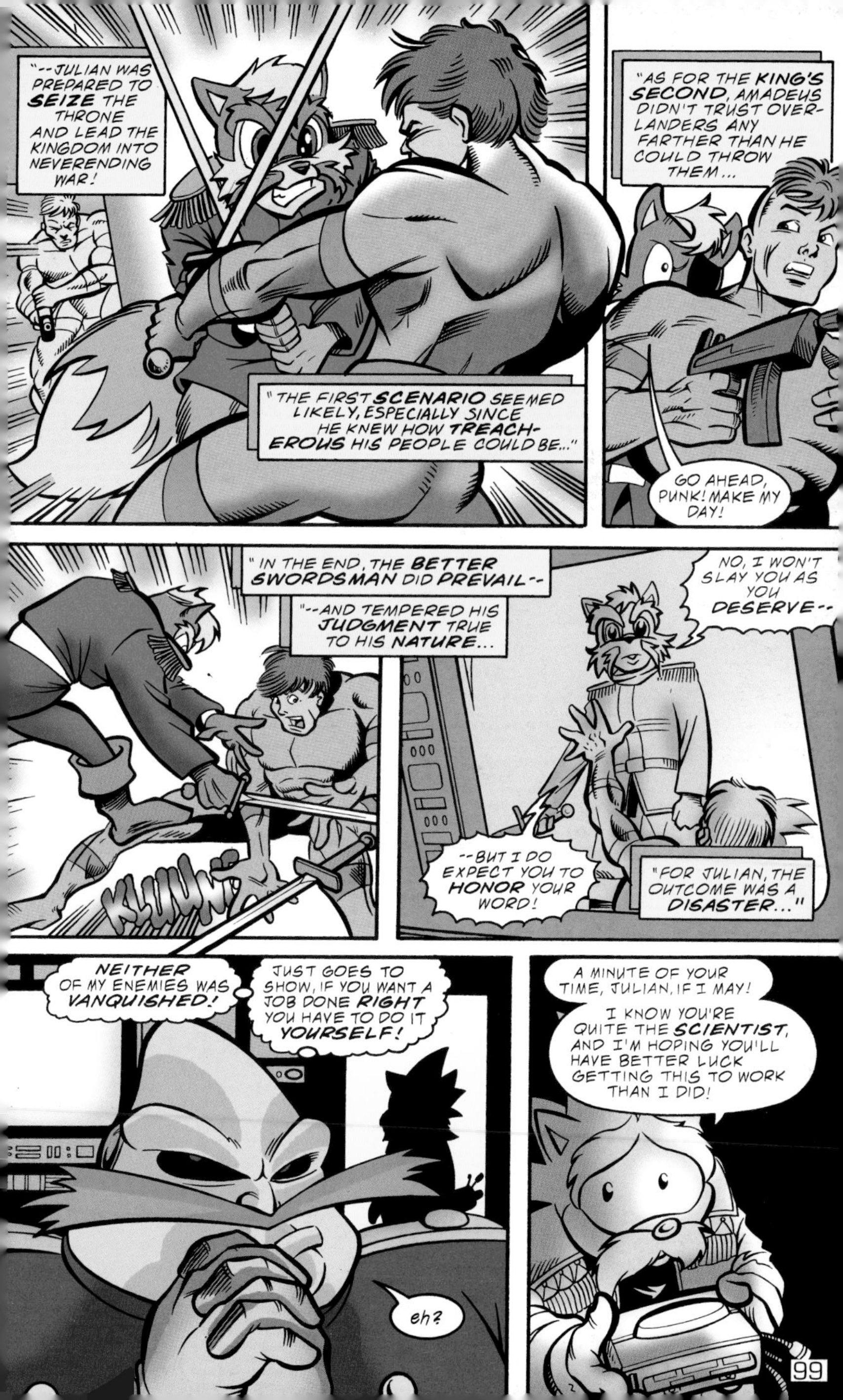
"--JULIAN WAS PREPARED TO SEIZE THE THRONE AND LEAD THE KINGDOM INTO NEVERENDING WAR!
"THE FIRST SCENARIO SEEMED LIKELY, ESPECIALLY SINCE HE KNEW HOW TREACHEROUS HIS PEOPLE COULD BE..."
"AS FOR THE KING'S SECOND, AMADEUS DIDN'T TRUST OVERLANDERS ANY FARTHER THAN HE COULD THROW THEM...
GO AHEAD, PUNK! MAKE MY DAY!
"IN THE END, THE BETTER SWORDSMAN DID PREVAIL--
"--AND TEMPERED HIS JUDGMENT TRUE TO HIS NATURE...
KLUUNK
NO, I WON'T SLAY YOU AS YOU DESERVE--
--BUT I DO EXPECT YOU TO HONOR YOUR WORD!
"FOR JULIAN, THE OUTCOME WAS A DISASTER..."
NEITHER OF MY ENEMIES WAS VANQUISHED!
JUST GOES TO SHOW, IF YOU WANT A JOB DONE RIGHT YOU HAVE TO DO IT YOURSELF!
eh?
A MINUTE OF YOUR TIME, JULIAN, IF I MAY!
I KNOW YOU'RE QUITE THE SCIENTIST, AND I'M HOPING YOU'LL HAVE BETTER LUCK GETTING THIS TO WORK THAN I DID!
99

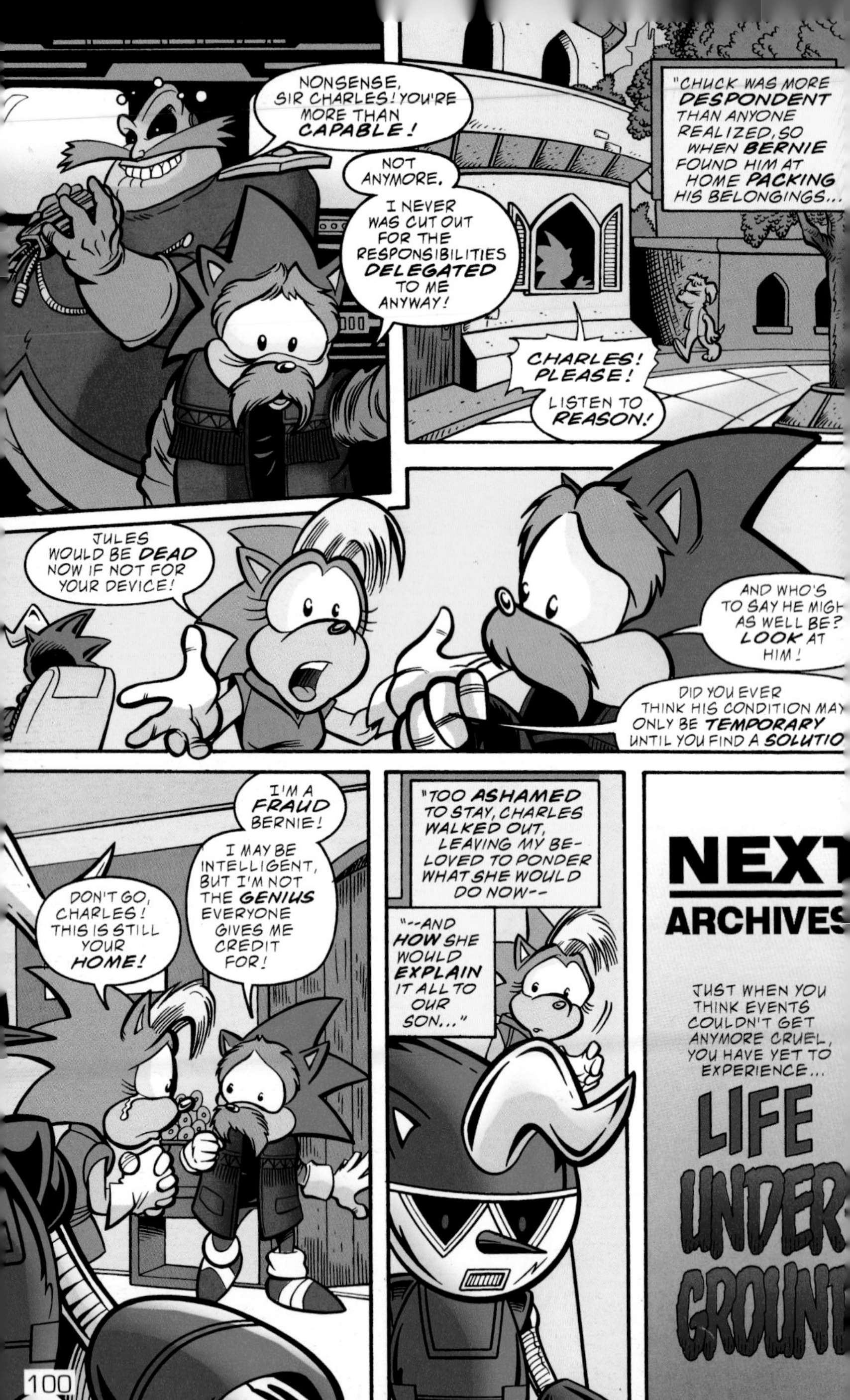
NONSENSE, SIR CHARLES! YOU'RE MORE THAN CAPABLE!
NOT ANYMORE.
I NEVER WAS CUT OUT FOR THE RESPONSIBILITIES DELEGATED TO ME ANYWAY!
"CHUCK WAS MORE DESPONDENT THAN ANYONE REALIZED, SO WHEN BERNIE FOUND HIM AT HOME PACKING HIS BELONGINGS...
CHARLES! PLEASE!
LISTEN TO REASON!
JULES WOULD BE DEAD NOW IF NOT FOR YOUR DEVICE!
AND WHO'S TO SAY HE MIGH AS WELL BE? LOOK AT HIM!
DID YOU EVER THINK HIS CONDITION MAY ONLY BE TEMPORARY UNTIL YOU FIND A SOLUTIO
I'M A FRAUD BERNIE!
I MAY BE INTELLIGENT, BUT I'M NOT THE GENIUS EVERYONE GIVES ME CREDIT FOR!
DON'T GO, CHARLES! THIS IS STILL YOUR HOME!
"TOO ASHAMED TO STAY, CHARLES WALKED OUT, LEAVING MY BE-LOVED TO PONDER WHAT SHE WOULD DO NOW--
"--AND HOW SHE WOULD EXPLAIN IT ALL TO OUR SON..."
NEXT
ARCHIVES
JUST WHEN YOU THINK EVENTS COULDN'T GET ANYMORE CRUEL, YOU HAVE YET TO EXPERIENCE...
LIFE UNDER GROUN

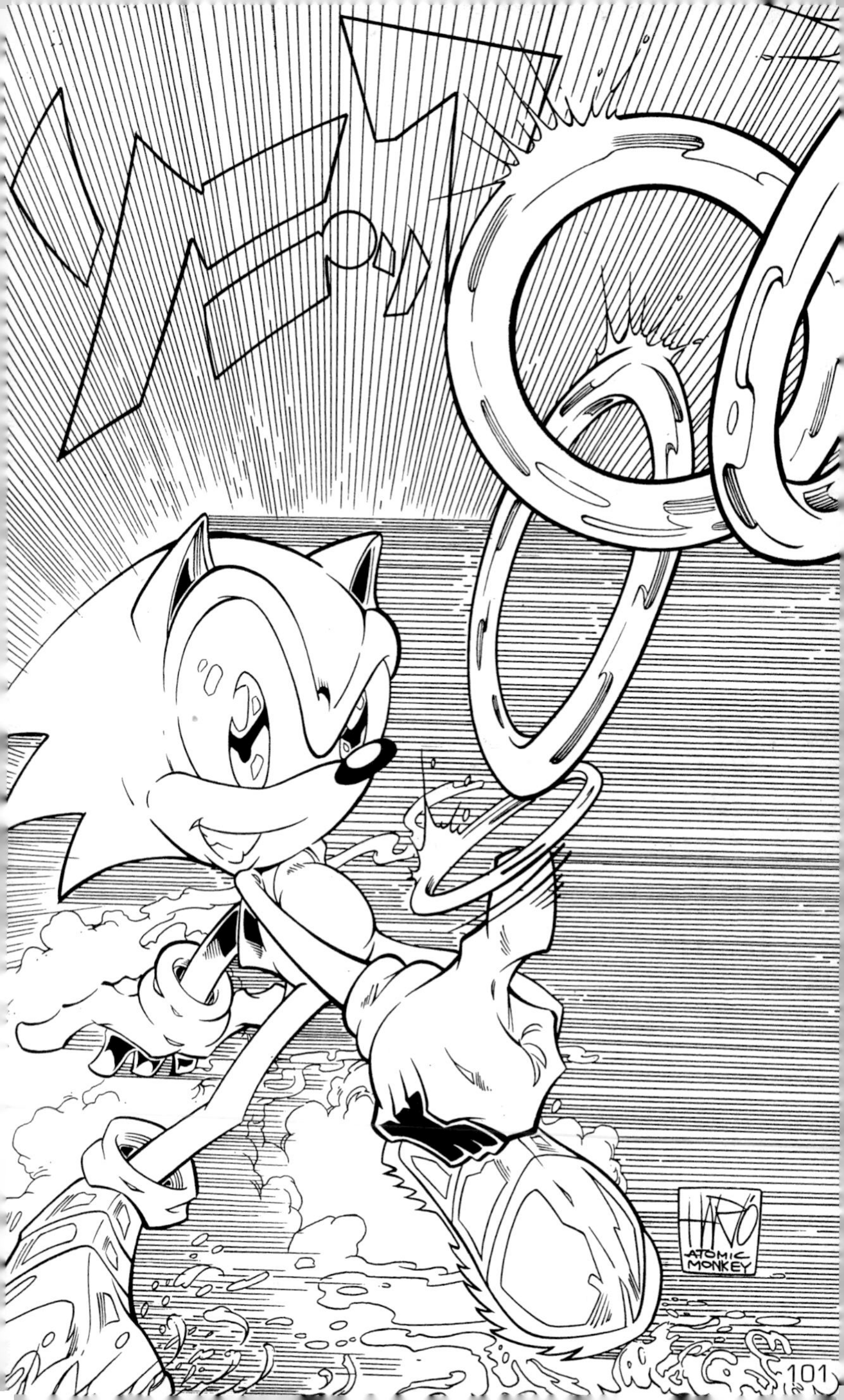
ATOMIC
MONKEY

SONIC THE HEDGEHOG™

Welcome to a brief who's who
of the Sonic universe. You have
just read some of the earliest
and most loved stories from the
Sonic comic. We thought
you'd like to learn a little extra
about a few of our
favorite Sonic characters!

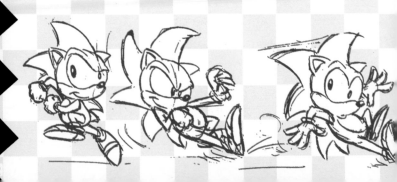

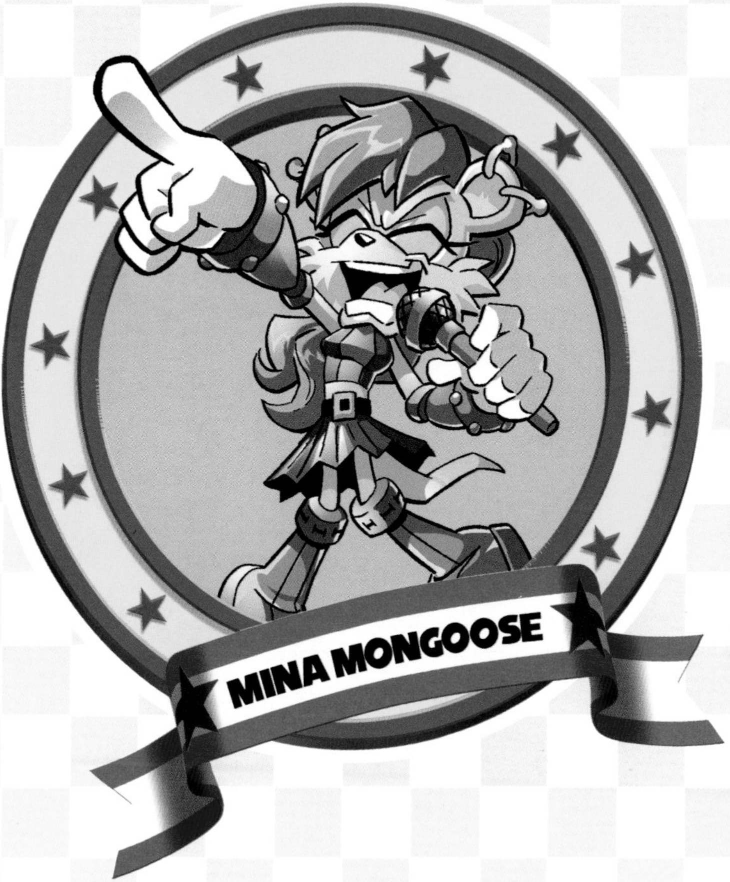
MINA MONGOOSE

MINA MONGOOSE

A scared girl with a powerful secret! Mina is full of potential, but is held back by her own self-doubt. Can Sonic's heroism give her the courage she needs to come out of her shell?

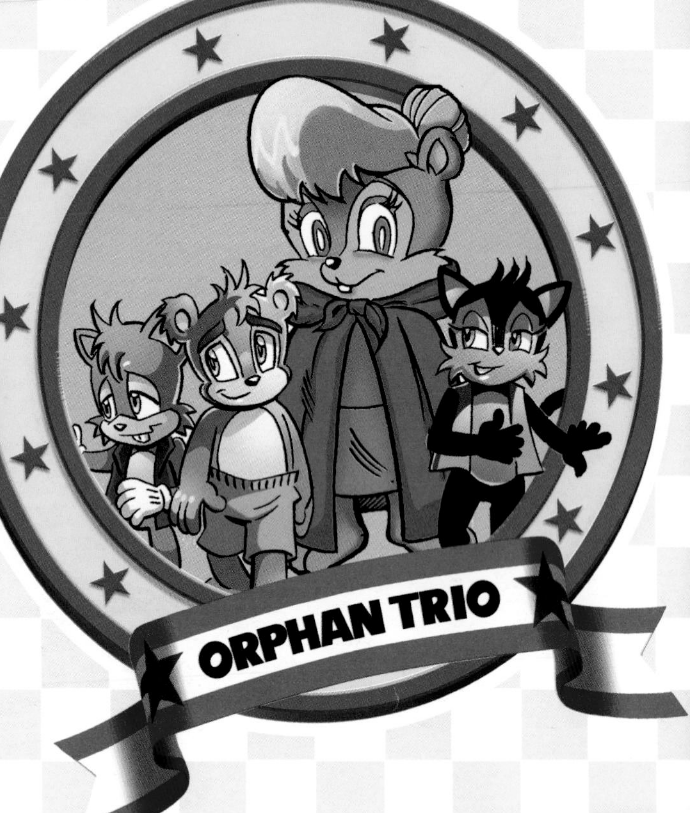
ORPHAN TRIO

ORPHAN TRIO

Rory the Bear, Sasha the Cat and Snaggle the Tiger are all young Mobians under the care of the wise and loving Rosie. They lost their parents to the violence of the First Robotnik War and are now caught up in the first days of the Second.

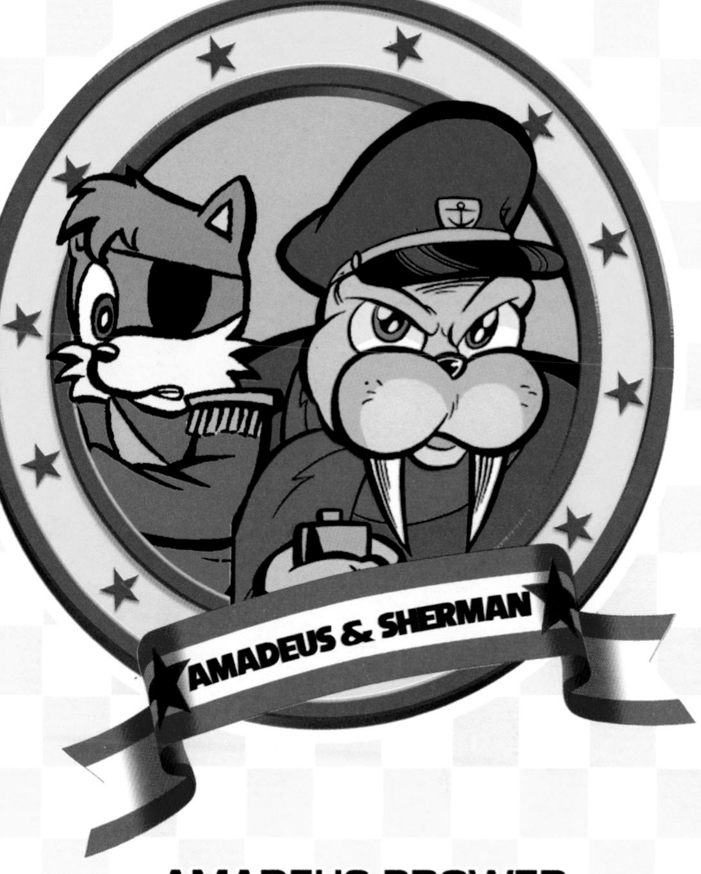
AMADEUS & SHERMAN

AMADEUS PROWER & SHERMAN WALRUS

Known as the "Conductor of the Battle Field," Tails's father is a celebrated hero from the Great War. Many served under his command, including Sherman Walrus, the brave pilot and father of Rotor.

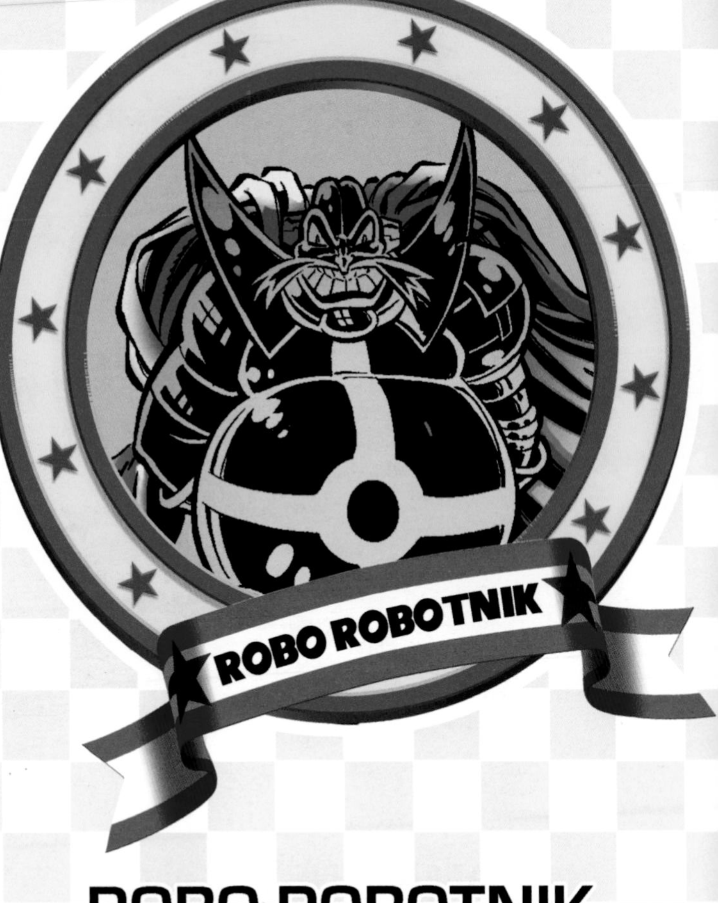
ROBO ROBOTNIK

ROBO-ROBOTNIK

He comes from across time and space – the Roboticized Robotnik! He conquered his dimension using technology recovered from the Giant Borg. Now he's traveled to his past – Sonic's time and world – to destroy Mobius again!

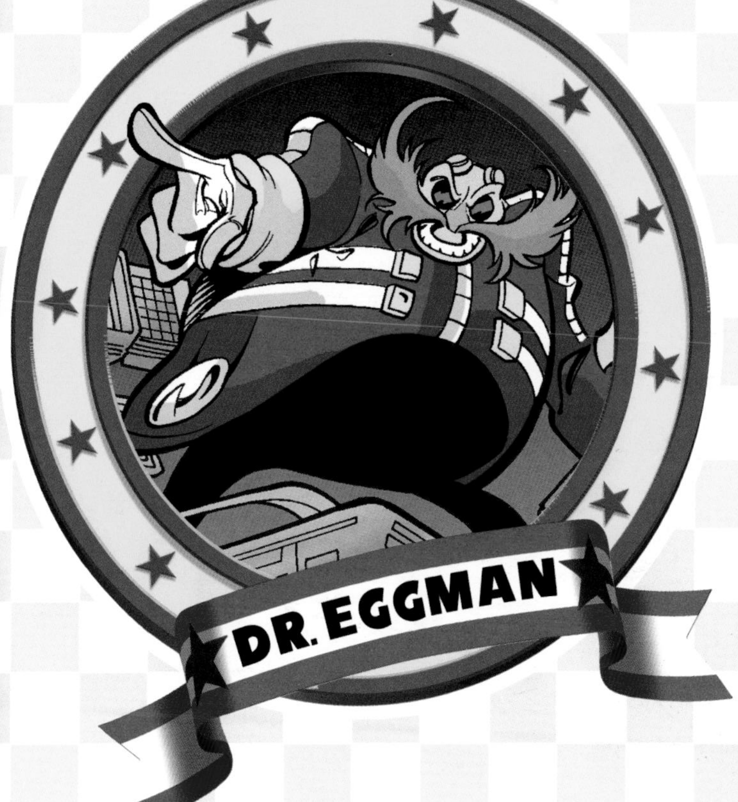
DR. EGGMAN

DR. EGGMAN

You can destroy his body, but you can't stop his evil! Robo-Robotnik downloaded his consciousness into a new robot shell. The Eggman Empire now has its modern-looking leader!

SHADOW BOTS

SHADOW-BOTS

Not to be confused with a certain black-and-red hedgehog, the SHADOW-Bots are advanced SWAT-Bots. Their dark armor is stronger, their weapons are more powerful, and their A.I. is fiercer. And look out for the towering SHADOW-Bot Deluxe models!

SONIC THE HEDGEHOG™

Welcome to a brief what's what
of the Sonic universe. You have
just read some of the earliest
and most loved stories from the
Sonic comic. We thought
you'd like to learn a little extra
about a few of the items and places
that make the Sonic universe so
awesome!

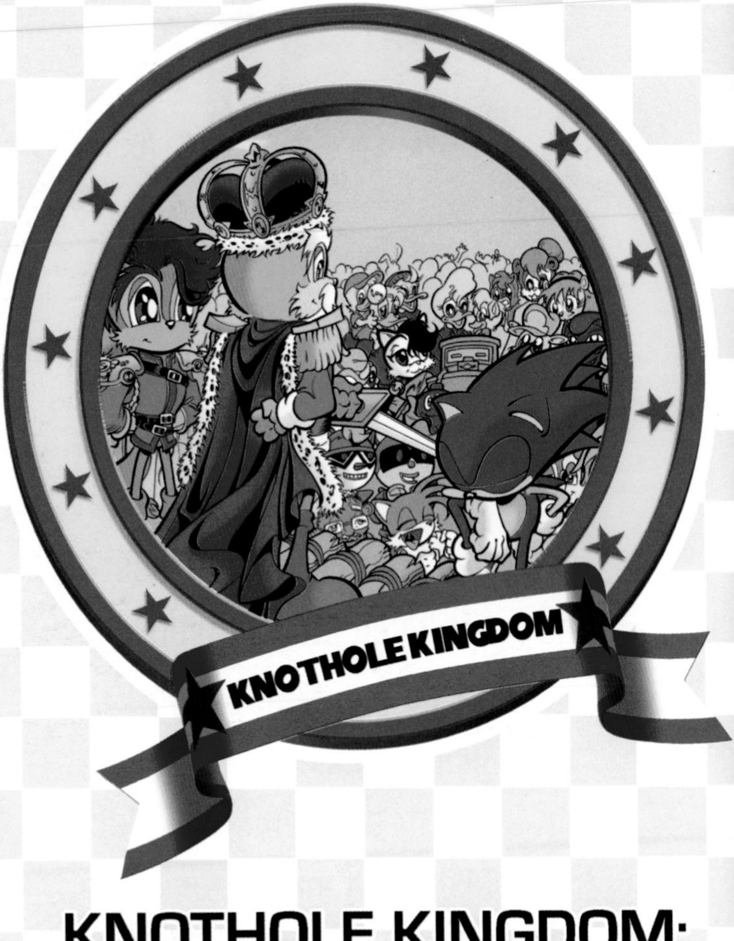
KNOTHOLE KINGDOM

KNOTHOLE KINGDOM: SEEKING REFUGE

Mobotropolis and the Kingdom of Acorn have fallen – again! What's a king to do? Pick up and begin anew – that's what!

KNOTHOLE KINGDOM

KNOTHOLE KINGDOM: A NEW HOME!

Knothole Village served as the beacon of hope during the First Robotnik War, so now the Kingdom of Knothole inspires Mobius through the second one!